Crawl

by

John McCormick

Visit us online at www.authorsonline.co.uk

An Authors Online Book

Copyright © John McCormick 2010

Cover design by Jamie Day © 2010

All rights reserved. No part of this publication may be reproduced, stored in a retrieval system, or transmitted in any form or by any means, electronic, mechanical, photocopy, recording or otherwise, without prior written permission of the copyright owner. Nor can it be circulated in any form of binding or cover other than that in which it is published and without similar condition including this condition being imposed on a subsequent purchaser.

British Library Cataloguing Publication Data.
A catalogue record for this book is available from the British Library

ISBN 978 07552 0609 4

Authors OnLine Ltd
19 The Cinques
Gamlingay, Sandy
Bedfordshire SG19 3NU
England

This book is also available in ebook format,
details of which are available at www.authorsonline.co.uk

Prologue

24 December 1989

A line of tall, craggy peaks looks south to see a line of high, green hills rolling back into the distance. In the valley, in between, a river widens its mouth into a broad, salty estuary. Clinging to the riverbanks and nestled snugly up against the hillsides, a city lies safe and protected, shielded on all sides by the mountains and by the sea.

A cosy place. A happy place. Belfast.

"Their balls! Do you hear me, Michael? I want their balls!"

"Yes, love," he mumbled automatically as he slipped the pistol into his overcoat pocket.

"It could be one of my Christmas presents," she suggested, and then giggled at the thought.

"Yes, love," he repeated, only half-listening. He could do without this, he thought, today of all days. As he walked to the front door he stopped suddenly and turned his head. "I'm sorry," he said, "but what did you just say?"

"Four wee testicles on a plate," she answered as she topped up her gin and tonic. "That's what I want for Christmas."

"Jesus!" he muttered to himself. He opened the front door and stepped out into the cold. "That'll look fucking lovely under the tree."

One

The pretty girls from the perfume counter at Boots were over in the corner murdering *The Little Drummer Boy*, while, behind the bar, a single strand of tinsel danced in the updraft of a microwave oven as Jamesy placed his first order of the day.

"A pint of Bass and a cheeseburger, please."

The barmaid, a slight, dark-haired girl, paused briefly before stepping into the kitchen to deliver the food order. She came back and began to pour the beer, at the same time casting surreptitious glances in Jamesy's direction. Jamesy was unaware of her covert attention as he struggled to keep his place at the crowded bar.

It was lunchtime, though the bar was much busier than normal. It was also a lot noisier. The perfume counter girls had begun to grapple with *Frosty the Snowman* as Jamesy's pint was placed in front of him.

"Your food's on its way," the barmaid told him as she looked directly into his eyes. Jamesy nodded and handed over a five-pound note. Taking it, the barmaid loudly informed the clamouring faces around the bar that they needed to hold their effing horses. She then turned and, giving Jamesy a coy smile, walked over to the till. Jamesy took a sip of his beer as he waited for his change and his food to arrive. He was in The Tudor Lounge, the upstairs bar of Hannigan's, in the city centre; the place where it had begun all those years ago and the place that had remained the starting point ever since. Despite the uncomfortable jostling of the crowd, Jamesy was feeling relaxed. Today was special, after all.

He straightened up as his cheeseburger arrived. The barmaid held out Jamesy's change and, dropping it into his open palm, she fixed him with what she felt was her most wanton gaze. Seemingly oblivious, Jamesy pocketed the money, picked up his beer and food and pushed his way backwards through the crowd.

"Men!" the barmaid fumed. She then turned her attention to an elderly gentleman who was wearing a pointed red hat with a white fur trim.

"OK, you!" she shouted. "Santa bloody Claus! What do you want?"

Jamesy made his way to where Sean and Joker were sitting. They had arrived earlier and had managed to acquire one end of a table by the door at the top of the stairs. A stern-faced woman, finishing off a glass of stout, occupied the other end.

There was no room for Jamesy to sit, so he placed his drink on the table and stood beside Sean as he ate. Joker had just finished his own cheeseburger and was raising his long arms in a leisurely stretch.

"All right there, Jamesy?" Joker said. "All set, are you?"

Jamesy swallowed a mouthful of food and took a sip of beer to wash it down. "Of course," he replied. "I've been looking forward to it."

A tiny, silver-haired man appeared at the end of the table and began gushing apologies to the stern-faced woman who simply nodded to her empty glass. Getting the message, he snatched up the glass and headed for the bar. Joker lit a cigarette and picked up his drink. Behind Jamesy, in the middle of the bar, some young men wearing smart business suits stood in a tight little group. Joker watched them with a smile; he could see they were building up the beer-filled confidence to make an approach on the perfume counter girls. The girls, meanwhile, were trying to pin down *Rudolph the Red Nosed Reindeer*. Rudolph, gamely, was having none of it.

"Is Ding-a-Ling not with you?" Jamesy asked Joker.

Joker shook his head. "Stayed up at his ma's last night," he said. "Should be on his way." Joker then knocked back the remainder of his drink and stood up. "I'm going to the bar, are you two OK?" He gestured to Sean and Jamesy's glasses. Jamesy held up three-quarters of a pint as an answer and Sean regarded his own half-filled glass. "You never heard of pacing yourself?" Sean asked Joker. "It's going to be a long day."

Joker rubbed his hands together and grinned down at Sean. "Pace myself?" he said derisively. "What sort of talk is that?" He then pushed his way into the throng around the bar.

"Joker's in good form then?" Jamesy said to Sean as he sat in Joker's seat.

"Yeah, it's funny that, isn't it?" Sean replied. "How the prospect of a day-long drinking session really perks him up."

The tiny, silver-haired man returned from the bar with a drink in either hand. He set the drinks on the table and manoeuvred himself into the empty chair that his wife had been saving. They both picked up their drinks and sipped silently, steeling themselves for a trip around the shops on the busiest day of the year.

Joker's height and physique made it easy for him to force his way through to the bar. The barmaid, though, was unimpressed. "Right, Baldy," she said. "You can just wait your turn."

Joker smiled. He loved Christmas Eve.

Jamesy finished his food and wiped his mouth with a napkin. He glanced down at the carrier bag by Sean's chair. "Have you done all your shopping already, Sean?" he asked.

"Not exactly," said Sean. "I still have some things to get, but I think I need a few drinks inside me before I can face the shops again."

Jamesy laughed. "Yeah, I know what you mean. It's already mental out there."

After a while, Joker reappeared with his drink in his hand. "Hard luck, lads!" he called over to the young men in smart business suits who were shuffling their way back to the middle of the bar. They had just been given some explicit instructions from the perfume counter girls that were not entirely in keeping with the spirit of the day.

Joker reached the table and motioned for Jamesy to stay seated. "I'm OK standing, Jamesy," he said.

"We're going now anyway, son," the stern-faced woman said as she and her husband got to their feet. "So there's a wee bit more room for you there."

"Oh, right, cheers!" Joker said, and sat down. He sipped his drink and then looked at his watch. Frowning, he turned to Jamesy and Sean. "OK!" he said. "So where the bloody hell *is* everybody?"

Two

A few miles north of the city centre lay a sprawling housing estate, made up mainly of small terraced houses placed in rigidly straight rows. A large part of this estate was cordoned off from the surrounding areas with high, ugly fences of corrugated iron. These fences had been hastily erected, many years before, by an exasperated British Army as they tried to keep the population of North Belfast from tearing itself apart. These 'peace lines' had sprouted up all over Northern Ireland and were seen as a temporary measure.

The housing estate in question was called Ardoyne, and its residents were mostly Irish Nationalists. They were separated from the surrounding areas, whose residents were mostly British Unionists. This led to a certain amount of disagreement between the two sides that, from time to time, would flare up into arguments that could often be heated and brisk.

None of this, however, was of any real concern to one particular Ardoyne resident at that moment in time. Snatter had troubles of his own, but, for today at least, or so he had promised himself, he would dwell on them as little as possible. He was waiting outside a large drinking establishment called The Crumlin Star. This was unusual in that, normally, he was to be found on the inside. Today, however, he was waiting for a lift.

The previous day Ding-a-Ling had phoned to tell him that Harry, Ding-a-Ling's brother-in-law, would be able to drop them off in town in plenty of time for the start of the pub-crawl. They would meet him outside the Star at eleven.

Snatter looked at his watch: it had just gone eleven, so he could expect them any time soon. He looked back on the few occasions that he had met Harry and realised that, apart from the obvious physical aspect of the man, he didn't know much about him. He knew him to see and would always say hello whenever he saw him, but they rarely met in social situations. He had heard stories, of course, but he had put most of those down to exaggeration. There were the nicknames as well, he recalled; things like 'Scary Harry' or 'Mad Dog', but they could be put down, quite easily, to a knee-jerk reaction to Harry's size.

For Harry was enormous. Not overweight or anything like that, just enormous. Enormous both up and down and from side to side. Brick shithouses, mused Snatter, could only aspire to be built like Harry.

Still, once you got past the intimidating physical presence, Snatter thought, then Harry was fairly quiet and unassuming. Judging books by covers, he decided, just as an old white Transit van pulled up.

Ding-a-Ling jumped down from the passenger seat and held open the door.

"You jump on up into the middle there, Snatter," he said. Snatter did so and, as Ding-a-Ling followed him in, they drove off.

"Cheers for the lift, Harry," said Snatter as he realised that Harry was even bigger than he had remembered. Harry simply turned to him and nodded.

'A man of few words,' thought Snatter quietly. 'Or indeed,' he thought, much more quietly, 'a man of fuck-all words.'

"Should be a good one this year, eh, Snatter?" said Ding-a-Ling, which made Snatter jump.

"Uhm, yeah, I can't wait. Been a while since we've all been out for a drink together. You spoken to Tone lately?"

"Yeah, he phoned the flat last week, making sure we're all still up for it. Said he could really do with a good piss-up." Ding-a-Ling giggled. "Tone does make me laugh when he's had a few."

Snatter grinned. "Yeah, he does tend to get a bit professorial the more he drinks."

"Nah," said Ding-a-Ling, "he just gets a bit gay. Joker's been really hyper the last couple of days as well."

"Mmmm?" Snatter was barely listening.

"Did you know he wants me to go over to Ibrox with him in the New Year?"

Snatter turned to face his friend. "Really?" he asked. "That should be an experience."

The van turned onto Ardoyne Road, which led down to one of the main roads into the city centre.

"Uhm, Snatter …" Ding-a-Ling seemed hesitant.

"What is it?" Snatter asked, although he sensed what was coming. He was dreading it.

"Well, apparently, Rosie was round our Karen's this morning and -"

"Why?" Snatter snapped, a little too forcefully.

"What the hell do you mean 'why'?" Ding-a-Ling was taken aback. "You know they're old mates, they were at Holy Cross together and -"

"Yes, yes, I know, OK … I just meant, well, what's your point?"

"Well, according to Karen, Rosie seems to think that you'll be round her sister's house all day today. Some sort of big family thing … I don't know, I was just wondering if anybody had bothered to tell *you*, that's all."

Karen was Ding-a-Ling's sister and Harry's wife. S
different, Snatter thought, from Harry. Where he was
huge, she was tiny. Where he was quiet, she could be
pretty vocal. Ding-a-Ling must have gone round there ...
Snatter realised his mind was trying to avoid the issue. He
turned to Ding-a-Ling.

"What did Karen tell her?"

Ding-a-Ling looked out at the row of shops on his left
as he considered his reply.

This was one of those rare occasions, he decided, when
the truth was perfectly acceptable as an answer.

"Well," he began, "I think she might have said that she
thought you were going into town with me today."

"Oh shit!" Snatter hissed. "What do you mean, you
'think'?"

Ding-a-Ling considered this. "Actually, not so much
'think' as 'know', because she told me that's what she
said. Although, to be fair, she did tell Rosie that she may
have got it wrong. Fuck, it wouldn't be the first time,
would it? No offence, Harry."

"Did Karen say how Rosie seemed when she left?"

Ding-a-Ling decided he had had enough of this truth
business for one day. "Yeah, she was dead on," he said.
"Really dead on."

As they drove past the shops a Royal Mail van pulled
up outside the Ardoyne Post Office, just ahead. On this
occasion, and despite the traditional IRA Christmas
ceasefire, the mail van had an army escort. A dark green
Land Rover pulled up behind the van and four soldiers
jumped from the back.

The Post Office was set in a long row of shops that was
situated a little way back from the road. There were crowds

'ng around, getting in last-minute shopping, ...ds and neighbours and exchanging festive ... The soldiers proceeded to secure the area. This ..olved them standing around and pointing their rifles, every so often, at nothing in particular, while the locals ignored them.

One of the soldiers, however, had spotted a potential threat. Moving traffic, it seemed, posed an unacceptable security risk, which the soldier took upon himself to neutralise. He stepped into the middle of the road and, with calm authority, raised his hand.

The car in front of Harry's van was a small blue Vauxhall and the driver saw the soldier just in time. He braked hard, causing the car to skid before coming to a halt only feet in front of the, now slightly nervous, soldier.

Harry was also alert to the situation and jumped on his brakes. Unfortunately, Harry's brakes, lacking the urgency of younger, more virile brakes, were too slow. The familiar sounds ensued; the sounds associated with an automotive collision. The crumple of metal, the pop of a headlight bursting, the soft crack of Snatter's forehead striking the windscreen.

Ding-a-Ling, sitting on the outside seat, which had been equipped with a seat belt, had felt no more than a sudden jolt and was able, therefore, to observe what happened next.

He watched the driver of the car, a balding, middle-aged man, leap furiously from his car to confront the stupid asshole who had gone into the back of him. As Harry stepped down from the van, Ding-a-Ling could see the car driver turn and point towards the soldier.

"It was his fault, mister!" he was shouting. "He did it!"

Ding-a-Ling watched Harry walk calmly past the driver and stop in front of the, now terrified, soldier. Harry then snapped his head forward, shattering the soldier's nose in a spray of blood.

"Oh, holy shit!" exclaimed Ding-a-Ling.

"What's happening?" Snatter lay crumpled in the passenger footwell of the van; his head was spinning and his tongue seemed to have swollen in his mouth.

"Shit, Snatter, are you OK?"

"I don't know ... I can't fucking see!"

'Probably not a bad thing,' thought Ding-a-Ling, looking through the windscreen. "Listen, Snatter," he said, "I think you're just a wee bit dazed, you're going to be all right, OK? Try lifting your face off the floor, see if that helps your vision." Ding-a-Ling looked outside to see that events had moved on. The soldier who had been directing traffic was now rolling on the ground clutching not only his nose but also his groin. Ding-a-Ling could only assume that it had received some attention from Harry as well.

Two of the other soldiers were hanging from Harry's neck while Harry appeared to be spinning around in the middle of the road. The fourth soldier was pointing his rifle at the car driver and screaming something that Ding-a-Ling couldn't make out. The car driver had his arms at full stretch above his head, but seemed to be trying to get his hands to go even higher. A crowd had gathered.

Ding-a-Ling turned to Snatter. "How are you feeling? Do you think you can walk OK?"

Snatter had managed to get back into his seat but was feeling very shaky; he was also having some trouble getting his vision to stay in focus.

"Uhm ... I suppose so ... why, what's going on?"

"Oh, nothing, it's just I think we may need to get the bus after all."

As Ding-a-Ling opened the passenger door of the van, the door of the army Land Rover also opened. After much soul searching and internal debate, the driver of the Land Rover had decided to enter the fray. By now the car driver, still with an automatic rifle pointed at him, was almost sobbing.

"I'm a school caretaker!" he began shouting. "I'm just a caretaker!"

This didn't help matters as the soldier who was covering him, in a highly emotional state, began to wonder if 'caretaker' was some sort of code name. Was this man confessing to be the IRA's commander in North Belfast?

Harry, meanwhile, wrestling with the two soldiers in the road and causing a bit of a traffic jam, managed to free his left arm just as a target presented itself. The Land Rover driver, now fully committed to action, didn't see it coming. Harry's fist caught him directly under the chin with such force that he was knocked instantly unconscious. This, at least temporarily, spared him from the knowledge that he had bitten off the end of his tongue. There was a ripple of applause through those sections of the crowd that knew a sweet left uppercut when they saw one.

"Harry, we're just going to head on here, if that's OK." Ding-a-Ling, along with a semi-conscious Snatter, was standing behind the soldier who had captured 'the caretaker'. The soldier, suddenly realising his rear was exposed, spun around and aimed his rifle at this new threat.

"Who the fuck are you?" he yelled in a lilting Geordie accent.

Ding-a-Ling seemed genuinely offended "What? Oh, we're nobody," he began. "We're just a couple of passengers who -"

Now the soldier was convinced that 'passenger' was a code word … Passengers? Weren't they the sort of baby-killing bastards who planted bombs on trains and buses?

"Get your fucking hands up!" he screamed.

"No, you don't understand," Ding-a-Ling protested.

"Fucking hands up! Now!"

Snatter, in a brief moment of clarity, found himself staring down the barrel of a gun and, in a panic, threw his hands into the air. This turned out to be a cure for his semi-consciousness.

He fainted.

Three

Bobby's face was arranged in such a way as to make him appear cheerful all of the time. His eyes had a constant sparkle while the corners of his mouth were naturally upturned, even in repose. It was a face that was open and honest and happy. A smiley face. A face that stood in stark contrast to the face that suddenly appeared behind his left shoulder. This was a much darker face. With sunken cheeks and hooded eyes and with a scarf covering its lower half, this was a face of menace; the face of a predator.

Bobby felt something hard dig into his lower back as a voice hissed in his ear.

"Just keep walking, you Orange bastard!"

Bobby kept walking. He was in Queen's Arcade, making his way along the enclosed alleyway of shops, heading for The Tudor Lounge. His pace didn't change and his face remained impassively cheerful. He turned his head, very slightly, to the left.

"All right there, Tone?" he said. "I hope those fingers aren't loaded."

Tone took his hand away from Bobby's back and plunged it into his coat pocket.

"Yeah, Bobby," he said, "you can act as cool as you like but you can't fool me. The shite was flying out of you there, wasn't it?"

"OK, Tone," Bobby sighed. "You really had me going there."

The crowd, in the narrow confines of Queen's Arcade, made it difficult for the two friends to walk abreast, so Tone remained a step behind and to Bobby's left.

"We're running a wee bit late, aren't we?" Tone remarked. "I thought you would have travelled in with Sean."

"Sean was up far too early for me; you know what he's like."

"Last-minute shopping?"

"Yeah," Bobby replied. "I could do with picking up a couple of things myself at some point. If I remember, that is."

They reached the end of Queen's Arcade and Tone fell into step beside Bobby.

"I'd say we're the last to arrive," he said, looking at his watch. "Joker and Ding-a-Ling are probably half-pissed already."

Bobby laughed. "We're not that late," he said. They came to a door that opened onto a tiny hall with another door to the left and a stairway straight ahead. The door on the left led to Hannigan's Bar, but Tone and Bobby climbed the stairs to The Tudor Lounge.

"And just what time do you call this?" Joker shouted as they came through the door. Tone ignored him. He unwound the scarf from around his neck, placed it over the back of a chair and sat down. "Merry Christmas to you too, Joker," he said. Bobby went off to find an extra chair. Jamesy got up, an empty pint glass in his hand. "I'll get this round," he said, and looked down at Tone. "The usual, I take it?"

"Good man yourself, Jamesy!" said Tone, and Jamesy set off.

Joker stood up. "I suppose I should give him a hand," he said, and followed Jamesy to the bar. Bobby returned with a chair and, having established to his satisfaction that the arrival of alcohol was imminent, he sat down.

"Well, how have you two been?" Tone asked, leaning

back in his seat. "Still a couple of parasitic drains on society?"

Sean sighed, rolling his eyes. "Not for much longer, Tone," Bobby said happily. "Big year coming up."

Tone said nothing, though Sean thought he could detect a growling sneer. "Oh yeah, Bobby!" Tone suddenly exclaimed. "Who were those dodgy-looking characters I saw you with earlier?"

"You mean Joker and Jamesy?"

"Oh, ha ha," said Tone. "No, it was at the City Hall. I was going past on the bus and you were talking to some real shiny buggers."

"Shiny buggers?"

"Yeah, they looked like somebody had come along and polished them. They -"

"Oh, right," Bobby said. "They were a bunch of Holy Joes, out recruiting for the Jesus Gang." Bobby smiled at Tone. "The girl was pretty, though, in a sterile sort of way."

Watching Tone, Sean could smell a rant. Too early for that, he decided. "Bloody Christians, eh, Tone?" he said. "Just trying to spoil Christmas for the rest of us."

Tone eyed Sean coolly. "I know you're being flippant, Sean," he said, "but essentially you're right. Christianity has no -"

"For fuck's sake, Tone, give it a rest!" Joker had returned from the bar, his two hands clasped around three pints. He carefully placed the drinks on the table and turned to face Tone. "Or at least wait till we're all too pissed to give a shit."

Tone feigned offence. "Where's my bloody cheeseburger, Joker?"

"It's coming. Don't panic." Joker went back to the bar

for the remaining drinks. Sean turned to Bobby. "Made up your mind yet about going to Solitude?" he asked.

"Yeah," Bobby said, "I don't think I'll bother. I've never had any great desire to have my head shoved up my own arse."

"Well, obviously you don't wear your bloody scarf!" Sean protested. "Just try not to smell like a Prod and you'll be OK."

"The Glens are playing at Solitude?" Tone interrupted.

"At the end of January," Sean told him. "Me and Ding-a-Ling are thinking of going; do you fancy it?" Tone thought about it. "Yeah, maybe," he said. "You going, Joker?" Joker was setting down the last two drinks on the table. "Wise up, Tone!" he answered as he took his seat. "The only ground in Belfast worth going to is Windsor; you should know that."

Jamesy arrived with two cheeseburgers. He handed one to Tone and one to Bobby and sat down. "Seems to get busier every year," he said, mainly to himself.

As Tone chewed his first mouthful he looked over at Sean. "What's this I hear about Snatter getting engaged?"

"What? Oh right!" Sean replied. "Nothing official, as far as I know."

"He hasn't been going out with her all that long, has he?" Tone went on. "Has anybody even met her?"

"Yeah, I know her from way back," said Sean. "She's, well she's …" he tailed off and took a swig from his pint.

"I've met her," Joker piped up.

"Excellent!" Tone cried. "So at least we know what her tits look like."

"Hey, that's not fair!"

"What colour hair has she got?"

"She's got hair?"

Tone took another bite of his cheeseburger and glanced around the table. "I think young Snatter has got some explaining to do," he said. "What about you, Joker? I heard you split up with Carol? So what happened? She sober up?"

"Yeah, very funny, Tone," Joker said. "No, she started getting all sleepy and weird, you know? I just can't handle that sort of crap."

"Sleepy and weird?" asked Tone.

Sean interjected. "Carol was having some problems with her blood pressure," he told Tone. "Nothing serious, like, but she started having dizzy spells; fainting and stuff."

Tone turned to Joker. "You broke up with her because she was sick?"

"Well, don't put it like that," Joker said. "You make me sound like a right prick."

Tone finished his lunch and put up his hands in protest. "On the contrary," he said. "I think you could well be in line for a sainthood. I could put in a good word for you." Tone held up two fingers, pressed together. "Me and John Paul are like that, you know." He then opened a packet of cigarettes and, passing a cigarette to Bobby and one to Joker, he lit one for himself. "Yeah, Joker," he continued. "You're a bloody prince, you know that? A real bloody prince."

"That a wee bit of Salinger there, Tone?" Sean asked with a grin.

Tone blew a smoke ring into the air and looked across the table at Sean. "You always were a bit of a smartass,

Sean," he said. "Yes, actually it is. I've been doing -"

"Look, Tone," Joker said, keen to plead his case. "There was more to it than Carol not being well, you know. We both knew it was never going to work. All that couple's shit isn't really me."

"So what exactly *is* you, Joker?" Bobby asked.

"Well, I'm too much of a free spirit, you see, a lone wolf, you may as well try and lasso the -"

"In other words," Sean said, "she was far too good for you."

"Well, fuck!" replied Joker, taking a sip of beer. "We all knew that!"

The lunchtime crowd had started to ease, leaving a few groups dotted around the room. The barmaid began to ferry stacks of glasses back to the kitchen.

"Anyway!" Joker said, turning to Tone. "What's this I hear about you screwing some bird down south?"

Tone regarded him with some amusement. "Your increasing flirtations with the vernacular, you know, may help to explain your current lone wolf status," he said.

"My current status is self-imposed. Just trying to get -"

"What's the plan here?" Sean broke in. "Are we staying for another?"

Joker voiced his enthusiastic approval of the idea. Tone looked at his watch.

"I suppose we could hang on for another one," he said. "See if these two dickheads manage to show up."

Sean went off to the bar and Bobby followed to help carry the drinks. Tone turned to Joker. "Here, is Ding-a-Ling OK?" he asked.

Joker looked puzzled. "OK? Yeah, why?"

"Oh, I don't know," Tone replied. "He just sounded a bit weird on the phone the other day."

Joker shrugged. "Nothing wrong as far as I know," he said. "Although he did have a bit of a funny phase a while back."

"What do you mean?"

"Well, he was trying to get his hands on some videos and -"

"OK, Joker!" Tone grinned. "I think we get the -"

"No, it's not that," Joker continued. "It was a kid's TV show, you know? *The Banana Splits*?"

"Oh yeah!" Jamesy said. "I remember that. He asked me about it too."

"*The Banana Splits*?" Tone frowned. "What the hell for?"

"I don't know." Joker shrugged. "Nostalgia? I mean, it was a bloody good show, wasn't it?"

Tone and Jamesy both nodded, smiling at the memories. "Not like the shite kids have to watch these days," Tone said ruefully.

"You sound like an old man there, Tone," Jamesy teased.

"Three words, Jamesy," said Tone, holding up three fingers. "Just three words. Timmy fucking Mallett."

Standing side-by-side at the bar, Bobby turned to Sean. "It's not like Snatter to be late," he said. "You can usually set your watch by him."

"True," Sean agreed.

"Of course, Ding-a-Ling on the other hand ..."

"Oh, I'm sure there's nothing to worry about," said Sean.

"You heard about Sticky Mickey, didn't you?"

Sean turned to face Bobby. "That was ages ago," he said. "And anyway ..." Sean looked thoughtful for a second and then shook his head. "Come on, Bobby! It's Christmas Eve, for Christ's sake! Not even Ding-a-Ling can get into trouble on Christmas Eve."

Four

"You shot him, you Brit bastard!"

No one in the crowd believed for a second that Snatter had been shot, but there was no harm in introducing a little bit of controversy into the proceedings. Ding-a-Ling was adding to the general confusion by playing to the crowd; he shook Snatter's shoulder and gestured to the soldier, who was becoming increasingly agitated; surrounded, as he was, by crazed terrorists.

"Now see what you've done?" Ding-a-Ling called out. "In his prime, he was. In his bloody prime -"

The soldier continued to wave his rifle around in a desperate attempt to impose some sort of order. "Just put your fucking hands up!"

Elsewhere, things were beginning to calm down. His anger having run its course, Harry raised his hands in quiet resignation.

"OK, OK," he said, then strolled over to the back of the Land Rover and sat down. He reached down and patted the shoulder of the soldier he had first attacked.

"You'll be all right there, mate," he said consolingly. "Nothing too serious."

The soldier didn't appear to be consoled though, and, still holding his nose, told Harry to 'Fugg off'.

Harry shrugged as the other soldiers crowded around him, a little uncertain about how to proceed. Sirens could be heard in the background.

Snatter started to come round and then wished he hadn't. Ding-a-Ling, now warming to a theme, continued to harangue the unfortunate soldier, informing him that he was the personification of British Imperialism.

Inspired by his audience, Ding-a-Ling pursued his lecture with some gusto. With impassioned and unimpeachable logic, he explained the unthinking evil of Britain, pillaging the world for wealth and power. He outlined the soldier's part in it all with such erudition that he knew the soldier could not fail to be persuaded. The unassailable veracity of Ding-a-Ling's argument was embellished, Ding-a-Ling believed, with lyrical flourishes of such heart-melting beauty that the soldier would be, not so much bludgeoned as caressed into submission. The soldier, Ding-a-Ling saw, was beginning to buckle under the force of the truths that were piling on top of him. His true role in the grinding machinery of Empire was being unveiled to him and Ding-a-Ling knew that the soldier, while having his eyes opened, was having his soul crushed.

"What the blind, bloody fuck is this guy yelling about?" the soldier was thinking.

Behind him, the car driver, still in the middle of the road, was almost jumping up and down to demonstrate just how fully his hands were, in fact, up.

Overhead, the familiar undulating rattle and drone of a helicopter whisking the sky accompanied the shouting and the car horns as the cacophony, with the approach of the sirens, rose to a crescendo. Snatter's head hurt, but his vision was clear enough to see first one, then another grey Land Rover pull up. The police had arrived.

Despite Ding-a-Ling's best efforts, most of the people in the crowd, having decided that the entertainment value of the day had diminished since Harry had stopped hitting people, were beginning to drift away. Several police officers were now spreading out to put a stop to any further shenanigans and calm was finally descending on the scene. Ding-a-Ling, however, continued with his diatribe; still playing to those few members of the crowd that remained. Snatter, in a prone position at Ding-a-Ling's feet, began to groan.

A slightly overweight policeman with a thick moustache stepped in front of Harry and took out a notebook. "All right there, Harry? How's it going?"

"Hiya, John," said Harry. "I've had better days."

"So I see, so I see," said John, not writing anything down and having no intention of doing so. "So what's the butcher's bill, then?"

At that moment an ambulance pulled up and the crew began to treat whatever injuries they could find. Harry nodded over to the soldier he had punched, who was just coming round.

"He'll be OK," he said. "May need a few stitches in his tongue. This guy's nose is broken. To be honest, though, it didn't look like it was the first time."

"No harm done, then," said John cheerfully.

"What the fu-?" the soldier began, but John waved him down.

"All right, all right now," John said, "everybody calm down here. I don't think it's very helpful to go around pointing fingers at this stage of the game. Now what's the -?"

"All right there, Harry?" Another policeman appeared behind John. "I bloody knew it was you when the call came over the radio. You're a shocking man, so you are." He grinned and pointed over towards Ding-a-Ling. "Who's your man there?"

"Oh, hi, Stephen," Harry said, as they all looked over

to where Ding-a-Ling was delivering his speech. "That's my brother-in-law."

"Your brother-in-law? Karen's brother, you mean?" asked John, not taking his eyes off the show. Ding-a-Ling was now gesturing at his stricken comrade with one hand while draping his other hand theatrically across his brow. It was, thought Ding-a-Ling, bloody good stuff.

"Bit of a wanker, isn't he?" John said finally.

Harry nodded. "Harmless enough, though," he said.

"Any way to shut him up?" asked John.

"You could shoot him, I suppose."

John seemed to consider this, then shook his head.

"Wise up, Harry, it's Christmas Eve. Think of the paperwork."

"Oh, aye, here we go," Ding-a-Ling went on, "the fucking lapdogs of the RUC are here to -"

"Gary!" said Harry in a voice that, Snatter imagined, could cure the chronically constipated. "Shut it!"

Ding-a-Ling was immediately contrite. "No problem, Harry," he said. "No sweat there at all, mate."

"Is your mate OK there?" John asked, nodding to Snatter.

One of the ambulance crew, who was dabbing something on the bruise on Snatter's forehead, turned around.

"Could do with taking him in," he said, "get it looked at properly."

Ding-a-Ling was appalled. He knew exactly what that would entail. They would end up sitting for hours in casualty before some doctor, who would, no doubt, look about twelve-years-old, told Snatter to take some Aspirin and to have a lie down.

"Nah, don't worry about it," Ding-a-Ling said quickly.

"He'll be OK, won't you, Snatter? It's just we have somewhere to go and we're a wee bit late already, you know? And we're going -" A scowl from Harry suggested to Ding-a-Ling that he should stop talking.

Harry turned to John and Stephen. "You'll be taking me in, I suppose?" he asked.

"You know the score, Harry," John replied. "Damage to Her Majesty's property and all that." He nodded over towards the soldiers. "We'll be as quick as we can, though; you'll be out in no time at all. Do you want us to let Karen know?"

Harry took a glance at the people milling around; he knew most of them to some degree.

"She already knows," he said.

John looked around and chuckled. "Yeah, I see what you mean. No secrets in Ardoyne, eh? Well, let's get this over with."

As the other policemen took statements from Ding-a-Ling, Snatter, the car driver and several other witnesses, Harry clambered into the back of one of the police Land Rovers with John and Stephen and was driven away. The soldiers and the ambulance crew left, Harry's van was pushed off to the side of the road, the Vauxhall driver, muttering curses under his breath, was able to continue his journey and peace was finally restored.

Snatter turned to Ding-a-Ling. "Harry really lost the bap there, didn't he?" he said.

"Yeah, he's got a bit of a short fuse and -"

"A short fuse?" Snatter asked in disbelief. "I didn't see any fucking fuse at all!"

"Well, anyway, that's why the cops know him. Familiarity, you know? In fact, there's even -"

"Ding-a-Ling?" Snatter interrupted.

"Yeah?"

"I need a drink."

"Yeah, you're right. Come on, let's go."

Snatter tentatively touched the bump on his forehead as they turned and made their way to the nearby bus stop.

Five

The Tudor Lounge had been an unusual choice and no one could ever quite remember who had suggested it. There had been so many of them, after all, that first year when a group of sixth-formers from a Catholic grammar school in the city had arranged to meet in town for a Christmas drink. For many it was the first date on a long-term relationship with alcohol and had proved to be an enjoyable occasion.

The meeting place, however, was surprising. In a city that boasted many famous bars, The Tudor Lounge was drab and unfashionable and, perversely, in a country known for its authentic bars, had aspirations to be an English country pub.

Dull horse-brasses and dark wood panelling, combined with furnishings of worn red velvet, gave the interior a gloomy appearance. The heavily leaded glass in the windows seemed designed to prevent as much daylight as possible from seeping through and the task of illuminating the room was given to a few uninterested table-lamps and some overhead light bulbs.

The sun-bright days of summer only emphasised the dejected feel of the place, prying into dark corners and exposing the true aspect of The Tudor Lounge: weary and unloved tawdriness.

It took winter, though, to transform that tawdriness into cosiness. The little coal fire in the corner, risible in summer, was suddenly welcoming. A place by which to sit, comfortable and safe, as the angry weather clawed uselessly at the reassuringly heavy windows. The glow from The Tudor Lounge may have been dim but, in a world of shivering darkness, dim was enough. On Christmas

Eve, The Tudor Lounge was perfect.

It lacked just one thing; there was no public payphone.

Jamesy stomped his feet and watched his breath steam up the little rectangular windows of the phone box in the pedestrian courtyard outside. He listened to Snatter's phone ring for a few more seconds before replacing the receiver in its cradle. Glancing at his watch, he was beginning to wonder if there may be some cause for concern. He had just spoken on the phone to Ding-a-Ling's father and had been informed that Ding-a-Ling had left earlier that morning with the intention, Jamesy guessed, of going directly to the pub-crawl.

Snatter's absence suggested that he and Ding-a-Ling were together and Jamesy was reassured by the thought. Snatter was dependable to the point of tedium and had often proved to be a steadying influence on Ding-a-Ling's more capricious tendencies.

Even so, Jamesy had to acknowledge, there was no sign of them.

He stepped out of the phone box into the cold breeze and at that moment caught the eye of an attractive girl who was passing. She almost broke stride as she smiled at him, glancing back every so often as she melted into the crowd. Jamesy was used to this: girls smiled at him all the time, from the very young to the very old. Jamesy certainly did not lack for female attention, and he knew the reason why.

Jamesy was good-looking in a conventional sort of way, but it was more than this. His personality, while not immediately apparent, was both earnest and engaging, but it was more than this too. It was his eyes.

'Junkie's eyes', Joker called them, even though Jamesy's one experiment with marijuana - which Joker had provided - had ended abruptly with some explosive vomiting and a vow from Jamesy to stick with beer in the future.

Joker, however, was not to be dissuaded. It was indecent, he argued, for anyone who did not harbour a severe and life-threatening chemical addiction to possess such eyes.

"Yeah," Joker would sadly inform anyone who expressed an interest, "your man there? He's got more chemicals in him than a packet of Spangles." Joker felt happier this way, more at peace with the world, for Jamesy's eyes were, indeed, strange.

They were a pale, almost opaque, milky-blue, which, coupled with Jamesy's naturally swarthy complexion, gave him an exotic appearance that women found captivating.

"Any woman could easily fall in love with Jamesy's eyes," an old girlfriend of Sean's had once remarked, "but once you get past the eyes then what else is there?"

Sean had split up with her shortly afterwards but, despite the casual cruelty of her observation, there were those who thought she had a point.

Not those who knew him well, of course, but even Jamesy was acutely aware of a certain personality trait that, to casual acquaintances, could make him seem arrogant or disinterested. It was simple: he was incapable of small talk.

The tiny droplets of conversation employed to cover over any awkward silences were beyond Jamesy, which, he supposed, would give the impression that he was a little aloof or maybe even ill-mannered. He just literally couldn't think of anything to say.

This was part of the reason for Jamesy's poor record with the opposite sex for, despite his physical attractiveness, all of his relationships happened to peter out after two or three dates. It may have been part of the reason, but was not, Jamesy knew, the entire reason. Physically, he was attracted to women, but whenever he tried to connect with a girl on a more profound level he would inevitably become exasperated. Women confused him. Maybe it just happened to be the particular women that he had, so far, been acquainted with, but he tended to find their conversations shallow and vacuous which, he was horrified to think, might make him some sort of intellectual snob.

Not that Jamesy was overly concerned by any of this, he liked to think, because, at this point in his life, he had decided, women were no more than a distraction, a diversion from the main focus of his life, and that focus was the world of academia.

Jamesy was born to be a student. He was born to immerse himself in study, to find joy in learning and to value few things more worthy than the acquisition of knowledge.

Jamesy could see a wife in his future at some point: a wife was certainly part of his vision of how his life would play out; he just assumed that when the time was ready it would, somehow, happen. At the moment, though, he felt no compulsion to force the issue. He was happy to wait.

As he walked back to the bar, watching the passers-by pull their coats more tightly around themselves as the wind suddenly became a little more vicious, Jamesy smiled to himself. Winter was his favourite time of the year. His idea of the perfect day was waking early on a weekend morning in mid-winter to find a cold, misty rain drenching the quiet little streets around the university, a day that could be fit for only one purpose, a day when there was nothing else for it but to light the fire, put the kettle on and to settle down for many pleasant hours in the company of books. The sunshine of summer would make Jamesy feel guilty for wanting to stay indoors, immersed in study; but winter gave him the perfect excuse to indulge his passion, cosseted away in studious hibernation.

Jamesy made his way up the stairs to the bar and, after suffering some sexual harassment from the perfume counter girls on their way back to work, he pushed open the door.

"For fuck's sake, Joker!" Bobby, who had his nose and mouth buried in the crook of his elbow, was berating Joker. "I mean, Jesus Christ, even the IRA have called a truce!"

"That's certainly a feisty wee odour you've made there," Tone added.

"Thank you, Tone," said Joker, glowering at Bobby, "it's nice to know that some people can still appreciate craftsmanship."

Sean looked up as Jamesy approached the table. "Any news?"

"No answer at Snatter's house," Jamesy replied. "And Ding-a-Ling's da said he left early this morning."

"So where the hell are they?" asked Tone as he put a light to his cigarette. "We're going to have to make a decision here."

Joker drained his pint and got up. "I'm going to the bogs," he said. "Let me know what's happening when I get back."

"Ding-a-Ling's da said he thought that Ding-a-Ling was getting a lift from his brother-in-law." Jamesy sat down and picked up the remainder of his drink. "If that's any help."

"We could try ringing Ding-a-Ling's sister," Bobby suggested. "Anybody got her number?"

"Well, I don't have it on me," Sean said. "Joker might, though."

Most of the drinks on the table were almost finished, so Tone made a decision. He picked up his scarf. "I say we move on; there's no point in hanging around here. If they do make it into town then they won't be expecting us to still be here at this time."

Everyone agreed. "I need to do a bit of shopping," Bobby said, "so where will I meet you?"

Although there was a limited number of bars that were visited every year, the itinerary for the pub-crawl was always fluid, with no fixed route; though there were a few exceptions, such as White's, The Botanic Inn and The Tudor Lounge, which were annual stalwarts.

Sean stood up as Joker returned. "I'll go with you, Bobby. I need to get a few things. Joker, do you have Ding-a-Ling's sister's number? Me and Bobby could give her a bell on the way."

Joker took out a small black diary, shuffled through it, and then handed it to Sean. Sean copied the number and handed the book back to Joker.

"Where to next, then?" he asked Tone.

Tone thought for a minute. "What about Kelly's?" he suggested.

"Sounds good," Sean and Bobby both agreed. "We'll see you there shortly."

As they headed for the door, Joker picked up his cigarettes and sat down. "I suppose we'll just have to wait for Jamesy to finish his bloody pint, then," he grumbled with good humour.

"Well, I'm going for a piss," said Tone. "Be ready to go when I get back."

Bobby and Sean stepped out into the cold. "Jesus!" Bobby exclaimed. "Bit bloody nippy, isn't it?"

"Yeah," said Sean. "I think it has something to do with the weather."

Bobby was used to Sean's dry humour and ignored it. "So what do you think the deal is with Snatter getting engaged?" he asked. They were walking along with teeth gritted against the wind.

"I don't know," Sean replied. "None of my business, really."

"Tone reckons it's the beginning of the end."

"The end of what?"

"Well … the pub-crawl for one thing."

Sean stopped and looked at Bobby. "Did Tone actually say that?" he asked, concerned.

"Well, no, but think about it. I mean, it's inevitable, isn't it?"

They walked on and reached a public phone box. They bundled inside and, now out of the wind, sighed with relief.

"Inevitable? Why?" asked Sean.

"Well, we're all going to have to settle down eventually. We're both going to be starting work properly in the New Year, aren't we? Haven't you thought about it?"

Sean fumbled for the piece of paper that had Karen's number on it. "Not as much as you, obviously," he said.

Bobby hesitated for a second. "I've been looking at engagement rings," he finally admitted.

"Seriously?" Sean was surprised.

Bobby became a little defensive. "It's the next step, isn't it? I mean, that's just the way things go."

"Not necessarily," said Sean. "Fuck me, are you saying that you have your whole life planned out one bloody step at a time?"

Bobby shrugged. "For me it just seems like a natural progression, that's all."

Sean stared at him as he dialled the number. "Jesus!" he muttered, shaking his head.

"Hello, is that Karen? Yeah, it's Sean here; yeah, Sean Thompson. I was just wondering if you'd seen Ding … um … Gary at all today. What? Yeah with Seamus, they were supp … What? Lifted? Who? Shit, I mean what happened to … shit … no, we were just wondering. Look, don't worry; no, I'm sure there's no problem, and you know Harry's going to be OK … No I don't think so. Look, I'll make sure he rings you or your folks when he shows up. What? What about Rosie? No, I don't know anything about it … Look, I have to go now, the money's running out and … No, don't worry!"

Sean hastily replaced the receiver and turned to face Bobby.

"Fuck!" he said.

Six

Seamus and Gary had been friends from birth. Or as close to birth as they could remember. Born within a few months of each other in the same Ardoyne street, it was only natural they would grow up together. The differences in their characters were apparent from the beginning, but they also proved to be complementary.

Physically, Seamus was stocky and solid with a serious face that bordered on solemn. In life he was naturally cautious.

Gary, wiry and athletic, was reckless to an almost dangerous degree. He had an insatiable thirst for experience and would frequently get both himself and Seamus into trouble. His twinkling boyish grin could not have contrasted more sharply with the sombre, almost worried, expression that Seamus wore. They were opposites and they had quickly become inseparable.

When they first started school, Seamus' mother had walked along with them for the first few weeks and then they were allowed to walk the short distance on their own. They walked, cocooned in their private world, past the smouldering carcasses of burnt-out vehicles, past the silent soldiers and the menacing bulk of armoured cars, the hooded men carrying milk crates filled with petrol bombs, the screaming graffiti, past the rubble, the broken glass and the bullet casings. This was Ardoyne. They were safe.

During their first year at school, as nicknames were allocated and they became Snatter and Ding-a-Ling, they met Sean Thompson, a smiling and confident boy in their class who they immediately christened Tommy Gun.

One day Tommy Gun told Snatter and Ding-a-Ling of a nearby pond that he knew to contain frogspawn. The idea of any sort of wildlife in Ardoyne was so ridiculous that Tommy Gun was told to wise up and he was branded a dirty liar until proof was forthcoming.

And so, after school, they set off, along with a few other boys from their class, toward the wasteland behind Etna Drive that led to the Bone hills.

There were a few pools of filthy water scattered in between the bushes and the mounds of rubbish, between the broken bricks and the patches of tarmac and the moss-covered earth, but Tommy Gun led them further into the waste ground until he came to a large, untidy hedge. There was a rusted rectangular bed frame off to one side that still contained many of its 'v'-shaped wire springs. These springs, the boys knowledgeably told each other, made excellent catapults, although that would have to wait for another time as Tommy Gun pushed aside a lower branch of the hedge and crawled inside. They all clambered in after him and there it was, just as Tommy Gun had described: a small, overgrown pond that, indeed, contained some frogspawn. To a bunch of scruffy, working class city kids, however, it was nothing less than miraculous: it was nature unveiled in all her glorious majesty.

Tommy Gun beamed in triumph as Ding-a-Ling and Snatter looked upon him with a new respect and at that moment the two became three.

Plans were made to race home and scavenge for jam-jars, to collect the precious frogspawn, to watch tiny tadpoles grow into frogs, to have the greatest pets ever. These plans would never come to fruition, however. A million other plans would just get in the way.

They lived in and out of each other's houses and they

lived life at frantic boyhood speeds, racing chaotically from football to play-fights and cycling trips to important expeditions into the unknown and building sleds in the winter and 'guiders' in the summer. And, occasionally, girls.

There were childish stolen kisses and crushes that came and went almost instantly. One memorable time saw Ding-a-Ling become dramatically inconsolable when the love of his life had to move away with her family and Snatter and Tommy Gun had to coax him out his torpor. They had teased him for days afterwards.

There were sunny Sunday afternoons when the three boys would sit on empty beer crates outside the Saunders' and sip Coke and gossip like old women while their das were inside drinking bottles of Red Heart and talking treason. Or wet weekends in winter when they would visit Toby's Hall in Butler Street to watch old Hammer horror movies and flirt with girls.

During the week they would spend almost all of their time together, both in and out of school. They would explore the burnt-out and deserted houses of 'old' Ardoyne, ancient cobbled streets that looked as if they had been abandoned for a hundred years or more. Once, in a narrow alleyway, they had found some bullet holes along a wall and had convinced themselves they had discovered the very spot where the British Army had shot James Connelly; their knowledge of the facts of Irish history being a little hazy.

They would roam far and wide, as far, even, as the 'waterworks' where they climbed trees and fished for 'spricks' and swam and were kids.

Snatter got up and switched off the television. He wasn't really concentrating on it anyway.

"You're living in the past, me old mate," he muttered to himself.

He took a swig from his can of beer, then lit a cigarette. Standing in the middle of the room, looking through the window, he could see the Christmas tree lights blinking in the windows of the houses across the street as the thoughts and memories swirled around in his head. He was fully aware of just how much he had relied upon his friends in the past and how much he would rely on them again. They had always been there, he thought, through the joys and the sorrows and through the unspeakable agonies. Agonies, he was convinced, that would have broken him into pieces had his friends not been standing by his side. He thought back to his first day of grammar school, waiting in the very spot where he now stood, waiting for Tommy Gun and Ding-a-Ling to call for him; waiting in his smart new uniform while his da leant against the mantelpiece, a stupid grin on his face and the tears tripping him.

Snatter had felt awkward and fearful of what his friends would say, for such raw displays of emotion were open to mockery. He should have known better, however, for they never said a word, not then, not ever, and he had loved them for it. Not that he could ever tell them that, of course; nor did it even need to be said.

A few years later his friends, Tone and Jamesy now included, had helped to carry his father's coffin up to the chapel on the hill and, later on, had dragged him away from the suffocating crowd of relatives to go and sit in the local park with a few bottles of illicit cider. They had talked away the evening, both joyful and morose, jeering, cajoling and tipsy. Doing what they had always done, thought Snatter: keeping me from falling apart.

Was it fair, he wondered, to need their support so much?

Maybe he had been through more troubles than most, or maybe he was just more pathetic than most. More needy.

He took a final draw from his cigarette and dropped the butt into his empty beer can. He went into the kitchen, took another can from the fridge and rolled it along his forehead before he opened it. He was feeling restless and uneasy. 'It's just bloody life, isn't it?' he thought to himself. 'Just when everything seems to be going well, just when the only obstacles ahead seem to be minor ones, just when there's a hint of calm and possible contentment, then along comes life to fuck everything up.' He let his mind drift again and found himself in the grim surroundings of the Department of Health and Social Services.

It had been a strange summer after their school days had all come to an end. As expected, Jamesy and Tommy Gun, who now insisted on being called Sean, had achieved the required exam results and were preparing for their fresher year at Queen's University. Tone, with typical contrariness, had applied for and been accepted to Southampton University and had left for the south of England soon after the exam results were released. Snatter and Ding-a-Ling had signed on the dole.

It had been no great surprise that they had both underachieved so dramatically for their final exams: neither Snatter nor Ding-a-Ling had ever really expressed any ambition or appetite for further education. Snatter, in particular, had seemed to become more and more weary of the constant learning and revision of things he had simply no desire to know. He was beginning to feel that life was passing him by and he felt eager to get on with things. What those things would turn out to be he had no idea, but he thought that going to university would only postpone them. Ding-a-Ling had just liked to get drunk most nights.

For a while they had both enjoyed being unemployed: after seven years in the strict confines of a Catholic grammar school, the unrestricted freedom now on offer was almost daunting. Soon, however, the days began to merge into one another as time became more and more meaningless. Quite often, mostly on Friday afternoons when lectures had finished for the week, Snatter and Ding-a-Ling would make their way up to the student union at Queen's to meet up with Sean and Jamesy. These afternoons would invariably extend into riotous evenings via some brief stops at the University Café for some stodgy food to soak up the alcohol.

Such interludes, though enjoyable at the time, only served to highlight the emptiness of the rest of the long days on the dole. Snatter, especially, was becoming increasingly despondent, which only deepened as winter approached.

'Jesus Christ!' thought Snatter, as he stubbed out another cigarette. 'Have I always been such a miserable bastard?' He got up again and went to the fridge. He wasn't even enjoying having a drink, but he took out another can of beer just in case that situation changed.

'Was I ever bloody happy?' he wondered. 'Was I even happy when the cheque came?'

Snatter and Ding-a-Ling had both been half-heartedly applying for various jobs since signing on the dole, although Ding-a-Ling was by far the more half-hearted of the two. Snatter had once watched in horror as Ding-a-Ling casually put down in his list of hobbies on an application form 'not giving a shit', but the lack of any real opportunities was starting to wear them both down. Then, in December, the cheque came.

Snatter had forgotten all about his claim; it was his uncle, after all, who had pushed him into applying for it, and then it was his uncle who had dealt with any subsequent paperwork. It was a compensation claim from the British government and it was a sizeable amount, sizeable enough for Snatter to generously thank his aunt and uncle for everything they had done for him. "Ach, we didn't do it for the money!" said his uncle, taking the money. He was also able to buy his parents' old house, which he did for no other reason than it just didn't seem right for strangers to be living there, so much had happened to him there. Too much, perhaps.

He then had enough money left over to acquire the lease to a small newsagent's shop in the centre of town, close to a busy bus stop and with excellent potential. On the first day that Snatter took over the shop, he and Ding-a-Ling were both nervous and excited at this new direction their lives had taken. In theory, Ding-a-Ling was Snatter's employee; though, as far as Ding-a-Ling was concerned, he was being paid to hang out all day with his friend.

Initially things went smoothly: the shop thrived and Snatter and Ding-a-Ling enjoyed the busy routine, joking throughout the day and generally being comfortable in each other's company. Eventually, though, it became impossible for Snatter to ignore the fact that his friend was becoming more restless as the routine turned to monotony and, although Snatter loved working in his little shop, he pretended to sympathise.

"Yeah, I know what you mean," he would say. "It's crazy, now that we can actually afford to go out and get pissed whenever we want, we never seem to have the time or else we're too bloody tired!"

"Yeah, seriously, we're going to have to do something; this is driving me up the walls."

They moaned about it to each other for a while until Snatter came to a decision that would have certain repercussions.

"We'll just have to take on someone else," he declared. "Take a bit of the strain off."

"Can you afford to do that?" asked Ding-a-Ling, trying to suppress his interest.

"Yeah, I don't see why not. We seem to be doing OK. What do you reckon?"

"Yeah, fuck it, go for it."

They were both energised by this new project and, after the advertisement was placed in the *Belfast Telegraph*, they constantly discussed what kind of personal attributes they expected to see in their new colleague.

"Seventeen-year-old girl, miniskirt, dubious morals … oh, and a good sense of humour," Ding-a-Ling would suggest, and Snatter would try to match it with an equally childish fantasy. In their minds they had drawn up a rough list of ideal candidates, at the top of which was a seventeen-year-old, miniskirt-wearing girl with dubious morals; and they eagerly awaited the applicants.

Had they taken their list to its obvious conclusion, then hovering around somewhere near the very bottom would have been a six-foot-four skinhead from Sandy Row.

Joseph Anderson was a six-foot-four skinhead from Sandy Row who also happened to be, unforgivably, a Linfield supporter. As soon as he had walked into the shop, Snatter and Ding-a-Ling had not only dismissed him as a suitable contender for the position but had also marked him down as a potential nutcase.

After ten minutes of an increasingly surreal interview, this opinion hadn't really changed, but it had quickly become apparent that they had found a soul mate.

"Call me Joker," said Joker, after being offered the job, and, so pleased were they all at having arrived at such a definite decision, it was decided to close the shop early and to go and have a drink to celebrate and to get to know each other better.

Snatter woke up later that evening on a public bench. In a train station. In Larne.

Larne, a busy port thirty miles from Belfast, was not normally the sort of place where Snatter would expect to wake up.

He was, at first, a little confused. In the background he could hear a strange noise that, in his addled state, he imagined sounded like someone kicking a pig. He had a vague recollection that he might be in Larne and thought, with the typical condescension of a city dweller, that maybe kicking a pig was considered top-flight entertainment around these parts.

"… king eejits?"

As Snatter's senses came more into focus, he was aware of a reddish blur just inches from his face; it appeared to be asking him a question. Also, it was wearing a policeman's cap.

"All right, son? You with these eejits?"

Snatter looked past the ruddy-faced police officer and was able to discover the source of the noise. Ding-a-Ling and Joker were standing, or rather swaying, on the station's platform, each with an arm around the other's shoulders. They seemed to have discovered a mutual love of the Beach Boys' music and were now treating the citizens of Larne to a rousing rendition of *The Sloop John B*, while several bemused police officers looked on.

Snatter couldn't help smiling at the memory. That was the first time he had ever spent the night in a police cell, although it wouldn't be the last.

That first day with Joker set the tone for how things would proceed from then on; it would require only the flimsiest of excuses for the shop to be closed and a drinking session to be instigated. It was after one particularly boisterous occasion, a celebration for Joker being nominated salesman of the month, having sold a Kit-Kat, twenty Regal and a can of Coke in one transaction, that Snatter realised that if things were to carry on like this then he would very soon be bankrupt. He came to a painful conclusion. The next morning he explained the situation to Joker and Ding-a-Ling.

"Look, I hate to say it, but things are looking bad here. I can see myself going out of business unless I do something drastic."

"This sounds ominous," said Joker.

"To be honest, I can't afford to keep either of you on. I really need to cut costs and the best way I can do that is to just run the shop on my own for a while. I'm sorry but -"

"Well, it's about fucking time!" Ding-a-Ling interrupted.

"What?"

"We were wondering how long it was going to take you to wise up," Joker added. "We thought we were going to have to say something ourselves."

"But -"

"Look, don't sweat it," said Ding-a-Ling; "we've

already got something sorted. I mean, we can't stay in this dump forever, now can we?"

"What?"

"Look," said Joker, "we're not fucking stupid." He glanced over at Ding-a-Ling. "Well, I'm not anyway," he continued. "We knew things couldn't go on the way they were; it was just costing too much. Anyway, we've both been offered jobs in that new electrical place in Royal Avenue. Ding-a-Ling's cousin got us in. Money's not bad either; certainly covers the old rent."

Joker and Ding-a-Ling had recently moved into a flat together on the Ormeau Road after Joker's girlfriend had kicked him out for being a 'drunken shit', and they were enjoying living the bachelor life.

"Electrical place?" asked Snatter. "Doing what?"

"Trainee salesmen," Ding-a-Ling replied. "We start next week."

Snatter didn't know what to say; part of him felt disappointed that his friends seemed to be deserting him, but mostly what he felt was overwhelming relief. Everything had reached such a satisfactory conclusion, in fact, that it was decided to close the shop early and go and have a piss-up.

During this session it was reckoned that such a momentous day would need to be recorded in some way for posterity and so Ding-a-Ling proposed that a poem should be composed to commemorate the occasion.

'The Sacking of The Lads' was a rambling and increasingly incoherent epic, pitching Snatter as a villainous landlord who heaps a series of torments and some rather inventive depravities upon the two stalwart heroes of the piece.

Joker and Ding-a-Ling were cast in the same heroic

vein as many other giants of Irish mythology, such as Cuchulainn, the Fianna and Billy Bingham. Snatter gleefully added some of the more colourful accounts of his villainy as the beer flowed and the day rolled off into the fog banks of his memory.

'This isn't helping,' Snatter thought as he drained his beer can. 'Maybe I should go to bed.' He remained in his seat. 'Maybe things were just going too well,' he thought.

After Joker and Ding-a-Ling had left to start their new careers, life for Snatter had settled into a comfortable routine. It wasn't long before the shop began to show a decent profit and, eventually, he was able to employ a woman called Moira to help out. Moira brought such efficient professionalism to the role that Snatter felt slightly embarrassed at the ease with which she was able to dramatically increase his takings. Slowly and quietly, things began to look up for Snatter, as everything now seemed to have been resolved in a very acceptable manner.

Everything, that is, apart from one small matter. Snatter, though, if he was being honest with himself, was looking forward to exploring that small matter with a mixture of trepidation and excitement. And then Rosie happened.

'How the bloody hell did that all come about?' he wondered. 'It all just happened so fast … I mean, what the fuck?'

To Snatter the last few months had been a bit of a blur. Rosie had suddenly burst into his life and had swept him along with her before he really understood what was going on. There was no denying Rosie's incredible beauty, but there was something about the woman that Snatter found genuinely frightening and now, as he sat bewildered in his chair, he was worried. What was he going to do?

'They do say tomorrow's another day,' he told himself. 'Hell, tomorrow is Christmas Eve; all the lads will be together again. The pub-crawl!'

He was cheered by the thought. He would forget about his worries for one day, at least.

Maybe he would even seek some advice. Tone could be pretty level-headed, or maybe Jamesy with his easy-going wisdom, or Bobby, perhaps? Snatter was aware that, even now, he was still relying on his friends, but he didn't care because tomorrow was Christmas Eve. Tomorrow was the pub-crawl. Tomorrow everything would seem so much better.

Tomorrow.

Seven

"No, it doesn't make you look like a fucking gargoyle! Will you stop whingeing?"

Snatter took his hand away from the growing bump on his forehead and accepted a cigarette that Ding-a-Ling was holding out. "Are you sure?" he asked. "It feels bloody huge."

Ding-a-Ling shook his head dismissively as he lit first Snatter's cigarette and then his own. They both took a long draw as they waited for the bus to arrive.

"Saw your da up in the Star the other night," Snatter said. "He was telling me about Sticky Mickey, among other things."

"Yeah? Well it's not something I'm really bothered about." Ding-a-Ling shrugged. "No point in worrying, is there?"

"So what's the deal with this job, then?" Snatter asked.

"Oh, yeah, Joker's uncle got us in," Ding-a-Ling replied. "We start in the New Year."

"Printing firm, isn't it?"

"Yeah, it's not far from the city centre. They're planning a big expansion next year and they're looking for a load of trainees."

"So, what'll you and Joker be doing?"

"Die-cutting, apparently. Whatever the fuck that is. Anyway, I suppose it's about time." Ding-a-Ling seemed a little more thoughtful than usual; in fact, Snatter would almost have said he seemed a bit low.

"What do you mean, 'about time'?"

Ding-a-Ling sighed. "Oh, well, maybe it's time I got

my life sorted out, you know? I just feel like it's been on hold for too long. Time to move on now; you know what I mean?"

Snatter nodded, though he hadn't the slightest idea what Ding-a-Ling was talking about.

"Here's the bus," said Ding-a-Ling, chucking his cigarette butt into the road.

"It's a Shankill bus," moaned Snatter.

"So what?" said Ding-a-Ling. "It's not a problem, is it?"

"No, I suppose not." Snatter was always nervous about getting on a Shankill Road bus at such an obvious Republican bus stop. He worried about who might be watching, taking notes, making plans as the bus took him further into the Loyalist heartland of the Shankill. Today, however, the bus was almost empty.

As Snatter and Ding-a-Ling climbed on board and moved towards the back, Ding-a-Ling spotted someone he knew. A small, greasy-haired man was sitting by himself near the back of the bus. On the seat beside him was a large holdall that appeared to be completely empty.

"All right there, Macker?" Ding-a-Ling asked as he and Snatter pulled themselves into the seat behind. Snatter was always amazed at the number of people that Ding-a-Ling knew. It didn't seem to matter where in the city they went, there would always be someone who Ding-a-Ling would nod to or wave to or stop and chat to. 'He certainly gets about,' Snatter thought to himself.

"Taking your bag for a walk?" Ding-a-Ling asked Macker, nodding to the holdall.

Macker looked all around him in a shifty manner that Snatter thought was a bit over-dramatic, given that the only other people on the bus were an old woman, who was sitting up at the front and who didn't look particularly dangerous, and the driver, who had his hands full. Of course, there was always the possibility that Special Branch was hiding under the seats. 'You can never rule that out,' thought Snatter. He was beginning to feel in a much better mood; his head still hurt a bit, but what mattered most was that it was Christmas Eve and he was on his way to the pub-crawl. He could almost taste the first pint.

"No," replied Macker, and then he began to tap the side of his nose with his forefinger, a gesture so ridiculous that Snatter almost burst out laughing.

"I'm on a wee score," Macker said in little more than a whisper.

"Oh yeah?" Ding-a-Ling asked, suddenly interested. Snatter rolled his eyes and looked out of the window as the bus pulled onto the top of the Shankill Road.

"Aye," said Macker. "I was talking to this guy in town last week; I sort of know him to see, you know? We both drink in the same pubs, you see. Well, anyway, it was late and we were both the worse for wear when he lets me in on this wee secret."

Ding-a-Ling moved a little closer to hear better. Snatter, who was not remotely interested in Macker's 'wee score', was wondering if they had stopped serving cheeseburgers by this time in The Tudor Lounge. He had a horrible feeling that they probably had. Still, he thought, they should be able to grab a bite to eat somewhere in town before they started on the beer.

"And you know where this spare key is?" Ding-a-Ling was asking Macker.

"Oh aye, he told me exactly where to find it, so, as long as I put it back where it was, nobody should be any the wiser," Macker replied.

"And there's really that much gear?"

"Tons of it," said Macker, "straight from the docks, you know? So, what do you say? Are you in?"

Ding-a-Ling rubbed his chin and thought about it. He was certainly tempted. He turned to Snatter, who was still staring out of the window. "What do you reckon, Snatter?"

"What?" Snatter asked, his reverie interrupted. "What do I reckon about what?"

"Macker here knows where we can get a load of free cigarettes, cartons of them, just there for the taking, just off the Shankill."

"Free? What do you mean, free? You mean steal them?"

"No, no, you don't understand," said Macker. "They've already been stolen; you can't steal something twice, now can you? Not just smokes, either; there's booze, clothes, electrical stuff, anything."

If Macker was expecting this appeal to mollify Snatter, then he was disappointed. "Oh, I see," Snatter said, "they've already been stolen? That's OK then. For a minute there I was worried. So we're talking about a safe house, are we?" Macker nodded. "We're talking about a safe house," Snatter continued, "full of stolen goods, just off the Shankill Road, is that right? I wonder why the letters UV, fucking, F have just popped into my head, eh? Now why do you think that would be, eh?"

"Look, it's no sweat," said Ding-a-Ling, suddenly an expert on the whole affair. "It's Christmas Eve, isn't it? Nobody's going to be there on Christmas Eve; isn't that right, Macker?"

"Aye, that's what I've been told." Macker nodded reassuringly.

"Ding-a-Ling, don't do this to me," Snatter implored, his panic rising. "I mean, do not fucking do -"

"What's the problem?" Ding-a-Ling asked, trying to ease Snatter's fears. "It's only a couple of stops away. We jump off, find the house, load up with free cigs and jump back on the next bus. Twenty minutes, tops. Just think of the look on the lads' faces when we start handing out free packets of fags."

Snatter groaned. "Ding-a-Ling, I sell cigarettes for a living."

"I know, and who the fuck can afford those prices? Technically, I'm still on the dole, remember?"

For a brief moment Snatter was tempted to let Ding-a-Ling go off on his own while he stayed on the bus and carried on into town, but he knew he couldn't do that. It wasn't just that he would never forgive himself if anything happened to Ding-a-Ling, but how would he explain to the lads that he'd just let Ding-a-Ling go wandering around the Shankill with nothing but a greasy stranger and an empty bag for company. Of course, he knew that Ding-a-Ling was more than capable of looking after himself, but still he knew he just couldn't let him go. Fuck it.

Ten minutes later the three of them were trying not to look conspicuous as they weaved their way through the maze of streets that clustered around the Shankill Road. He couldn't tell what Ding-a-Ling's or Macker's thoughts were at that moment in time, but Snatter was sure of one thing: he had never felt so far away from his comfort zone in his entire life.

Eight

They shivered as they became acclimatised to the cold; then Tone, Jamesy and Joker strode off in search of the next beer.

"Well, something must have happened," Joker was saying. "Ding-a-Ling was really looking forward to today and Snatter's never bloody late for anything."

"I'm sure they'll turn up," Jamesy said.

"Yeah," Tone agreed. "They're bound to show up at some point in the day."

They walked through the crowds of busy shoppers towards Royal Avenue, and then turned onto the city centre's main thoroughfare for the short walk to Kelly's Cellars. Joker saw them first. A small crowd of young people standing outside the Bank Buildings, smiling and chatting and passing out leaflets; a few at the back were singing carols. There was something about born-again Christians, Joker was thinking, that made them stand out; perhaps it was the strangely sinister exuberance that seemed to flow from them, with their broad smiles and shining eyes. Yeah, that would certainly make them stand out in the centre of Belfast on Christmas Eve, where everyone else looked as if they could cheerfully murder every last person on the planet.

Joker glanced at Tone. "Easy, tiger!" he said.

Tone ignored him. "They're the ones who were hassling Bobby earlier at the City Hall."

"So what?" Joker protested. "That's got nothing to do with us, has it?"

"Well, I just want to hear what they have to say, OK?"

"Bollocks," said Joker. He had been looking forward

to the warm and friendly atmosphere of Kelly's. And the beer, of course; especially the beer. Now it looked as if that pleasure would have to wait a little while longer.

Tone walked up to the little group, with Joker and Jamesy reluctantly following. There was a young man and woman at the front who appeared to be the main point of contact. They were both impeccably dressed and, as Tone had hinted at earlier, so clean they almost sparkled. The young man seemed to have a permanent smile on his face. He appeared pleasant and approachable, and Tone despised him instantly. The woman, in comparison, was a little more subdued, perhaps a bit shy, as she let the man do most of the talking. As she saw the three friends approach, however, she gave them a warm smile.

"Merry Christmas to you, friends," said the man, whose name turned out to be Greg. Tone would have bet money on it being Greg, or Nigel, or Simon, or bloody Samuel.

"Afternoon," said Tone gruffly. "So what is it you're selling here?"

"I'm sorry? Selling? We're not selling anything. We're simply celebrating the birthday of Our Lord, Jesus Christ."

"Born around this time, was he?"

Greg smiled. "Of course, no one can say for certain what the exact date was of Jesus' birth, but the 25th of December is as good as any other day. Remember, we celebrate the birth itself, not the date."

"You're aware of the significance of that particular date, are you?"

"Oh, yes," said Greg, laughing, "it's an old pagan festival, isn't it? Well, it makes sense, I suppose, if you want to spread the word of God then it must be a lot easier to use the existing festivals. It would make for a smoother transition, don't you think?"

Greg was turning out be a little more clued up than the usual idiots that Tone would confront. 'Not that it makes any difference,' Tone thought.

"Can I ask," Greg went on, "if any of you have been born again?"

"Nah." Joker shook his head. "I suggested it once but my ma told me to fuck off." Joker tutted at their blank expressions. 'Way over their heads,' he told himself.

"Of course, you are aware, aren't you, that Jesus Christ died for all of our sins?" Greg went on.

"No he didn't," Tone said.

Greg was stupefied. "I beg your pardon, it's clearly -"

"You Christians don't believe that," Tone argued. "Isn't it true that you believe, and I quote, 'Jesus ascended into heaven to be seated on the right hand of God'?"

"Yeah," said Joker, trying to lighten the mood, "you'd think God could have knocked up a couple of chairs." Everyone ignored him.

"Well, of course," Greg explained. "The fact that Jesus rose from the dead forms the whole basis of Christianity. It shows us that -"

"So, to be more accurate, in other words," Tone interrupted, "you would have to say that Jesus died *temporarily* for our sins, isn't that right?"

"It clearly states in John 3:16 that 'God so loved the world that he gave his only begotten son'."

"Shouldn't that be *lent* his only son? Doesn't have quite the same impact, does it? Not so much of a sacrifice when you really think about it. The all-powerful, all-knowing, all-seeing creator of the entire universe spends a total of three earth days not existing before scuttling off to spend the rest of eternity in paradise. Hardly a big deal at all, now, is it?"

"Yes, but -"

"Anyway, God's *only* son? John clearly hadn't read his scriptures now, had he?"

"What?"

"Genesis 6:2," said Tone. " 'That the sons of God saw the daughters of men that were fair; and they took them wives of all which they chose.' Seems that God had loads of sons, and they were horny buggers too. Don't start quoting your book of fairy stories at me, mate. I've read it, so I know what a pile of crap it really is."

"Well I just -"

"And another thing, why would God choose to be born as a human baby at a time and a place which he knew - he's all-knowing, remember - would lead directly to the slaughter of all those infants? In fact, why bother with anything at all? Even before God created the earth he would have known every detail of how human history would play out, but still he goes ahead with it! He would have known that sending himself down to earth as his own son would achieve nothing more than the creation of more religion and, therefore, more suffering and persecution; but still he goes ahead with it! I'm sorry, but this God of yours only seems to be interested in human misery."

An atmosphere had descended on the scene; the carollers had stopped singing and were listening anxiously to the exchange. The young woman, who was quite pretty in a sterile sort of way, looked worried. They were all used to suffering casual abuse and shouted insults from passers-by, it came with the territory, but there was something more sinister in Tone's measured calm. His quiet assurance seemed to suggest a hint of menace while his tall, bald companion definitely suggested a hint of menace.

Greg was still smiling, though now it seemed a little forced. "You have some interesting points to make," he said, rather condescendingly, Tone thought, "but it's really rather pointless for us, and we are only mortals, remember, to try to make sense of or to even try to comprehend the full majesty of God's eternal plan. I know it can be difficult at times and there are times when we all have our faith tested, but as long as we keep our trust in the Lord Jesus Christ then eventually all shall become clear and we shall have all the answers that we need."

"It's the old get-out clause, isn't it?" Tone sneered. "Whenever the questions get a wee bit too difficult, all you religious types have the same old chestnut to fall back on: 'man cannot know the mind of God' or 'God works in mysterious ways'. Well, that's just the same as closing your eyes and putting your hands over your ears."

"But it's the truth," Greg protested. "How can you be so dismissive of the truth? How can anyone claim to know the mind of God?"

Joker was becoming restless, though he sensed that Tone was only warming up. The young woman shuffled uneasily and stared at the ground.

"But that is exactly what you do claim," Tone insisted. "When you stand here and tell people about God, do you let them know that you are only proffering your own personal opinion and that the actual intentions and desires of God cannot possibly be known by any mere human?"

Greg smiled, even more smugly than before, Tone thought. "God, in his wisdom, has provided us with all the guidelines that we need. If we follow the Holy Scriptures then the path becomes clear," he explained calmly. "God has obviously made those scriptures with our level of understanding in mind; the full intricacies of his design are simply beyond our comprehension."

Tone, to Greg at least, seemed to assume a faintly demonic air. The breeze tugged at his long black overcoat and at the lurid splash of red that was wrapped around his neck. His long black hair became ruffled and the deep darkness of his eyes seemed to become even more piercing. "So, the Bible is a perfectly clear set of guidelines? Is that what you're saying?" Tone asked sweetly.

Greg, however, was not to be trapped so easily. "It's true," he admitted, "there are many ways to interpret the scriptures, perhaps that is the clearest proof of their divinity, but I would say that they are all variations on a common belief. The underlying message of our salvation through the love and sacrifice of Jesus Christ is the fundamental basis of all denominations."

"All *Christian* denominations," Tone corrected him.

"Well, yes, obviously."

Tone, as usual in these circumstances, was becoming angry and, as usual, this annoyed him. Anger, he was perfectly aware, did not get him anywhere; if anything it only served to weaken his arguments. "OK, then why bother with different denominations at all?" he asked as he tried to keep his anger under control. "Are you really saying that one denomination is just as valid as the next? Are you saying that the beliefs of Quakers, of Mormons, of Seventh Day Adventists, of Jehovah's Witnesses, even of Catholics, are all perfectly acceptable in the eyes of God? Of course you're not; if you were then you wouldn't be standing here pushing your own narrow views. In your mind *your* beliefs, and only your beliefs, are solid facts that need to be forced upon everyone else for them to be saved. As you try to convince everyone that your wee Jew on a stick is somehow a third of a God and at the same time just the one God, you offer them a simple choice, don't you? Except, if you examine it, it isn't simple at all, is it? You have the -"

"Come on, Tone, for fuck's sake!" Joker had had enough and was pulling Tone by his arm. "Come on now, leave the nice Christians alone. We have somewhere to be, remember?" Tone let himself be led away, although his anger was just coming to the boil. Jamesy slowly followed.

"Your man said 'shall' a lot; did you notice that?" Joker was saying.

"Closed-minded … bloody myopic … bloody fuckwits," Tone fumed. He angrily threw the end of his scarf around his neck.

"I mean, what sort of bloke says 'shall' all the time? Bit creepy, if you ask me," Joker went on. "Oh yeah, Tone, bloody hell! Jew on a stick? Even I was a bit offended by that."

"Yeah, well, that's understandable," Tone said. "The reason you feel offended, Joker, is because you've been brainwashed from birth to accept, without question, the whole pile of bloody nonsense. It's hard to shake off that sort of conditioning. Isn't that right, Jamesy? … Jamesy?"

Jamesy, however, wasn't listening because Jamesy, to his astonishment, had just fallen in love.

Nine

Everything, to Snatter at least, was taking on a more menacing aspect. The area they were in was becoming more derelict; there was suddenly no one around and more of the houses were either burnt out or simply abandoned. There was an eerie quietness to the place as Macker eventually led them to a little row of houses that was desolate, overgrown and devoid of any signs of life. All of the houses were boarded up to one extent or another, but Macker went to a house in the middle of the row and gave the door a shove. Nothing happened.

"Oh, right," he said to himself and, crouching down, swept away a small pile of rubbish to reveal a large bolt lock. He pulled back the bolt and tried the door again. This time it opened with a creak that almost snapped Snatter's already taut nerves. Just inside the door there was another door, which was padlocked. Macker looked up to see a baton of wood jammed haphazardly above the door; it blended in perfectly with the rest of the desolation but, as Macker reached up, he realised it formed a ledge. He felt around for a bit, then turned around and smiled. He had found the key.

"OK now," he said to Snatter and Ding-a-Ling as they squeezed through the open door, "as far as I know, all the gear is stashed upstairs." He then carefully pushed the first door closed.

They made their way into the house and gingerly climbed the stairs. At the top there was a small landing with three doorways leading off it. The first room they looked in turned out to be the bathroom and beside it was a back bedroom, which had a gaping hole in the wall where a window had once been. Ding-a-Ling walked over and took a look down into the back yard. The door to the yard was long gone and the walls had crumbled in places. Plants were growing wildly all over the place. Ding-a-Ling turned to Snatter. "Reminds me of old Ardoyne," he said. "Remember when we were kids?"

Snatter's nerves were still at breaking point; he could feel his heart pounding in his chest. "Can we just get a bloody move on?" he implored.

"Yeah, OK," said Ding-a-Ling. They both went through the third door to find Macker standing in the middle of the room; he was rubbing his hands. "What did I tell you, lads? What did I tell you?" He grinned.

"Jesus Christ!" Ding-a-Ling exclaimed.

It was just as Macker had described. All around the room there were goods piled as high as the ceiling, mostly cigarettes and cases of spirits, but also video recorders and heaps of clothing.

Macker reached up and took down a case of whiskey. "I think I'll do all my Christmas shopping here," he said, as he opened the case.

"Fuck," said Ding-a-Ling, "we never thought to get a hold of some bags from somewhere."

"Look, we'll just take what we can and then split," Snatter told him. "This place is freaking me out."

"Ah, you worry too much," Ding-a-Ling said as he ripped open a carton of Benson and Hedges. "You always have done."

"Can you see any Regal?" Snatter asked, looking round. 'Be stupid to leave empty handed,' he told himself.

A sudden noise from downstairs made them all freeze. And then a man's voice. "Hey, this fucking door's open!"

"Aye, look, the lock's just lying there on the floor." Another voice.

"Do you think anybody's still here?" A third.

"Listen, you run and get Big Dennis and some of the lads. Tell him to bring a rod!"

They heard footsteps quickly disappear down the street. Snatter stared at Ding-a-Ling, his eyes wide with panic.

"Look!" Ding-a-Ling whispered. "I think there's only two of them; we could rush them."

Snatter felt a sudden urge to strangle his oldest friend. "Have you gone fucking mad?" he demanded. He looked at Macker, who was literally shaking with fear. "Rush them?"

"Seriously, they won't be expecting it. We'll just push past them and away we go. Come on. I'll go first."

Ding-a-Ling ran quickly to the end of the landing; the top of the stairs lay around the corner to his left. Suddenly, with a yell, he launched himself down the stairs. Seconds later he came sprinting back. "Nah, there's fucking loads of them!" he shouted. "Leg it!"

They could hear footsteps rushing up the stairs as Snatter and Macker followed Ding-a-Ling into the back bedroom and, without any hesitation, all three jumped in unison through the hole in the wall and into the back yard. They all landed heavily, but otherwise unhurt. As they scrambled to their feet and bolted into the narrow alleyway beyond, they could hear the shouts behind them. "Quick, round the back!", "Block off the entry!", "Don't let them get away!"

Sheer panic spurred them on to the end of the alley, where Macker took off to the right. "Scatter, lads," he shouted.

Ding-a-Ling and Snatter sprinted in the opposite

direction, which took them past some more derelict houses until they came to a large expanse of waste ground. They paused for breath as they crouched behind a low wall. Ding-a-Ling pointed to a clump of bushes on the far side of the waste ground. "If we could make it to the bushes over there, we could lie low for a bit till things quieten down," he suggested.

Snatter didn't like the look of it. "We're going to be bloody exposed on that waste ground," he pointed out.

"I know! That's why we need to move quickly, before they get here. Come on!"

They both jumped up and ran toward the bushes.

The waste ground they were running across had been used for many years as the location for the local twelfth of July bonfire and was strewn with old and charred pieces of wood. One of these pieces had once belonged to a wooden pallet that was broken and burned to the extent that now all that remained was this last little piece, featuring a long and rusted nail that pointed straight up to the heavy grey sky.

Snatter hit it at full pelt, driving the nail through the sole of his favourite trainer and into the sole of his right foot. There was a tiny moment of shocked silence before he went down in a flurry of expletives.

Ding-a-Ling stopped and turned round. "Stop acting the fucking maggot, Snatter!" he cried. "Come on, we're going to get ... Oh, shit!" He suddenly saw what the problem was. He rushed over and pulled the wood from Snatter's foot. This caused an increase in the volume and intensity of Snatter's swearing as Ding-a-Ling then pulled him onto his one good foot and helped him to hobble the remaining distance to the bushes. They stumbled and pushed their way through the bushes and collapsed, panting, sweating and swearing, onto the ground.

Ten

Kelly's Cellars pub had been there from the beginning of the eighteenth century and it wasn't going anywhere. Hence, when the Victorian architects, over a hundred years later, wanted to build a vibrant, modern city, they had no choice but to build around it. The buildings the architects produced were designed to reflect the fact that Belfast was the beating, industrial heart of nineteenth-century Ireland. The solid, imposing buildings would stand in testament to the city's prosperity and demonstrate how progressive the city had become.

Kelly's was prepared to bide its time. The tall Victorian interlopers that now crowded around it, forcing it into the shade of its own little alley, would eventually be gone. Kelly's, as always, would persevere.

Tone, Joker and Jamesy walked along the alleyway towards the stubborn little bar. As they approached, they could hear the muffled buzz of conversation and laughter, suggesting that Kelly's was busy.

Tone was already feeling his anger fade, Joker was anticipating the cold touch of lager on his lips, while Jamesy wanted to throw up.

"Keep up, Jamesy!" Tone called over his shoulder. "There's a good lad."

This doesn't make sense, Jamesy was telling himself. Love at first sight? That's just nonsense, isn't it? Jamesy had always prided himself on his pragmatism when it came to emotional matters. He had never given much credence to the traditional notion of romantic love. The image of the tragically lovesick, unable to eat or sleep, pining and swooning the days away, had, to Jamesy, always seemed faintly embarrassing. Physical attraction, he would say, can be explained in terms of chemical reactions that are born out of biological necessity. 'Cast a cold eye' begins the epitaph of W B Yeats, and it was a phrase that Jamesy took to heart. There is nothing, he liked to pontificate, that cannot be explained by reason and scrutiny. Even love can be rationalised and broken down into components that show it to be no more mysterious than a bowel movement. Jamesy, needless to say, didn't get a lot of sex.

So what was going on? Why was his stomach churning? Why couldn't he think straight? Yes, the girl had been pretty, he accepted that, but he had seen pretty girls before. He had seen exceptionally beautiful girls before and he knew that he appreciated their beauty in the same way that he could appreciate a sunset. It was a simple matter of aesthetics.

But a sunset had never made him want to vomit. A sunset had never made him feel torn with irrational, joyous despair. For Jamesy, this was something new. The more he tried to 'cast a cold eye' on his feelings, the more he was faced with a conclusion that, to his dismay, seemed inescapable. He was in love. And he hated it.

The indistinct conversational buzz became a low roar as Tone pushed open the door into Kelly's. It looked to be standing room only as Jamesy, still in something of a daze, pushed his way through to the bar. Over to the left, in a far corner, a fiddler and an accordion player were preparing to add to the noise. The smell of a turf fire mingled with the usual smells of beer and tobacco smoke. Tone, who had now calmed down completely, scanned the room. He suddenly spotted something and turned to

Joker. "This way," he said. "Jamesy, we'll be down the back!" he shouted over to the bar, though Jamesy seemed to be in a world of his own. Tone and Joker made their way through the crowd to a table where a young man and woman were hunched in conversation.

"All right there, Ed?" Tone asked the man. "Thought it was you."

Ed, surprised, seemed slightly wary as he looked up. "Tone?" he stammered. "Uh, yeah, how's it going?"

"Oh, not too bad. Here, do you think we could squeeze in? You know Joker, don't you?"

"Hiya, Joker," Ed said. "Uh, I suppose so. Could you move around a wee bit there, love?"

Ed's companion looked to be a little put out, but she pulled her chair closer to the wall, which left some room for a few more chairs to be placed at the table. Ed shifted along the bench that ran along the wall and Tone squeezed in beside him. Joker found an unused chair and pulled it in beside the girl. He turned to her and leered. "Bout ye, love," he said, exaggerating his Belfast accent. Then, with his most salacious grin, he held out his hand.

Tone tutted loudly and kicked Joker under the table. "You'll have to forgive him, I'm afraid," he said. "He's had a blow to the head."

"When?" Joker asked.

"We'll just have to see," Tone replied curtly.

Jamesy appeared carrying three pints and Tone noticed that he seemed a little distracted. As he placed the drinks on the table, Tone was about to say something, but Jamesy turned and disappeared back into the crowd.

"Of course!" exclaimed Ed, slapping the table. "How could I forget? It's the pub-crawl, isn't it?"

"The very same," said Tone, lifting his pint.

At that moment Sean appeared, carrying some plastic carrier bags. "All right there?" he asked. "Ed! How're you doing? Long time no see."

Jamesy came back with two chairs. "All I could find," he said.

"Bobby's at the bar," Sean said as he took a seat.

"Ah, yes," Tone said, turning to Ed. "Two more weary participants in the mind-crushing tedium of existence."

"Ever thought of becoming one of those motivational speakers, Tone?" Sean asked drily. "I reckon you'd be a natural."

As Tone found himself in mid-swig he had to reply visually to Sean, using one of his fingers.

"Seriously!" Sean continued. "I'll bet people would pay a lot of money to be told that their lives are pointless and they should all just fuck off and die."

At his side Joker sensed Ed's companion squirm slightly at this. 'If she's prudish about the language,' he thought to himself with a smile, 'then this should be fun.'

"Just think of the applause," Sean added.

"All joking aside, Sean," Tone replied. "I'll bet that you're absolutely right. Nihilism has become the new apathy, you know. I could clean up."

Bobby arrived from the bar with a pint each for him and Sean. "No fucking seat?" he asked with mock disgust.

Joker was disappointed that there seemed to be no reaction from the girl at his side, then he realised that she was trying hard not to stare at Jamesy. Joker shook his head sadly. 'Junkie's eyes,' he thought.

Tone managed to push up a little, which squashed Ed against the end of the bench. "Cheers, Tone," said Bobby, squeezing in. Joker passed some cigarettes around. "So, is this the full complement for the pub-crawl these days, then?" Ed asked as he struggled to reach the table to retrieve his beer.

"We've got two missing at the minute," Bobby answered. "You know about the pub- crawl, then?"

"I was on the first two," Ed replied proudly. "But then, well, you know," he said, glancing at his girlfriend, "things come up. So who's missing?"

"Snatter and Ding-a-Ling," Tone said.

"Oh, yeah," said Sean. "I spoke to Karen; seems there was a bit of an incident involving our happy wanderers which ended up with Harry helping the police with their enquiries."

"Shit!" said Joker. "What happened?"

"Not too sure. Karen was a bit hysterical, you know, Christmas Eve and all, but it sounds like Snatter and Ding-a-Ling ended up getting the bus."

"So they *are* on their way, then?" Tone asked.

"As far as I could tell."

"Ding-a-Ling … Ding-a-Ling." Ed seemed deep in thought. "Now just what the hell did I hear about Ding-a-Ling?"

"That he's a total wab?" Joker offered.

"No." Ed shook his head. "No, it was something I hadn't heard before. What was it? It was a while ago, not even sure where I heard it from. Oh yeah, wasn't it that Ding-a-Ling got castrated?"

They all turned to look at Ed. "What the fuck are you talking about?" Tone asked him.

"It was probably just one of those rumours," Ed said defensively, "but I'm sure that's what I heard. Not true then?"

"Well, I'm sure that's something that Ding-a-Ling would've mentioned," Sean said. "You know? It's just the sort of thing that might pop up in conversation. I don't know where the hell that rumour came from."

Tone seemed to ponder this, then he smiled to himself. "Perhaps," he declared grandly, "I might be able to shed some light on this grubby little subject." They all looked at him.

"You will remember, I am sure," Tone began, "Ding-a-Ling's excursion to Majorca earlier in the year."

"Yeah, too bloody right," Joker lamented. "I was meant to go as well, but my fucking great auntie died." He took a draw from his cigarette and leant back in contemplation.

"Yes, well that's unfortunate," said Tone, "but to -"

"Bitch," Joker muttered into his pint.

"Yes, I remember," Bobby said. "It was just after we got back from Anfield, wasn't it?"

"Anfield?" Ed looked puzzled.

"Aye," Joker said. "I mean I bloody hate Liverpool, but we all thought we should go and pay our respects, you know? Put down a wreath and all."

"Oh, yeah, of course," said Ed.

"What was the name of your man that Ding-a-Ling went on holiday with then?" Bobby asked.

"Marty," Sean answered. "I think it was Marty who actually organised it."

"Is that Marty from Andytown?" Ed asked.

"Yes," Tone interjected, trying to regain control of the conversation. "Indeed it was Marty who got in touch with Ding-a-Ling with the idea of going on one of those Club 18-30 deals. No doubt he was inspired by the delicate subtlety of the bilingual wordplay that Club18-30 employed on their advertising hoardings at the time."

"That's right!" Sean laughed. "Beaver España, wasn't it?"

"Exactly," said Tone. "Now I seem to recall that when Ding-a-Ling got back he mentioned something about being the victim of some sort of knife attack."

"Oh, yeah," said Bobby, thinking back.

"Rings a bell," Joker agreed.

"Of course, no one took a blind bit of notice, given Ding-a-Ling's rather nebulous relationship with the truth," Tone continued, "but I bumped into Marty up in Renshaw's not too long ago and he told me the whole story." He paused to take a drink and to check that he had everyone's attention. "It turns out that Marty and Ding-a-Ling, whilst partaking of some refreshing beverages, fell into conversation with some like-minded souls from Glasgow who were there to celebrate the impending nuptials of one of their own. Well, as it transpired that they all shared some very similar interests, it was decided that they should pursue those interests together in a vigorous and manly manner." Tone took another drink and lit a cigarette.

"So," said Joker, "in other words, they all got pissed together."

"To put it bluntly, yes," Tone agreed. "Then, some time later, as the group was careering along the town's paseo, one of the Glasgow contingent decided that Marty and Ding-a-Ling just had to have a look at a new pocket-knife that he had recently acquired. Apparently, it took a considerable effort for this rather wobbly character to extricate the knife from the pocket of his shorts and presumably Ding-a-Ling was becoming a little impatient, for this is where the incident occurs. Seeing that the poor man was struggling to then free the knife blade from its housing, the bold Ding-a-Ling leapt to his aid. At some point during the frantic fumbling that ensued, the blade was freed and somehow managed to nick Ding-a-Ling on the finger. Then, with the exaggerated reactions of the inebriated, he jumped backwards, slipped on some local vomit and fell, cracking his head on a public bench."

Tone paused to drain his pint glass and take a draw from his cigarette.

"Where, exactly, are you going with this, Tone?" asked Sean.

"Well, I put it to you," Tone went on, "Ding-a-Ling didn't press the whole knife attack business too much with those who know him well, now, did he?"

"That's true," Joker nodded.

"But Ding-a-Ling has a lot of passing acquaintances all over Belfast, doesn't he? And doesn't Ding-a-Ling have a tendency to over-dramatise situations, to embellish the facts to a certain degree; to, basically, talk a load of old bollocks?" Everyone around the table nodded, recognising Ding-a-Ling from the description.

"So, it's likely, is it not, that a variety of people around town are under the impression that Ding-a-Ling, while on holiday, was the victim of a vicious attack by a knife-wielding maniac, which probably happened as Ding-a-Ling heroically intervened to save a bus load of disabled orphans? With me so far?" Tone took the blank stares to mean yes and carried on. "You're all familiar with Chinese whispers, aren't you? Well, the chances are that the story was passed around and distorted by any number of different people."

"Feel free to arrive at a point any time soon, Tone," Sean interrupted.

Tone held up his hand. "Well, perchance, there were some people," he continued, "more given to drollery, you understand, who simply said that Ding-a-Ling had been stabbed in the Balearics."

"Oh, for fuck's sake!" Sean groaned. Joker and Bobby laughed and Ed smiled uncertainly. Jamesy stared at his pint.

"It's my round isn't it?" Tone said as he stood up. "Ed, you two OK for drinks?"

"Yeah, no problem, Tone; you go ahead."

"Don't get me one either, Tone," Jamesy added. "I seem to be struggling a bit."

Giving Jamesy a quizzical look, Tone turned and forced his way through the crowd to the bar. At the other end of the room a grey-haired lady, who looked to be in her seventies, had acquired a microphone from the musicians and was delivering an enthusiastic rendition of *Santa Claus is Coming to Town*. As she reached the chorus, virtually everyone in the pub joined in. And even Tone, standing at the bar, had to smile.

Joker had been watching Jamesy. "What's up with you, Jamesy? You've a face on you like a slapped arse."

"What?" exclaimed Jamesy, suddenly self-conscious. "Oh, nothing, just thinking, that's all."

"Ah, you don't want to get involved with any of that thinking business; it can only lead to trouble," said Joker with an air of authority. Jamesy smiled weakly. He wasn't accustomed to how he was feeling at that moment and he had decided it would be wise to seek some advice; it made sense, he thought, to consult with someone who had more experience in the, suddenly very confusing, matters of the heart. He had swiftly dismissed the idea of Joker as a possible confidant, for although Joker possessed many admirable qualities, the ability to dispense tactful and sage advice was not, Jamesy feared, one of them. Tone had once referred to Joker as an abstract collection of noises and smells and the fact that Joker had taken this to be a compliment summed up, for Jamesy, Joker's cavalier approach to life.

Jamesy had also discounted Sean and Bobby for, great guys though they were, he had always thought they were a little too self-absorbed to fully appreciate the dilemmas of anyone else. Snatter would have been Jamesy's preferred choice, but as Snatter had, so far, failed to show up, that just left -

Tone appeared at the table with a tray of drinks. "I'd better make this a quick one," he said. "I forgot to get some tobacco for my da when I was in Queen's Arcade, so I have to nip back."

"Mind if I tag along?" asked Jamesy. "I could probably do with some air."

"No problem, Jamesy. Drink up." Tone turned to Sean. "So, where will we meet up?"

Sean shrugged. "I don't think we'll have time for The Morning Star this year; how about White's?"

"Yeah, OK, though we might pop into The Globe for one first, just to see what the crack is."

Tone knocked back his pint in a few gulps and stood up; Jamesy tried as best he could, but still ended up leaving half a pint. He pulled on his coat as he stood and then followed Tone to the door.

"Well, Tone seems in better form from the last time I saw him," Ed remarked to Sean when Jamesy and Tone had gone.

"What do you mean?" Sean asked.

"I saw him a while ago at the top of the New Lodge. We were just standing there, chatting away, when I told him I was on my way to Mass. All of a sudden he calls me a credulous moron and storms off. I thought what the bloody hell was that all about?"

"That," said Sean with a sigh, "is a long story."

Eleven

Bournemouth was showing off. Tone got that impression as he let his old Ford Fiesta coast past the Royal Bath Hotel towards the seafront. It had been a mediocre summer on England's south coast; but now, as September was coming to an end, the weather had decided to make up for lost time. The sun was hanging at just the right angle to skim rays of light across the surface of the sea and let them cascade into the coastal pines and rhododendrons that tumbled down the hillsides to meet the shore. With the sky forming a solid blue background and the impossibly pretty local girls filling in the details, the overall effect was dazzling.

Tone tried not to notice. It had been a long, hot drive from Southampton and he was eager to reach his destination. He was driving to a hotel in West Cliff, where his friend, Douglas, had arranged a meeting with a young playwright named Matthew Patterson. Tone had recently received, from Douglas, a copy of Matthew's manuscript, which told the story of the early struggles of a Christian group that had been founded in Bournemouth in the nineteenth century. It was not a subject that would normally have interested Tone, but it had been written so well and with such gentle humour that Tone could already see a lot of possibilities with it. He thought he could use it for his second-year project.

Since Tone had watched, as a schoolboy, a performance by the Royal Shakespeare Company, his main ambitions had all involved the theatre. He wanted to write for the theatre, he wanted to direct in the theatre, he wanted to thrill and entertain and educate and provoke in the theatre, and so for his university drama project for the year he was planning to direct his first play.

Tone had met Douglas at Southampton University the previous year, a shared passion for drama bringing them together. It had been Douglas' final year and he had already been offered a lucrative position as assistant casting director for a company in London.

"Not going to take it, though," he had told Tone. "Can't see me working for a bunch of poncey twats up in London. Besides, I'd always planned to move back to Bournemouth when I finished here."

He had got a job with the local arts council and was helping to discover and develop new talent. Tone had kept in touch and had let him know that he was going to need an interesting project for the coming year. It looked like Douglas may have found the very thing.

Tone drove past the new conference centre and, as he approached the West Cliff Road, he spotted the sign for the hotel, just up ahead, almost lost in a forest of hotel signs that blanketed the West Cliff. It was hot in the car and Tone was looking forward to a pint of cold lager in the hotel bar. Douglas had actually invited him to afternoon tea, but Tone had simply assumed that 'afternoon tea' was some kind of Dorset euphemism. Douglas, he well knew, was a huge fan of alcohol. Tone had even seen him put beer on his corn flakes one breakfast-time and, sure enough, as he pulled into the hotel car park, Tone could see, through the window, Douglas standing at the bar.

'Afternoon tea,' Tone chuckled to himself. 'Yeah, right!'

"Was that two sugars?"
"Yes, thank you," Tone answered. "Two sugars would be great, thank you very much."

As Matthew went over to a side table to pour the teas, Tone looked at Douglas and raised an inquisitive eyebrow. Douglas pursed his lips and gave a slight shake of his head. 'Just let it go,' was the message Tone received. Matthew returned with three cups of tea and a plate of scones on a tray.

"The hotel was my idea," Matthew explained as he passed around the teas. "I just think they do such wonderful teas here; you really should try the scones, you know, the best in Dorset, I would say."

Tone had taken a liking to Matthew right away; he was a good-looking and well-dressed young man who was open and friendly. He made Tone feel immediately at ease.

Douglas, Tone thought, looked out of place in this dainty little side room; his shock of chaotic red hair and unruly beard betrayed his Scottish ancestry and gave the impression that his head was in the process of exploding. He'd look more at home, Tone thought, on an ancient Scottish battlefield, swinging a claymore and smiting the Sassenachs. As Douglas reached down for his tea, he gripped the delicate handle between his thumb and forefinger and, with his little finger pointing into the air, he raised the cup to his lips. Tone suppressed a smile.

"So, where did the idea for your play come from?" he asked Matthew.

Matthew dabbed at the corner of his mouth with a napkin. "Well," he said, "it's really just my way of spreading the Lord's message. I don't know if you had ever heard of our little community before you read the play?" Tone shook his head.

"No, I'm not surprised." Matthew laughed. "You have heard of Jesus Christ, though?"

"The name rings a bell," said Tone.

"Tone's a bit of a Godless heathen," Douglas pointed out.

"I'm a Catholic."

"Yeah," said Douglas, "that's what I meant."

Matthew laughed again. "My father was the one who gave me the idea," he said. "He has been concerned of late about the dwindling numbers of our little community. So I thought, as I'm studying English at college, I might be able to combine the two and come up with something to help."

"So it's like some sort of recruitment drive, then?" Tone asked.

"I like to think it simply provides information about us in, hopefully, an entertaining way. And, perhaps, it might lead some people to want to know more."

"Well, with your words and my masterful direction, I'd like to think that we can manage that," Tone said, and they all laughed. They carried on talking, working out various details, for another hour or so and then Matthew said he had to go.

Tone and Douglas walked him to the front door and, once they had waved him off, they both turned and bolted to the bar.

"Fuck!" Douglas exclaimed as he handed Tone a cigarette. "I never knew how bloody hard it would be to be on your best behaviour for so long."

Tone had just ordered two pints and now he sat on a stool at the bar and took a puff of his cigarette.

"Yeah, why though?" he asked. "Why were we so bothered about offending him?" Douglas shook his head. "Don't know," he said. "It just wouldn't have seemed right, do you know what I mean?"

"Yeah," said Tone. "He just seemed like such a nice bloke, it would have been like kicking a puppy."

"Exactly, he is a nice guy, isn't he?"

Tone nodded as he took a sip of beer. "Yeah," he said. "I mean, as queer as a bottle of chips, of course, but …"

"No, no, no," Douglas protested. "He can't be, you see; his God doesn't allow it."

"He should get himself a new God, then, shouldn't he?"

"It doesn't work like that with these religious types," Douglas explained. "They tend to be stuck with whatever God their parents give them."

"Spoken like a true cynic!"

"That's me," Douglas said cheerfully. He took a large gulp from his pint and wiped his beard with the back of his hand. "Anyway, what sort of timescale do you have in mind for this?"

"Not sure, exactly. Off the top of my head I'd say a short run in the spring."

"Sounds OK," said Douglas. "I'll scout out some venues."

"Casting?" Tone asked.

"I've a few people in mind," Douglas told him. "Sarah might be a bit of a bitch, though."

Tone nodded. "Yeah, I'd thought that myself. He's written her like a cross between Florence Nightingale and Attila the fucking Hun."

Douglas laughed. "We'll sort something out." He finished his drink. "You're staying at my place tonight, right?"

"If that's still OK."

"Of course," Douglas said as he ordered two more beers. "So, how have you been, Tony? It's been a while."

"Yeah, not too bad," Tone answered. "You know, the usual, settling back into the routine and all."

"Seen Adrian lately?"

"Yeah, I called round the other day; he seems well enough."

"That's good." Douglas took a long drink and turned to Tone. "So, have you any plans for the rest of the day?"

"Well," Tone replied, "after you've bought me dinner I thought we could trawl through the decadent fleshpots of Bournemouth."

And that's what they did.

Tone spent the next few weekends travelling back and forth between Southampton and Bournemouth, meeting with Douglas and Matthew and slowly bringing together the components that would make his directorial debut a success.

One evening, during the week, Tone received a phone call from Matthew. He was ringing to invite Tone to lunch with his family on Saturday. It was to be at their family home in Canford Cliffs. Tone wasn't entirely keen on the idea, but he accepted the invitation and told Matthew that he was looking forward to it. 'At least Douglas will be there as well,' he thought.

"Douglas can't make it, I'm afraid," Matthew informed Tone as he arrived at the house. "Bit of a dodgy tummy I'm afraid. He rang earlier."

'Bastard,' thought Tone. 'Why didn't I think of that?'

Matthew led the way into the house, which was an impressively large, detached building.

"Nice place," Tone commented.

"Thank you," Matthew smiled. "It's been in my mother's family for a long time." There was a stairway straight ahead as they entered the hall and a doorway to the left and one to the right. Matthew opened the door on the right and led Tone in to meet the family.

The introductions, Tone thought, were a little formal. Matthew's father sat in an armchair, while his mother sat on a couch with a younger girl beside her.

"Anthony," Matthew said, "I'd like you to meet my father, Samuel." He gestured to the man in the chair, who gave a polite nod. "My mother, Jessica." Another nod. "And this is my sister, Emily." Emily also nodded, but with a smile.

"Nice to meet you all," Tone said, feeling a little uncomfortable. He continued to feel uncomfortable right up until they all sat down for lunch.

They had to wait for prayers to be said before they could eat. Tone thought they went on for a bit - Samuel even read passages from the Bible - but eventually they could make a start on the soup course.

"Matthew tells me that you are a Roman Catholic," Samuel said to Tone as they ate their soup.

"Not a very good one, I'm afraid," Tone replied with a smile. Samuel shook his head sadly. "So many misguided people," he said, "so, so many." He then continued to eat his soup, leaving Tone feeling a little bewildered. Samuel appeared to be a sombre man. 'Can't imagine him kicking back with a spliff and having a fit of the giggles,' thought Tone.

"You do know that idolatry is a terrible, terrible sin?" Samuel suddenly asked, turning to Tone.

"Aye, well, I've been trying to cut down on that, lately," Tone answered, having been taken by surprise. Samuel continued to stare at him for a few seconds and then turned back to his soup. 'Jesus!' thought Tone.

"Anthony's been having some wonderful ideas about 'The Congregation'," Matthew spoke to ease the awkward silence. "It's all beginning to look very professional; you really must come and take a look some time."

Samuel shifted in his seat. "I'm still not at all sure about this," he said gruffly. "Parading around on the stage seems disrespectful to me."

"Well, that's where Anthony has been so clever," said Matthew, smiling sweetly. "I think that he's given it just the right touch of gravitas; it's all very respectful."

Samuel did not reply. He finished his soup and leaned back in his chair. His wife, Jessica, got up and took his bowl back to the kitchen.

"What do you know of our faith?" Samuel barked suddenly. He was staring intensely at Tone. Tone was, again, taken by surprise. "Well, to be honest, only what I've gathered from the play. It's an interesting story."

"I doubt that the full account of our founding can be conveyed in a single play," Samuel said. "Although I have every faith in Matthew." He paused; then, still staring at Tone, continued. "The Catholic Church has been guilty of dreadful sins throughout history; do you not feel the burden of guilt upon you?"

"Well, like I said, I've never been a very good Catholic. Although, to be fair, the Catholic Church has been trying to improve things over the years. I mean, we're only allowed to sacrifice a baby when there's a full moon nowadays." Tone grinned.

"You make jokes?" Samuel asked incredulously. He kept his gaze on Tone for a few more seconds and then pointedly turned away. Tone shrugged and let his gaze stray over to settle on Emily.

Jessica returned to clear the rest of the bowls and to

prepare for the next course. She was a strong-featured woman, though maybe a little serious. There seemed to be a strange mixture of strength and sorrow in her, which only enhanced her looks. In this, Emily was similar.

"Matthew," Tone said thoughtfully. "What do you think of Emily for Sarah's role?" Emily stared at her bowl and blushed furiously. Her lips were pressed tightly together as she tried to control her expression. Matthew handed his bowl to his mother and took a long look at his sister. "My goodness!" he declared. "I never would have thought of it but, yes, I can see what you mean."

"Emily has her studies," Samuel said firmly.

"Oh, but father," Matthew argued. "It won't take up too much time and she really would suit the role."

Tone could see Samuel's features soften and he reckoned that Matthew probably got his own way a lot in this family. He certainly possessed a persuasive charm. Samuel gave a slight nod. "Very well," he said. "If Emily wants to -"

Emily could hold it no longer and her smile erupted, giving her, Tone thought, a curiously elfin look. He smiled along with her.

Later that afternoon Tone and Matthew took Emily to the Community Hall where they had been rehearsing in order to get a first glance at her potential. She proved to be a natural. Tone and Matthew were both delighted and a problem that had been bothering Tone for a while was resolved. He had found Sarah.

Over the next few weeks Tone watched as Emily's confidence grew. It seemed strange for such a slim and delicate figure to dominate the stage, but Emily had undeniable presence and a real flare for acting. During one rehearsal, Emily gave a performance that was so assured, so filled with passion and so flawless that the rest of the cast simply stood and stared. Tone was stunned.

"What did you think?" Emily asked nervously.

"Oh, it was …" Tone thought it was best to be sparing with his praise, not wanting to place too much pressure on Emily. "It was probably the greatest thing I have ever seen in my entire life," he said. And everyone laughed.

One Sunday Douglas and Tone were invited to attend a gathering of the Dorset Congregation and, having failed to think of a reasonable excuse not to go, they both went along. They had found it to be the most excruciatingly tedious hour and a half of their lives, unaware that Samuel had been watching them intently, taking in every stifled yawn, every roll of the eyes and every mocking smirk; and, in Samuel's mind, each gesture became magnified tenfold.

"What did you think? Did you enjoy it?" Matthew and Emily were both excited.

"Wonderful," Tone lied. "Very moving."

"Yes," Douglas agreed. "I found it very humbling."

To return the favour or to retaliate, as Douglas put it, Tone and Douglas persuaded Emily and Matthew to accompany them on a night out in Bournemouth. The night-life in the town was suitably lively as they visited the various bars and clubs such as The Vaults, The Third Side and Midnight Express. They met Teds reliving the fifties, Mods reliving the sixties and punks reliving two weeks in the summer of 1976. They saw peroxide blondes, Mohicans and dreadlocks. They met New Romantics, Futurists, Hippies, Poseurs and grunting skinheads. Technobillies, Psychobillies and Oriental Rockabillies.

They even met the 'Clash girl', a local celebrity who had run away from school to follow The Clash around the country.

Matthew and Emily dropped off Tone and Douglas on their way home. "What did you think?" Tone asked. "Did you have a good time?"

"Oh, yes, yes," they assured him. "Absolutely!" But alone, on the drive back home, they were in agreement: Bournemouth was overflowing with sinners.

William Makehurst and his wife Sarah had founded the little denomination of The Dorset Congregation in Bournemouth towards the end of the nineteenth century. They were part of a growing number of Christians who believed that the doctrines of the mainstream Church of England were becoming diluted and vague. It was felt that a more defined set of guidelines for what it meant to be a Christian was needed. Everyone, of course, had differing opinions on what those guidelines should be and lots of opposing little faiths were springing up around the country.

William and Sarah believed strongly in God's direct influence on earth; they could see his will everywhere and in everything. Therefore, when, as a result of a riding accident, Sarah lost the use of her legs, their faith allowed them to accept it as part of God's plan and their evangelical mission continued with as much fervour as before. They became a recognisable and popular couple as they preached around the south coast.

It was when Sarah's parents became involved, however, that the official doctrine of the new church would become fully galvanised. They came to see William and Sarah to let them know of a wonderful new physician who had started practising in Salisbury.

"His healing powers have been described as miraculous," Sarah's mother had gushed.

"Yes, I feel we should pursue every course available to us in aiding your recovery, Sarah," her father had said. "You will let us take you now, won't you?"

And so, despite William's misgivings, Sarah travelled with her parents to Salisbury where the miracle physician examined her. The physician told her he was confident that a simple operation to her spine would restore the power to her legs and there should be no complications. He was wrong and William never saw his wife alive again. Through his grief, William realised he had been given an unmistakeable message from heaven. 'Do not dare to oppose my design,' God was telling him and the foundational doctrine was laid for The First Church of The Dorset Congregation where, it would be decreed, the will of God was never to be challenged.

Samuel had spent the day in his study, which faced onto the drive at the front of the house. He knew the history of his faith intimately and he firmly believed in William's interpretation; it was only through prayer that God could be swayed for, although God's will was everything and absolute, it was possible for interventions to be made, through the Saviour, Jesus Christ, and only with the power of prayer.

Samuel had been reading the Holy Scriptures for most of the day, absorbing the moving passages of the Gospels, immersing himself in the beauty of God's plan and of God's justice. "And the Lord said, Simon, Simon, behold, Satan hath desired to have you, that he may sift you as wheat." Samuel could feel the words of Luke seep into his soul. "But I prayed for thee, that thy faith fail not." God was speaking to Samuel and, as Samuel opened himself to the divine revelation, the conclusion he arrived at was unmistakeable. Anthony, Samuel was now convinced, had been sent by Satan.

He stood and watched through the window as Anthony's car pulled up and Anthony, Matthew and Emily got out. He watched as Matthew shook Anthony warmly by the hand and then walked, smiling, towards the house. He watched as Emily smiled into those dark eyes, before rushing forward to jump up and plant a tiny kiss on Anthony's cheek. Blushing, she then turned and ran after her brother. Anthony waved after them as he climbed back into his car and drove off. Samuel watched him go and he felt his grip tighten on the leather-bound Bible. He knew with certainty what Satan was trying to do to his family and, as he heard his children's laughter out in the hall, Samuel got down on his knees and prayed to God.

"Belfast?" Emily asked. Tone thought she looked a little crestfallen, but then dismissed it as he nodded with a smile. "For how long?"

"Oh, it's just till after Christmas," Tone told her. "I'll be seeing my folks and, also, there happens to be a pub-crawl with my name on it."

The pub-crawl that year was memorable for many reasons: Tone met Joker for the first time and, later, a friend that Sean had met at Queen's, Bobby, became attached to the group. Everyone was in high spirits. Tone especially, it was noted, was in good form. He joked and laughed throughout the long day and at the end, as everyone staggered home, the feeling was unanimous. It had been a fine pub-crawl.

Tone finally had to admit to himself the reason for his feelings of euphoria; it was blatantly obvious anyway. He could not get Emily out of his head. He thought about her constantly and, as such, he was constantly smiling. The Christmas and New Year celebrations came and went and still he pictured her elf-like smile, her infectious laughter and her touching, wide-eyed innocence. 'You're wasting your bloody time,' he told himself. 'An innocent, God-fearing wee girl like that? And what are you? A jumped-up scruff from the slums of Belfast, that's what. Dream on, son. Dream on.' And he did.

By the time he settled into his seat in the coach at Stranraer for the long, overnight trip down through Scotland and England, Tone was already filling his head with silly fantasies. Of glittering opening nights where everyone would be enchanted by the beautiful pixie at his side, or of a far-flung beach at dusk where they would stroll and Tone would point something out and make a witty remark and Emily would laugh and tease and run a little ahead, and above and behind them both an ebbing sun would splash the sky with scarlet.

'Jesus!' thought Tone as he turned over, trying to get comfortable. 'How gay am I?'

Emily had not been feeling well for a while now. It was an unfamiliar, frightening and wonderful sickness that would see her hit peaks of joy and troughs of despair in equal measure. She had never been in love before and she was finding it all a bit intimidating. Just thinking of Anthony would make her pause to catch her breath as she felt her heart race.

Her father had dismissed Anthony as having no faith and this had worried her for a while. At first she had fretted over Anthony's immortal soul, but slowly she decided that, as a good person, Anthony would eventually find room in his life for the Lord. She was aware that she was thinking less and less about the Lord as other thoughts and feelings became all-consuming, but she couldn't help it. She was in love.

And Anthony *was* a good man, despite what her father said; she was sure of it. Then one day in mid-January she found out just what kind of man Anthony really was.

Tone phoned Matthew to tell him that he wouldn't be able to come to Bournemouth at the weekend due to some serious car trouble.

"Then I'll come over to you," Matthew had insisted. "I've done those rewrites we discussed and I'd like your opinion on them."

"No problem," said Tone as he looked around the house that he shared with three other students. "I'll give you the address of a coffee shop we can meet at."

Emily had insisted on tagging along and they set off for Southampton on Saturday morning with Emily struggling to contain her excitement. She had never revealed her feelings for Anthony: she was afraid of what his reaction would be; but just to spend some time in his company was enough for her.

The coffee shop was situated on The Avenue, not far from The Common, and Tone was already there when they arrived.

"We can get lunch here," he told them, surprised and delighted to see Emily. "It's a pretty decent menu."

It did, indeed, turn out to be a pretty decent menu and they had an enjoyable lunch, discussing various aspects of the play. After lunch, Matthew declared that he wanted to visit the city centre. "There's a shop that stocks rare books that I'd like to investigate," he said, then he laughed as he saw the look on Emily's face. "Don't worry," he told her. "You don't have to come. I can meet you back here, if Anthony doesn't mind, that is."

"Not at all." Tone shrugged casually. He resisted the urge to punch the air.

"I should only be about an hour," Matthew told them as he got up. "I'll see you both later." And he left.

Tone and Emily smiled shyly at each other and, at first, their conversation was a little stilted. It was their first time alone together and they were both feeling awkward and unsure of themselves. Soon, however, they began to open up and it wasn't long before they were laughing and feeling more relaxed in each other's company. Emily, especially, was feeling a warm and simple contentment as she gazed across the table at Tone. He was telling her about his studies and about his elaborate plans for the future, when suddenly Emily heard, behind her, the door to the coffee shop open and someone enter.

Tone glanced over Emily's shoulder and said loudly, with a sneer in his voice. "Look at that bloody spastic!"

Curious, Emily turned around and was almost physically sick with shock and embarrassment. A woman had just entered. She was pushing a wheelchair in which was a young boy, his body contorted and misshapen, his hands held like claws against his chest. The woman had heard Anthony's remark and was staring at him. Emily felt frozen in her seat and time seemed to slow; she could not believe that this was happening. With a rising feeling of panic, she sensed Anthony get up from his seat and walk towards the newcomers. She stared helplessly as he stopped in front of the wheelchair and glowered down at the boy.

"So, where the hell have *you* been, you wee bugger?" Tone asked the boy as he knelt to face him. He was patient as the boy, trying to keep a smile off his face, twitched and stammered a reply. "Far too busy for the likes of you, Normo!"

"Oh, is that right?" Tone began; he glanced up at the woman. "Hiya, Margaret, how's it going?"

"I heard you'd moved to Bournemouth, Tony," Margaret said. "Can't remember who told me that."

"No, it's just something I'm working on. I have to spend a lot of time down there." Tone turned back to the boy. "Right now, matey boy," he said, "you're well overdue an ass-kicking. I hope you've been practising."

"He's never off that little Spectrum thing you got him, Tony," Margaret said. "It's given him a new lease of life; isn't that right, Adrian?"

"So you must be getting pretty good, then?" Tone asked.

"No time for chess," Adrian said. "Programming now."

"What?" Tone cried. "You're writing your own programs? I don't believe you?"

"It's true," Margaret said with a laugh; "he's becoming a real whizz-kid."

"I'm impressed," Tone said. "Are you going to sit down?" he asked Margaret.

"No, Tony," she replied. "We're going to The Common. We just came in to get some sandwiches and drinks."

"Well, pick what you want and I'll get it," Tone said, reaching for his wallet.

"Don't be silly, Tony," Margaret argued.

"Look, I don't want to have to get violent with you, but -" Tone began, and Margaret laughed. "Oh, go on then, you daft sod!"

After Margaret and Adrian had left, Tone sat back at the table, facing Emily. "That was Adrian," he said. "A wee mate of mine. His ma's a cleaner at the halls of ... What are you grinning at?"

"Nothing," Emily replied, her heart soaring. "Nothing at all."

Twelve

Snatter had taken off his shoe and sock and was staring at the little circular hole in the sole of his foot. "That's going to go septic, isn't it?" he said. "I mean, who knows what was on that nail."

Ding-a-Ling was lying on his stomach, peering through a small gap in the branches. "I can't see anybody," he said, "but I can still hear some people shouting. I think we might have upset them."

"Some people can be so touchy," Snatter said. "Any idea what happened to Macker?"

"No, but fuck, did you see him go?" Ding-a-Ling answered. "He took off like two men and a wee lad. Never would have thought he'd have it in him." Ding-a-Ling crawled back to crouch beside Snatter. "I don't like the sound of that Big Dennis bloke," he said. "Sounds like a right laugh."

"Shit, it's starting to go purple!" Snatter moaned.

"What? Oh, will you stop whining about your bloody foot."

"Well, excuse me, but it happens to be extremely bloody painful."

"I'm sure you'll live," Ding-a-Ling reassured him. "We need to figure what we're going to do here."

"Why don't we wait till Big Dennis gets here," Snatter replied sulkily. "We could always ask *him*."

"Ha, bloody, ha," Ding-a-Ling said. "Anyway, maybe the 'Big' is used ironically."

"Yes, I'm sure you're right," Snatter told him. "I'm sure Big Dennis will turn out to be a one-legged midget with a passion for musical theatre. Yeah, I'd forgotten that's one of the things the UVF is known for, isn't it?

Paramilitary violence, racketeering and a playful sense of irony; that's right, isn't it? I mean -"

"Look, we don't even know if it *is* the UVF." Ding-a-Ling had had enough of Snatter's complaining.

"That's a good point, actually," Snatter conceded. "It could be the UDA. Well, if that's the case, then we're fucking laughing, aren't we? Or maybe it's the Salvation Army with a controversial new fundraising initiative, or the Boy Scouts, or the Little Sisters of fucking Mercy!"

"You know something, Snatter?" Ding-a-Ling snapped. "You've had a real shit attitude all day; from the minute we picked you up you've been in a real mood. Just what the fuck is the problem?"

Snatter was momentarily speechless. "Nothing," he mumbled. He started to pull on his bloodied sock. "There's nothing wrong," he went on, as he gently pulled on his trainer and began to tie the lace. "It's just that it's Christmas Eve, for fuck's sake! I should be sitting in a warm bar with a cold beer, but instead I'm bruised and bleeding and stuck under a bloody bush on the Shankill Road with the UVF or whoever on one side and this … this … Actually, what *is* this?"

Ding-a-Ling pulled aside some undergrowth to reveal a heavily corroded section of corrugated iron.

"It looks like … Shit, Snatter, it's the peace line! We're right at the fucking peace line."

"So?" asked Snatter.

"So, it's got to be the Falls Road on the other side, hasn't it? We just have to get to the other side and we're home free; we can jump in a black taxi and we'll be in the town in no time."

"I could do with calling at the hospital," Snatter said. "Get this foot looked at."

"What about the pub-crawl?"

"What about fucking blood poisoning?"

"Oh, for fuck's sake," said Ding-a-Ling. "I'll buy you some TCP."

"TCP? Isn't that throat medicine?"

"Oh, it's good for everything, don't worry: throats, feet, elbows, anything."

"Doesn't matter anyway," said Snatter. "I mean, this iron is rusted to fuck and all, but it still looks solid enough to me."

Ding-a-Ling did not reply. He was staring at the peace line and, as his gaze moved slowly upwards, Snatter suddenly realised what he was doing. He was looking for hand and foot holds.

"You must be joking, Ding-a-Ling; we're not climbing a fucking peace line."

"Why not?" Ding-a-Ling asked. "We've climbed harder stuff than this in our time, haven't we?"

"We were a lot fitter then, remember; there's been a lot of beer and fags since."

"Oh, it's mostly about technique, and look, this hedge thing nearly reaches to the top, so we'll be hidden most of the way up, just in case anybody's watching."

"Still," Snatter argued, "climbing a peace line? It just isn't done, is it?"

"Well, have you got any better ideas?"

Snatter had to admit that he hadn't. The fact was that if they tried to negotiate the maze of narrow streets to try to reach the relative safety of the main road, they would almost certainly be spotted and caught. They had stumbled across, and therefore compromised, what appeared to be a major criminal operation. It was also obvious that the sort of people involved would not require much of a reason to put a bullet in the back of their heads. 'Fuck, they'd do it for fun,' Snatter thought. "All right," he sighed, as he finally conceded. "Let's go."

Thirteen

It was a warm and sunny day at the beginning of May as Tone sat on a hillside above Poole harbour and gazed out to sea. In his hand was a half-bottle of vodka from which he would absent-mindedly take an occasional swig. It was the day of Emily's funeral, but he had decided early on that he wouldn't be going. He was sure he wouldn't be welcome anyway.

He watched, in the distance, the gulls hover and swoop around the chalk stacks of Old Harry's rocks and imagined he could hear their cries carried on the spring breeze.

It was a blood vessel, apparently. A blood vessel, Tone had learnt, that had expanded in Emily's brain. That was the medical reason; the cold and clinical, factual reason why Emily was dead, but Tone knew better. Tone knew that it was no aneurysm that had ended Emily's life. He was convinced she had been killed - murdered - by her own family.

They had been window-shopping in Bournemouth when Emily began to complain of a headache. She was smiling as she informed Tone. It wasn't a big problem: she just didn't feel that she could do much more walking and thought it would be better if she could go home and get some rest. As Tone walked her back to the car, he asked her if she wanted him to pick up some painkillers, but she declined.

"I do get these headaches from time to time," she told him, "but they usually go away on their own."

Tone drove her home, walked with her to the front lounge and helped her to lie down on the sofa. Jessica, Emily's mother, came into the room and immediately went to her daughter's side. She barely gave Tone a glance, which didn't surprise him; he had become used to being treated with a detached coolness lately from both of Emily's parents. After speaking briefly to Emily, Jessica then hurried out of the room and came back with a blanket that she draped over her daughter and tucked beneath her as if Emily were a small child. Once Jessica was satisfied that Emily was comfortable she stood and, facing Tone, gave a curt nod. Tone almost laughed aloud as he realised he was being dismissed. 'Fine,' he thought with amusement. 'Your presence is no longer required.' He turned and called to Emily on his way to the door. "I'll call later to see how you're getting on. Hope you feel better soon." Emily smiled and waved her goodbyes and Tone was gone.

He phoned Emily that evening from Douglas' house. She seemed a lot better. "Are you still up for driving to the Purbecks tomorrow?" Tone asked her.

"I think so," Emily replied. "What time are you calling round at? Eleven, wasn't it?"

"Yeah, I'll see you then. I'm just going out with Douglas for a few drinks tonight so I'll speak to you tomorrow."

That night Douglas and Tone found a reasonably quiet bar and settled in for a few beers and a chat.

"All ready for the opening night, then?" Douglas asked.

"As ready as we'll ever be," Tone replied. "It's looking bloody good, if I do say so myself."

Douglas laughed. "I think you're right. That dress rehearsal last week was impressive. Emily's a real star in the making, isn't she?"

"Yeah." Tone smiled. "I certainly think so."

"You two seem to be getting very cosy. Any gossip I should know about?"

"Not really; she's way out of my league, don't you think?"

Douglas threw his head back and laughed. "Are you serious? I used to think you had a bit of sense, Tony, but, trust me on this, you are totally fucking blind."

"What the hell are you talking about?"

"Oh, nothing," Douglas roared. "Nothing at all."

The next day Tone and Emily strolled along the clifftops of England's Jurassic coast. There was a strong wind coming off the sea and Emily clung tightly to Tone's arm. It felt natural, he thought, to have Emily so close, to feel her body pressed against him. "I think I can feel some spots of rain," Tone said. "We should probably start heading back to the car."

Emily looked out to sea; the waves were beginning to crash more vigorously onto the shore, the spray occasionally obscuring Durdle Door, which was off to their left. The sky above had darkened suddenly and Emily instinctively pulled a little closer to Tone. "I think there might be a storm coming," she said.

"Yeah, we'd better go." It was a long walk back to the car and, at first, Tone thought they would make it in time. The raindrops, however, soon became bigger and heavier as the storm rushed off the sea and raged around them. Tone searched for some shelter, but the landscape seemed bleak and empty. Not even a bloody tree, he thought. They struggled on towards the car: the wind tore at them while the rain was incessant and torrential. Tone noticed a large rock up ahead that was soaring at an angle out of the ground and he pulled Emily towards it. Breathless and drenched, they huddled beneath the rock, which loomed overhead and gave them some protection from the deluge. Tone looked into Emily's face and was surprised to see her eyes wide with excitement. She was grinning wildly as she threw her arms around Tone's neck and pulled him to her. Her lips were pressed to his ear but still, with the wind howling around them, he almost didn't hear it.

"I love you."

"What?" Tone cried as he pulled back to stare into Emily's eyes. All of a sudden she looked frightened and confused; she blushed and tried to look away.

"I … I … nothing … I just -"

"No, don't!" Tone shouted to be heard above the storm. "Don't do that! I feel the same, Emily. I feel the same. I love you!"

She stared at him and Tone could see the confusion in her eyes flicker and die and there, beneath an overhanging rock battered by a channel storm and with the rain disguising two sets of tears, they kissed.

Back at university, during the week, Tone was finding it difficult to concentrate. He had tried a few times to call Emily on the phone, but Matthew had answered and told him that Emily wasn't feeling well. Her headaches had been getting worse.

"Has she seen a doctor?" Tone asked.

"No, Anthony," Matthew told him, "but with God's will I'm sure that she will be fine. Don't worry, we are all praying for her."

Tone wasn't reassured and he began counting the seconds until Friday afternoon when he could finally get back down to Bournemouth. He arrived in the evening and drove straight round to see Emily. Samuel met him at the door and glared at him with undisguised hostility. He looked as if he was going to deny Tone entrance to the house, but he eventually moved to one side and allowed

Tone to step past him. Matthew met Tone in the hall and shook his hand. "Emily's in her room," he said. "In bed. I'm afraid there hasn't been much change."

"Can I see her?" Tone asked.

"Absolutely not," Samuel said as he closed the front door and walked past Tone into the lounge. Matthew smiled awkwardly; Tone walked past him and stood in the lounge doorway.

"Just for a minute," he said to Samuel. "I need … I just want to see how she is. Please."

Samuel said nothing; he didn't even look in Tone's direction. Matthew stepped into the lounge. "What harm can it do, father?" he pleaded. "Anthony has been a very good friend to Emily. I'm sure it would cheer her up if she could see him."

Samuel seemed to consider it and then finally relented. He nodded almost imperceptibly. "Just for one minute, remember," he said. "Emily tires easily."

Matthew led Tone up the stairs to Emily's bedroom. Tone was surprised at the simple austerity of the room, the only decoration being a wooden crucifix attached to the wall above the bed. Emily's mother was kneeling by the bedside when they walked in. She gave them the briefest of glances before lowering her head again and going back to her prayers.

"There is always at least one person praying by Emily's side," Matthew whispered to Tone in order to assure him that everything was being done that needed to be done. Tone, however, didn't hear him. He was transfixed by the figure on the bed.

Emily was barely recognisable. She was even more pale than usual, a ghostly white with a sheen of perspiration covering her face. Her eyes were open only slightly as if she were drifting off to sleep.

"Emily." Tone's voice was nothing more than a croak. Emily's eyelids flickered and she turned her head a little to the side; a thin, almost skeletal, smile appeared on her lips. Tone didn't hesitate: he turned and fled from the room. He took the stairs two at a time and clattered noisily into the hall, skidding across the polished floor. He reached a little table, upon which stood a telephone. Tone snatched the receiver and began to dial, nine … nine … the receiver was torn from his hand and was replaced, with a bang, in its cradle.

"Just what do you think you're doing?" Samuel was furious. Tone stared at him in disbelief.

"I'm calling for an ambulance, what do you think I'm doing? Emily needs to get to a hospital as soon as possible; don't you realise that? Why the hell haven't you called for a doctor or done *something*, at least?"

"Everything possible is being done for Emily." Samuel could barely conceal his anger. "She needs to be here, at home, with her family."

"But surely a doctor -"

"This has got nothing to do with doctors!" Samuel almost shouted. "It is in God's hands!"

"Listen," said Tone, "I know you must be very upset, but Emily really needs to get to a hospital. This is serious."

"It is not up to us," Samuel said coldly. "It is up to God. All we can do is pray for her in order to let God come to his own decision."

Tone was beginning to feel uneasy. "I understand that you are a man of faith, but I don't see -"

"Faith?" Samuel hissed. "Just what do you know about faith, Irishman? I know whose orders you follow, don't you think that I don't!"

"What?" Tone was thrown into confusion. "What the hell -"

"God has answered my prayers; you have been thwarted, Irishman! Don't you see? And now God has seen fit to test my faith and, trust me, that faith will not be found wanting."

"Look!" Tone was almost starting to panic. "Beliefs are all well and good, but this is real life, this is your daughter's life, this is -"

"Would you dare defy God?" Samuel demanded. "Do you really believe that these doctors, who are nothing more than men, can stand in defiance of the will of God? They are nothing but specks; you are nothing but a speck, and you have failed, Irishman."

Tone was astonished to see a smirk of satisfaction appear briefly on Samuel's face before he stared into Tone's eyes and said in a cold voice. "Leave this house, Irishman. You are not welcome here. You will never be welcome here again. Do you understand?"

"But -"

"Anthony." Matthew had appeared at the bottom of the stairs. "I think you'd better go. There's nothing you can do here." Matthew gently led Tone to the front door. "It's all right," he said. "I'll let you know if there's any news."

Tone left the house in a daze but, as he drove round to Douglas' house, he still didn't feel too concerned. He felt that, eventually, even Samuel would concede that Emily had to go to a hospital. Surely he couldn't sit and watch his daughter suffer for much longer.

Tone was back in his house in Southampton when Matthew rang. He told Tone that there was nothing that anyone could have done. God had decided to take Emily to him and she now dwelt with Him in eternal happiness.

There was no need to be sad, Matthew had said; that isn't what Emily would have wanted. Tone put down the phone, walked into the kitchen and vomited into the sink.

As he sat and watched the few white clouds floating over the harbour, Tone could feel the demons that were fuelling his grief and his anger begin to tug at him. They were tugging him away from here, tugging him out of the sunlight and into the dark places where his nightmares could feed. They dragged him into the drug-cosy warmth of the bedsits of London, the dripping, stygian alleyways of Manchester, of Liverpool, of Glasgow. Eventually, his rage subsiding, they dragged him home. To Belfast.

Fourteen

"Jesus, Mary and Saint Joseph, can you believe them two fucking eejits? I swear to God, when I get a hold of our fucking Gary, I'll … I'm really sorry, Rosie, love, if I'd only known earlier what them two fucking half-wits were up to; I mean, going off fucking alcoholicking all over the town when you're waiting there like a stupid dickhead, I just don't know. I mean, I'm fucking scundered for you, Rosie love." Karen had been round at her mother's house all day, supposedly to help out with the preparations for Christmas Day. In reality, though, she had spent the day moaning about how unfair it was that Harry, once again, had ended up in police custody. While doing so she had also managed to consume several very large vodkas, which was why Harry was now driving her car.

Harry was not in a good mood. When he had been released from the police barracks in town he had waited in the queue for a black taxi to take him back to Ardoyne. This hadn't bothered him too much as he was planning to go home, get something to eat and then head round to The League for a few Christmas drinks with his mates. He reckoned he deserved a few drinks after the day that he had had.

On arriving home, he realised that Karen must have gone to her parents' house and he had set off to find her. He had just wanted to let her know that he was back and what his plans were for the rest of the day. As he pushed open the gate into his in-laws' front garden, he could hear Karen's voice from inside the house, thirty feet away, which made him hesitate. He could be fairly certain that Karen wasn't upset about his brush with the law earlier, as she normally took that in her stride, but she was ranting about something and experience had taught him that it was best not to get involved. Harry, however, was not a man to shirk his responsibilities and, with a deep sigh, he strode up to the house and pushed open the front door. Karen was standing by the fireplace. Her friend Rosie McCann, Harry was surprised to see, was sitting on the sofa beside Karen's mother.

"Harry! Thank God!" Karen's mother exclaimed. "Thank God you're here!"

"Why?" asked Harry. "What's happening?"

"Will you take your bloody wife back to her own house? She's been doing my head in all day! Not you, Rosie, love; it's lovely to see you again."

Karen ignored her mother and turned to her husband. "Aye, Harry," she began, "just wait till you hear what -"

"Tell you what," said Karen's mother, "why don't you all head round to your own house, tell Harry all about it, Karen, and I'll see you all later." She got up and managed to bundle Karen, Harry and Rosie out the front door. "Good bloody riddance," she muttered when they were gone, and she went off to finish preparing her soup vegetables for the next day.

As Harry accompanied the two girls back to his own house, he could sadly see remainder of his Christmas Eve slip away. Once they got back home he started preparing some food for the three of them while he listened to their story.

Rosie, once she had realised that Seamus was not going to show up, had gone to find Karen to see if she knew where he might have gone. She had eventually found Karen at her mother's house and explained that she really needed to find Seamus. Karen, seeing how upset Rosie was, had told her not to worry.

"We'll find the fucking two of them," she had said. "I'll get Harry to drive us into town. He won't be long, he's only with the Peelers." She had then embarked on the rambling rant - on what a couple of useless bastards Gary and Seamus were - which Harry had interrupted.

So now, instead of drinking with his mates round the club, Harry found himself stone cold sober, chauffeuring a couple of hysterical, semi-pissed women around the town. He wasn't in a very good mood at all.

"So what exactly is the plan here?" he asked Karen.

"Well, I think they only go to certain pubs," she replied, "so if we split up - Harry, you take some pubs, and me and Rosie will take some - we should find them in no time. We'll meet back at the car. Is that OK, Rosie, love?"

Harry watched Rosie nod in his rear view mirror and thought, not for the first time, what a good-looking woman she was; though the obvious anger in her face gave her a slightly mean look.

Harry also thought he could see something other than anger in her eyes. Harry was familiar with the look of fear, he saw it quite frequently, and he could be pretty sure he was looking at it now.

Fifteen

"So it's love, is it?" Tone asked the back of Jamesy's head as they walked to their table. The Globe was situated down a narrow alleyway, or 'entry' as it's known in Belfast. It was a family pub and was crowded with weary parents taking a break from the frantic last-minute shopping. Children, fuelled by sugary drinks and Christmas, ran between the tables, shrieking with excitement. Tone and Jamesy weaved their way through it all until they reached an empty table. They set down their drinks and settled into the chairs.

"Well, I would have to say yes. I mean, I do seem to be exhibiting all the traditional symptoms."

"So, what's the plan?"

"That's the problem," Jamesy said. "I'm just not sure what I should do."

"Yeah, it's a tricky one," Tone agreed, "what with her severe mental problems and all."

Jamesy sat back in his chair and sighed. "I don't have a big problem with religion, Tone. She can believe whatever she wants. I meant that I'm not sure what sort of move I should make, you know? I'm not exactly experienced at this sort of thing." At that moment Tone spotted Joker coming through the door; he raised his arm and Joker nodded in acknowledgement before heading to the bar. Tone turned back to Jamesy. "I suppose it depends on how far gone she is," he said.

"What do you mean?"

"Well, if the brainwashing has really taken hold, then I'd say you've got no hope. She's probably too obsessed with Jesus to even give you a second glance."

"No, I don't think she'd be like that, would she? She seemed normal enough to me."

"Aye, they all do, Jamesy," Tone said wisely.

Joker arrived with a pint in his hand. "They're still fucking nattering away back in Kelly's there." He took a seat. "So what's happening then?"

"Jamesy's in love," Tone said as he handed Joker a cigarette and lit one for himself.

Joker nodded. "That wee Christian girl?"

Jamesy was amazed. "How did you -"

Joker held up his hand to interrupt. "My perspicacity is often underestimated," he said. Tone and Jamesy stared at him. "I mean, well … you know." Joker was suddenly flustered. "Well, fuck, I'd ride her."

Tone sighed. "Joker, I know you want to stay in touch with your roots, but do you not think you can go too far? I mean, you're back in the fucking Stone Age at the minute."

"It's people like you, Tone, trying to scramble into the middle classes, that forget one thing: you can take the boy out of the slums, but you can't take -"

"Excuse me!" Jamesy interrupted. "I thought we were talking about me for a change."

"Oh, aye, sorry, Jamesy," Joker said. "What are you going to do then?"

"I'm getting a pram for Christmas." They looked down to see a young girl of about eight or nine holding a doll. She was staring at Jamesy.

"That's brilliant," said Jamesy. "I bet you can't wait."

"Are you going to put your wee doll in it?" Joker asked her. She turned and looked at him as if he were some kind of simpleton.

"She's too old for a pram," she informed him. "She's nearly seven."

"Yeah, Joker, you spo!" Tone laughed. "He's a tube,

isn't he, love? Thick as champ, he is." The little girl giggled and ran off.

"Well, she's going to make some poor bastard's life a misery one day," Joker grumbled.

"Anyway, what about this woman of Jamesy's?" Tone said. "I'm trying to picture what she looked like. I didn't really take much notice of her."

"Did you not see her smile?" Jamesy asked in disbelief. "I mean, bloody hell, you could melt icebergs with a smile like that."

"Uhm, Jamesy?" Joker seemed concerned. "I think you're starting to go a wee bit gay there."

"As much as it appals me," Tone added, "I have to agree with *Homo erectus* here. You're the dry academic type, remember? Such outbursts of lyricism just don't suit you. Anyway, what about arse-face, needs-his-teeth-kicked-in, Greg?"

"Don't you think Greg looked like Fred from *Scooby-Doo*?" Joker asked.

"Yes, thank you!" Tone exclaimed. "That was bugging me; yes, that's exactly what he looked like."

"But getting back to me again," said Jamesy. "What's your point?"

"Well, they might be an item: they certainly looked the happy couple."

"I don't know. I didn't really get that impression. Don't suppose it matters anyway," Jamesy said miserably, "it looked like they'd gone when we passed."

"I saw them on my way here," Joker told him, before taking a long drink of beer. Jamesy stared at him expectantly. "Well?" he asked.

"Looked like they were setting up round by White's. Loads of sinners round there."

"Right, that's it," Jamesy said decisively. "I'm going to go for it."

"Good man, yourself!" Joker raised his glass. "Go for what?"

"Yeah, that's the point," Jamesy said, suddenly dejected. "I'm not very good at this sort of thing. I'm open to suggestions."

"I'm your man, Jamesy," Joker told him. "You can rely on me. What you do, right? You walk up to her, dead confident like, look into her eyes, maybe a wee bit of a smile, and just say to her, 'All right there, love? Any chance of a wee feel?'"

Jamesy turned to Tone. "Any ideas, Tone?"

"I don't know, Jamesy," Tone said. "I mean you just dismissed Joker's advice out of hand."

"Seriously," Jamesy pleaded.

"All right," Tone said, finally relenting, "here's what you do. First thing, get some mints or something to take the smell of beer off your breath. Then just go up to her and make out that you want to say sorry. Say something like, 'I want to apologise for my friend's behaviour earlier. It wasn't very nice, was it? It's just that he tends to value logic and reason over made-up, supernatural bullshit, the infantile mythology of a desert tribe from the fucking Bronze -"

"Yes, yes, I get the gist," Jamesy broke in. "Then what?"

"Well," Tone continued, "Delaney's is round there isn't it? Just tell her you want to buy her a coffee to make up for my antics. Be persuasive: don't ask her, just tell her. Insist, if you have to. Once you're sitting down with her over a cup of coffee then, I'm sorry, Jamesy, but you'll just have to rely on your own winning charm."

"Yeah," said Joker, scratching his chin, "I suppose that could work too."

Jamesy thought for a second. "That's not bad, Tone. That's not bad at all." He stood up. "Bugger it! I'm going to do it. Wish me luck."

"Yeah, go for it. All the best, mate," said Tone.

"A legend like you, Jamesy, doesn't need luck," Joker added.

"Right, well, I suppose I'll see you in White's afterwards. Hopefully I'll have a bit of a smile on my face." Jamesy steeled himself and headed for the door, pausing only to have his head blown off by a six-year-old with a ray gun.

"Think he's got a chance?" Joker asked when Jamesy had gone.

With a sigh, Tone looked over at Joker. "Is the Pope Japanese?"

Sixteen

Rosie McCann possessed a beauty that was inspiring and terrifying in equal measure. Her hazel eyes were flecked with gold, while her full, dark hair shone like a frame of ebony around her pale, unblemished complexion. She was undeniably beautiful, but it was a harsh beauty, a beauty that seemed unforgiving, an angry beauty, a beauty that had never been allowed to achieve its full flowering. The sullen bitterness in those stunning eyes bore witness to the fact that Rosie McCann's young life, so far, had not been easy.

Rosie was almost seven-years-old on the morning her world had ended. She had been excited about her upcoming birthday and, as it was also the summer holidays, her life could not have been much better. She was a happy child and she had much to be happy for. She had an older sister, Ellie, who she worshipped, and a younger brother, Jack, who she teased. Her parents loved their children and each other. Her mother, Shauna, worked part-time at the local boys' primary school, which meant she had plenty of time to spend with her kids.

'Never lie and never steal,' was Shauna's mantra that she taught to her children. She would repeat it to them often. 'Never lie and never steal,' it became their little slogan. Shauna's happiness was often infectious; there would be days when her children would laugh along with her as she would suddenly break into a song and drag her daughters up to dance with her around the room. There were few clouds in the sky of Rosie's early childhood.

And then the soldiers came.

It was a summer's dawn that promised a beautiful day with the sky already a pale blue. Rosie woke to see two soldiers drag her father past her bedroom door and down the stairs. She wasn't sure what had shocked her the most: the fact that he was just in his underwear or the unrecognisable mask of terror on his face. She never remembered hearing her mother's screams.

Martin McCann was a quiet, hard-working man who lived for his family. He made a good living at the nearby bus depot, keeping the bus engines in working order, and nothing gave him more pleasure than the joy he saw in his children's eyes when he could spend a little money to give them some small treat. He considered himself a lucky man in many ways; he had a job that he enjoyed, he had no real money worries and he had a family that he adored. He had watched in genuine dismay as Northern Ireland began to tear itself apart, and had determined to do the best that he could to shield his family from the worst of the violence. Northern Ireland's troubles were nothing to do with him and he wanted no part of them. There was nothing he could do, however, when Northern Ireland's troubles came to kick down his front door and drag him out of bed.

Internment was the British Army's attempt to, once and for all, destroy the growing threat of the provisional IRA. The idea was simple. At the same time, all across Northern Ireland, the army would swoop down on the homes of suspected Republican activists and take them off to holding centres, where they could be held indefinitely. For this idea to be effective, it was necessary to maintain absolute secrecy in the period leading up to its implementation, and so the only people who were aware of the plan were the British Prime Minister and selected members of his Cabinet, a few senior figures in Whitehall, the army top brass and, filtering down through the ranks, those who were to be involved in the actual raids. And, unfortunately for the British, the leadership of the provisional IRA.

The lack of secrecy, though, was not the only problem with the plan; there was also the fact that the intelligence the army was acting on happened to be hopelessly out of date. One example of this was the case of Michael 'Big Mick' McCain. Big Mick had fought against the Free State forces during the civil war that had followed the partition of Ireland and had remained a staunch and vocal Republican for the rest of his life. His views, inevitably, meant that he had come to the attention of the Northern Ireland security forces and, unknown to him, his name and address were noted and he was placed on a list of 'Known Republicans'.

Big Mick died at his Ardoyne home at the age of eighty-four; he had no family and his death was unexceptional. No one, certainly, thought to note the fact on his security file, and so, even in death, Big Mick was a 'Known Republican'.

The young McCann family moved into Big Mick's house with great excitement. It was their first proper home and Martin McCann could not conceal his pride. A real family home, where he and his wife could watch their three young children grow, was the final fulfilment of his modest dreams. He had no idea, of course, that it would be that very home that would bring his dreams to an end.

Had there been a trial, then the mistake would, more than likely, have come to light. The beauty of internment, though, was that the whole uncertain business of trials was simply removed from the process. To be a suspect was a good enough reason for you to be incarcerated; or, as a rebel song of the time pointed out, 'being Irish means you're guilty'.

Martin McCann, as far as the British Army was concerned, was indistinguishable from Michael McCain, and so Martin was taken to an army base and then transferred to a custom-built concentration camp on the outskirts of Belfast where the British Army could try out all of its latest torture techniques.

One small, poignant moment occurred when Martin was being taken from his home. A photograph on the wall at the top of the stairs caught the eye of the young officer who was supervising the operation; it was a black and white picture of a group of young men smiling for the camera. They had their arms around each other's shoulders and they were dressed in British Army uniforms. It was dated May 1944.

Martin McCann had always been proud of that photograph. "Oh, aye," he would boast to visitors, "that was taken just before my da and his mates went and got tore into the Nazis over in France."

The young officer turned away and caught a brief glimpse of a pink nightdress, a mess of black hair and Rosie's haunted eyes. Eyes flecked with gold and shining with tears.

The McCann family struggled to recover from the shock. Shauna tried everything she could to find out what was going on but, as families from all over Northern Ireland were going through the same thing, there didn't seem to be anyone who could help. As the days and weeks wore on with no word, Shauna realised that she was going to have to find more work, just to put some food on the table. She managed to find a variety of part-time jobs that brought in just enough to keep the family ticking over. The neighbours did what they could to help: they would look after the kids and help with any washing or cooking that Shauna couldn't manage, but still Shauna felt that the everyday struggle was becoming harder to bear.

It took three years before the system had finished with Martin McCann and he was allowed to return home. Shauna and the children were overjoyed, but it was soon apparent that the years away had taken their toll on the mind of Martin McCann. Before he was taken by the army, Martin had been tolerant and easy-going. When he returned, however, he was prone to sudden and violent outbursts. He would fly into a rage for the smallest of reasons and he now seemed incapable of holding down a job. The children learned to avoid the father they had once idolised; then, one day, Rosie came home from school and heard a strange noise coming from the kitchen. She took a tentative peek through the open door and saw her father lying, curled up on his side on the kitchen floor, wailing, as if in torment, through floods of tears.

"That's not my da in there," Rosie told herself as she slipped quietly from the house. "Not any more it's not." And she went to find a shoulder to cry on.

Martin McCann was committed to Belfast's main hospital for the treatment of mental illness, suffering from severe depression, and the McCann family's troubles continued. The children soon found themselves being teased and bullied by the other children of the area. To have a father held captive by the British was a badge of honour, but to have a father who had gone insane was seen as a weakness, a taint on the whole family.

Shauna was rarely at home as she struggled with several jobs, trying to ease the financial pressures of raising three children on her own. Her visits to see Martin became less frequent, mainly due to time constraints, but also because she found the visits heartbreaking. He barely acknowledged her presence.

Although Shauna tried to keep things at home as normal as possible for the sake of her children, it became increasingly difficult to disguise a growing sense of hopelessness as despair threatened to overwhelm her. The children, Rosie especially, would find refuge from the other children's taunts and the uncertainty at home in children's television programmes. Saturday morning, in particular, became a favourite time to hide away from their crumbling world.

Eventually, Shauna had to admit to herself that the current situation simply couldn't last. Whatever money she earned just went to pay off debts and still it wasn't enough. There were times, she knew, when her children would go to bed hungry and the fact they never complained just made her weep all the more. In desperation, she turned to her brother, Mark, for help.

They had never been very close. He had moved to Derry, years before, with his new wife and any subsequent contact had been sporadic. Shauna knew that Mark's wife had left him when it became apparent the marriage would remain childless and, as far as she knew, he still lived alone.

He seemed pleased to hear from her when she phoned and he listened carefully as she poured out her problems. After several more phone calls, back and forth, it was finally decided that Shauna and the children should move to Derry to live with him. Shauna hated to leave the home she had come to love, but she knew she had no choice. One thing that worried her was how the children would react, but when she told them they seemed to be fine with the idea: they even told her it would be an adventure. This came as a huge relief to her, but what she didn't know was that Rosie cried herself to sleep every night until they left.

At first it was fine. Mark said he was glad to have some company for a change; he'd been lonely since his wife left. He was making a reasonable living working at a nearby bakery, so Shauna did not feel under so much pressure to earn money. She managed to get work at a large textile factory and was able, to some extent, to choose her own hours. Rosie and Ellie started at the local girls' secondary school and Jack settled into the boys' school, which was a little further away. Shauna would work the early shift in order to pick up Jack after school, while Mark, who worked nights, took the kids to school in the mornings. Life settled down into a comfortable, if unexciting, routine. At school Ellie excelled while Rosie, although considered to be bright, never seemed to be out of trouble. Shauna was constantly being called to the school to discuss Rosie's attitude. "We know she has the ability," Shauna would be told, "but she just can't seem to settle."

Such worries, however, were mere niggles compared to the financial troubles that Shauna had previously faced and, in general, life went on without much drama. Ellie completed school with decent grades in her 'A' levels and went to Coleraine to study nursing; Jack was planning to leave school at sixteen in order to become an apprentice mechanic at a local garage; while Rosie, to Shauna's surprise, did well in her 'O' levels and decided to stay in school until she was eighteen. 'She's finally settling down,' Shauna told herself with relief.

Rosie had been a source of concern for Shauna ever since they had moved to Derry. Shauna knew that Rosie had become withdrawn after her father had been taken away, but it seemed to worsen after they had left Belfast, with Rosie becoming moody and quick-tempered.

Perhaps now she was over that, Shauna hoped. She hoped because she was feeling weary; she didn't feel that she could face any more disruptions in her life. She wanted to see her children grow up and embark on lives of their own; only then, she felt, would she be able to take it easy. She was definitely feeling more tired than usual and often found it hard to catch her breath. She looked forward to the day when, her work all done, she could sit down, put her feet up and not have a care in the world.

Then the IRA intervened.

Where the rumour had started, no one knew, but it was soon common knowledge. The bakery that Mark worked for was secretly supplying bread to the British Army bases in Derry, which, to the IRA, meant collaboration with the enemy. The bakery was subsequently firebombed and Mark found himself out of work. With the whole country in recession, Derry was hit particularly hard and Mark struggled to find another job that paid as well as he had been used to. As the household debts began to mount, Shauna agreed to work longer hours at the textile factory to help out and this meant that they could just about meet their financial commitments. The strain on Shauna, however, was becoming apparent. Her once lively face had aged dramatically and her eyes were dull and lifeless; she could find no joy any more, even in her children, as life became a treadmill of work and bills. It was with an overwhelming sense of despair and exhaustion that Shauna finally gave up. One early morning, as she walked home from a night shift, Shauna slumped to the pavement, her heart no longer pumping; her worries were over. Her work, at last, all done.

A lot of tears were shed at Shauna's funeral. Ellie, her heart broken, sobbed relentlessly. Jack tried hard to keep his emotions in check but, as his mother's coffin was lowered into the ground, big tears rolled down his cheeks and he had to wipe them away. Even Mark wept openly for the sister he had come to admire; it was only Rosie who didn't cry. She was saddened, of course, and shocked and upset; but, more than anything else, Rosie felt betrayed.

Rosie's anger at life erupted at school and eventually she was expelled. She no longer seemed to care about anything. Mark watched helplessly as she grabbed some clothes and left home to move in with a boy she had met. They lived on dole money and spent most of their time drinking, taking drugs and arguing. It took a year before they were both sober for long enough to split up and Rosie moved into a house, paid for by the dole, with some friends, and her partying continued. Ellie, Jack and Mark had all tried to get her to see sense, but it was only when Ellie moved to Belfast to work as a nurse that Rosie agreed to come and live with her. And so, finally, Rosie returned to Ardoyne.

Ellie had tried to find out what had happened to their father, but all she was able to discover was that there had been an arson attack on the hospital a few years before and many of the long-term patients had been transferred to specialist facilities in England. During the upheaval, a lot of the hospital records were either lost or destroyed, and no one was able to ascertain what had happened to Martin McCann.

"He can't have just disappeared," Ellie said to Rosie. "He's bound to turn up somewhere." Rosie pretended to sympathise, but as far as she was concerned she had lost her father when she was six and that was the end of it.

One of the first things that Rosie did when she arrived in Ardoyne was to track down her best friend from primary school, Karen Lingfield.

"It's Hegarty these days," Karen told her, clearly overjoyed to see her old friend. "Jesus! Would you look at you! You're fucking gorgeous! Come in, come in and tell me fucking everything."

Rosie told Karen all that had happened since she had left for Derry. Karen cried when she heard about Shauna and shook her head when she heard how Rosie had gone spinning off the rails. "I'm not fucking surprised, Rosie, love; what you've had to put up with." Rosie told her Jack was doing well for himself back in Derry. "Got himself a girl now, I hear," she said.

"And Ellie's a nurse now?" Karen asked. "You know, I think I can remember, even when she was a kid, she'd go on about being a nurse."

"Yes." Rosie smiled. "It's all she's ever wanted to do."

"And she did it. Well, fucking good for her."

"And what about you? Married and all?"

"Aye," Karen said with a sigh. "He's a fucking nuisance, but he's my fucking nuisance, if you know what I mean?"

Rosie laughed. "So what's been the gossip in Ardoyne?"

"Oh, the usual, for fuck's sake." Karen went on to tell Rosie all the gossip about the people she would remember from childhood. "And our Gary, he's living up the Ormeau Road now."

"Oh, really?"

"Aye, he lost his job a couple of months ago, so the dole's paying for his flat. He's living with this mad skinhead, Joseph. He's a geg, like, but he's fucking mad. The two of them are."

"Gary's on the dole then?"

"Aye, but he seems happy enough. Life of fucking Riley, if you ask me. He still knocks about with Seamus and Sean; you remember them, don't you?" Rosie nodded. "Aye, well, Sean is still at university, something to do with engineering. I don't really see much of him, like; he lives up by Queen's these days. Seamus, though? He moved into his ma and da's old house. Bought it outright, I heard. He owns his own shop in the town, or leases it, or whatever, and is doing very well for himself." Rosie raised an eyebrow. "He's lovely, Seamus: very polite, always says hello whenever I see him. Our Gary says he's on his way to being a millionaire."

"Is that right?" asked Rosie. And her sights were set.

"Seamus? It *is* Seamus, isn't it? You probably don't remember me but -"

"Rosie! Rosie McCann! Of course I remember you. I heard you were back in the district. How are you doing?"

"Oh, not too bad, you know? I'm staying with Ellie; you remember my big sister, don't you?"

"Course I do, and wee Jack as well. How are they doing?"

"They're doing great. Jack's still in Derry, doing well for himself. So, what about you? What have you been up to?"

"Oh, this and that; you know how it is."

"Here, you must come out for a drink sometime; we can both catch up on all the gossip."

"Yeah, that sounds good."

"I'll hold you to it, now."

"OK, I'll look forward to it."

And now Rosie would wake in the night, sobbing in disbelief at the bitch she had become. But it wouldn't last. She would shake it off and wipe her eyes, hardening her feelings. 'Never lie and never steal? Isn't that what you used to tell us?' she would ask her dead mother. 'Well, remember, I had to watch you work yourself to death. Where did your empty slogan ever get you, eh? A miserable life and an early grave? Well, I've got my own slogan now, 'No child of mine will ever starve'.'

'And what about love?' a tiny whisper would echo in the depths of her soul.

'Well,' she would coldly reply. 'Fuck love.'

Seventeen

Tone leaned forward to light Joker's cigarette, then put a light to his own. They puffed away in quiet contentment, enjoying the atmosphere.

"What'll we do then, Tone?" Joker said at last. "Finish these and head on?"

"Might as well," Tone replied. "Jamesy's probably in White's already. Drowning his sorrows."

"Oh, you never know, you miserable old bastard. Young love and all that crap."

Tone shrugged. "I hear you got a job," he said.

"Yeah, me and Ding-a-Ling," Joker told him. "Can't fucking wait, to be honest with you. I'm bored shitless on the dole. It's some printing firm my uncle works for; should be a good laugh. We start in the New Year."

"Ding-a-Ling was saying you've been having a bit of trouble with some hoods," Tone said. "What happened?"

"Aye, for fuck's sake! It was a couple of weeks ago. Ding-a-Ling's da was over at the flat and he'd left his car outside." Joker stubbed out his cigarette. "Anyway, Ding-a-Ling had to nip out to the shop and he caught a couple of wee bastards trying to break into his da's car. He chased them off and gave one of them a boot up the arse. We just thought that would be the end of it, but a couple of days later me and Ding-a-Ling got jumped by a crowd down at the back of the BBC. They were just kids, like; teenagers, you know? We slapped them about a bit and told them to fuck off, but there was one wee fucking slobber that I shoved and he tripped and fell." Joker paused to take a drink. "Broke his fucking arm, apparently, but he still got up and backed away, still giving it all this." He opened and closed his hand to mimic a mouth. "Shouting something about his brother-in-law and how me and Ding-a-Ling would be got."

"His brother-in-law?"

"Well, it turns out his sister is married to some bloke who's meant to be some sort of top hood. All the hoods around the Lower Ormeau answer to him. He reckons that even the paramilitaries can't touch him. Michael McClelland? You heard of him?" Tone shook his head.

"He's known as Sticky Mickey; heard of him now?"

"No." Tone laughed. "Sticky Mickey? Is he covered in jam or something?"

Joker smiled. "Something to do with sticky fingers, I suppose. Anyway, he's meant to be after me and Ding-a-Ling for breaking his brother-in-law's arm. Haven't heard anything for a while though."

"I'm sure it'll all blow over; these things usually do."

"Hope so." Joker took a drink. "Look who it is."

Sean and Bobby had just come in; they spotted Tone and Joker and came over. "Where's Jamesy?" Bobby asked. "Bogs?"

"No," said Tone, "he had to nip out. He'll catch up with us in White's."

Sean sat down and eyed up the drinks on the table. "You're nearly finished," he observed. "Are we going to move on then, or what?"

"I'm easy," Tone said. "I don't mind staying for another one here."

"Yeah, fuck it," said Bobby. "While we're here we may as well." He went off to the bar and Joker followed to give him a hand.

"So, guess who's been looking in jeweller's shop windows," Sean said to Tone.

"What?" Tone stammered. "What did you say?"

"Bobby! Apparently he's been looking at engagement rings." Sean decided to ignore the unmistakeable flash of panic he saw in Tone's eyes. "He seems to have it all planned out."

Tone lit a cigarette. "Yeah? Well, Bobby's the type, you know?" He had regained his composure. "He's probably already allocated an appropriate amount of time for an engagement and an exact date for the wedding. Have you ever met his girl?"

"Yeah, once," said Sean. "So has Jamesy."

"What's she like?"

Sean shrugged. "OK, I suppose. Do you want to know Jamesy's verdict?"

"Yeah, go on."

"He said she seems nice and she suits Bobby."

"Aye, that sounds like Jamesy. Mr fucking controversial; he doesn't give a shit, does he, that lad? Doesn't care whose feelings he tramples all over. Just comes right out with whatever's on his mind and bugger the consequences."

Sean laughed. "It'll happen to us all sooner or later. Getting into a serious relationship, I mean. Bobby seems to think it'll mean the end of the pub-crawl. What do you reckon?"

"He's got a point. What sort of woman is going to let her bloke go out on the rip with his mates on Christmas Eve?"

Bobby and Joker came back from the bar, arguing. "Marine Boy was not fucking gay!" Bobby protested. "He had a girlfriend."

"What? You mean that fish thing?"

"She was a bloody mermaid!"

"Oh, right!" Joker scoffed. "Isn't that the perfect girlfriend for a gay bloke? A woman with no genitals?"

"Fuck off!" was Bobby's deft riposte. "Anyway, what are you? Some sort of homophobe?"

"No, I'm just saying that Captain Scarlet would knock Marine Boy's bollocks in."

"Oh, you can be so bloody childish, Joker, you know that?" Bobby said as they both sat down.

"So, you're thinking of settling down, Bobby?" Tone asked. Bobby nodded as he accepted a cigarette from Joker. "Yeah, as I told Sean, I think it's the next step."

"That's a bit of a regimented way to look at life, isn't it? What date have you got your funeral booked in for, Bobby? I'll stick it in my diary."

"What the fuck's wrong with having plans?" Bobby protested. "I just like to know where I stand, that's all."

"Oh, I'm only messing you," Tone said. "I agree with you, it's more than likely going to happen to us all at some point, so it makes sense to prepare for it."

"You won't catch me getting married," Joker asserted.

"Yeah, well," Tone said, "you're the last of your species, aren't you? So you don't really have much choice."

"Hey, Bobby," said Sean, "you're not actually talking about getting married next year, are you?"

"Fuck, no!"

"It's just that there's been some talk about Snatter getting hitched pretty soon and I was wondering if this is going to turn out to be the last pub-crawl. I mean, if the -"

"You wash your fucking mouth out, Sean," Joker snapped. "And would you all stop talking about fucking marriage. Nobody's getting married. Marriage is for homos and that's all there is to it."

"As usual, Joker makes a concise and eloquent point," Tone said. "All this talk of marriage is getting a bit depressing; this is the pub-crawl, remember?"

"We could discuss the political situation," Joker said with a smile. "That always gets a laugh." Sean and Bobby groaned.

"Actually, that's not as stupid as Joker made it sound," Tone said. "Do you remember those two Dutch guys from last year? They wanted to know the history behind the Troubles?"

They all nodded. "Well," Tone continued, "they concluded, fairly enough, I suppose, that Northern Ireland was created because you Prods didn't want to live in a country that would effectively be ruled by the Catholic Church, right?" He directed this to Joker and Bobby.

"Yeah, so?" Bobby asked. "What's your point?"

"No, I'm not making a point; I'm just curious, that's all. I understand the whole Catholic Church thing, and I'm with you on that one, but there's a growing movement in the South that wants to see more of a separation between church and state. Obviously, there's a long way to go before a total separation, but what if, at some point in the future, the Irish people manage to free themselves from the stranglehold of the Church?" Sean rolled his eyes. "What if the Irish Republic was completely secular, with the Catholic Church having no more influence than any other faith? I was just wondering if a united Ireland would be any more acceptable from a Protestant point of view if it was a non-religious Ireland."

"Hang on," Bobby said. "You've always insisted that the divisions in Northern Ireland were first and foremost political; you've always tried to downplay any religious aspect."

Tone shrugged. "It's impossible to ignore the religious side of it. Put it this way, if all traces of religion were removed from the entire British Isles, then would you feel more of a connection with the rest of the people that you share an island with or with the people on the British mainland."

"It's a cultural thing as well," Joker said.

"Yeah, but isn't that tied to religion?" Tone asked.

"Not necessarily. It may have been at the beginning, but I think it's become more tribal."

"In what way?" Sean joined in.

"Well, how do you feel when you see a Union Jack?" Joker asked him. "Offence? Disgust? Hatred?"

"Pretty much, yeah."

"Well that's a conditioning thing, isn't it? And on the Unionist side we feel the same when we see an Irish tricolour. That's got nothing to do with religion, has it? It's tribal colours."

"Like football supporters, you mean?" Tone suggested.

Joker thought about it. "In a way, yeah, but it's on a different scale. In Northern Ireland it's been institutionalised, and yeah, religion has played a big part in it, but I think it's become a lot more than that."

"So, Unionism has become more of a cultural identity thing?" Sean asked. "You see yourselves more as British than Irish?"

"That's being over-simplistic," Bobby said.

"Yes, but, essentially, you can never envisage a united Ireland, can you? Under any circumstances?"

"I see myself as working class," Joker said. "That matters more to me than any king or queen or any fucking nationality."

"That's a different issue," Tone told him, "and something that you may need therapy for."

"No, seriously, Tone. You, Sean, Jamesy and Ding-a-Ling and Snatter are all from working class ghettoes, right?"

"Well, I wouldn't say that we -"

"And so are me and Bobby, right?"

"Hey!" said Bobby.

"Oh, for fuck's sake, wise up, Bobby. The Shore Road? All I'm saying is that I feel I have more in common with you Taigs than I ever had with the pricks I went to school with."

"That's very touching," Tone said, "but, to be honest, there's hardly anybody that would have anything in common with the pricks you went to school with. Anyway, what the hell was I talking about?"

"Don't ask me," Joker told him. "I wasn't listening. I just couldn't concentrate, you see? My mind was distracted by the bizarre properties of this glass. It's such an unusual aspect that I don't think -"

"OK, OK, I'll get the fucking round in!" Tone stood up. "Sean? Any chance of a hand?"

"No problem, Tone."

While Sean and Tone were at the bar, the old Slade song, *Merry Xmas, Everybody*, came on the sound system and someone behind the bar decided to turn up the volume. The entire room erupted. The little kids running around between the tables all began to dance, which seemed to involve them jumping up and down a lot. All the grown-ups joined in: they got to their feet and began to bop around to the music. It was Christmas, after all. Everyone was laughing; Tone could see Bobby standing on his chair, waving his arms in the air; Joker was jiving with the little girl who had been so condescending to him earlier. The crowd around the bar had forgotten about their drinks and were dancing and swaying en masse; even Sean was joining in. Tone, unable to wipe the smile off his face, shook his head, turned to the bar and ordered another round.

A little while later, Tone watched the glasses around the table gradually empty. It was turning out to be a much less-flowing pub-crawl than previous years, he realised, as they hung around for longer in each bar, constantly expecting Snatter and Ding-a-Ling to arrive. He knew it was a pointless tactic, of course. Snatter and Ding-a-Ling could just as easily be waiting for them in the next bar, and so he made the suggestion that they should move on.

"We're normally in White's about this time," he said, "so maybe they're already there."

"Yeah, you're right," said Sean. "We're meeting Jamesy there, aren't we? Where has he been, anyway? He can't have been shopping all this bloody time, can he?"

"He's away chasing some wee Christian girl," said Joker. "The one that was hassling you, Bobby."

"What?" Bobby exclaimed.

"And you let him go, Tone?" Sean asked. "Did you not even give him a lecture about the evils of Christianity?"

"Why should I? It's Jamesy's life; it's got nothing to do with me," Tone protested.

"Jesus, Tone, if I didn't know any better I'd say you were starting to get mellow in your old age," said Sean.

And Sean had a point. Because lately, for Tone, life was beginning to seem a lot less bleak and a lot less meaningless than it had seemed before. Tone found himself smiling more. He was less irritable and, even though he was still easily roused to anger, his anger didn't seem to last as long as it used to or to have the same intensity. Maybe, just maybe, Tone could see a ray of sunshine in an otherwise dull, grey sky.

Her name was Claire.

Eighteen

"Yes, I know it's a pain in the ass, but there's nothing I can do about it." Tone was standing in the lobby of his Dublin hotel, on the phone to Ding-a-Ling.

"Yeah, well if there's nothing you can do." Ding-a-Ling sounded disappointed. "Still, it's a bit of a shame; it should be a good party."

"I know, I'd been looking forward to it, but this asshole can only see me first thing in the morning before he goes back to Kerry. Joker's going, though, isn't he?"

"Yeah," said Ding-a-Ling, "though I think Carol will be there as well. Sean and Bobby are away on a course and Jamesy says he's too busy. Can you believe it? Too busy for a party? What the hell is the world coming to?"

"What about Snatter?"

"Oh, he's all fucking loved-up at the minute. I can't seem to get in touch with him at all these days."

Tone was surprised at the venom in Ding-a-Ling's voice, but he dismissed it as he continued. "Look, I'm sure you'll have a better bloody night than me, sitting on my todd in a hotel bar with a book! Not my idea of a fun Saturday night."

"You ever get the feeling we're all getting old?" Ding-a-Ling asked.

"Speak for yourself. Anyway, I'd better go. Have a good time at the party and try to keep Joker out of trouble."

Ding-a-Ling laughed. "I will," he said, "and I'll see you later."

"Yeah, see you," said Tone as he put down the phone. His plan for the evening was to go out and grab something to eat, something quick, like a burger or pizza, and then go back to his room for a shower before settling down in the bar with a book for a few quiet drinks and probably an early night. Despite what he had said to Ding-a-Ling, he was actually looking forward to it. 'Maybe Ding-a-Ling was right,' he thought, 'maybe we *are* all getting old.'

"Any good?"

Tone was engrossed in his book, quietly sipping his beer and minding his own business, so the interruption startled him.

"I'm sorry?"

"Your book. Is it any good?" the girl repeated with a smile. Tone's normal reaction would have been to tell her to piss off and stop bothering him, but there was something about her that made him pause.

"Yes, well, *I* think so," he told her.

"Bit of a pose, isn't it?"

"What?" he asked, a bit thrown.

"Sitting in a Dublin bar, on your own, reading Beckett." She was still smiling, which seemed to be her natural expression. It was highly contagious.

Tone, despite himself, was being drawn in by the openness of her expression, by the freshness of her smile. "It happens to be one of my favourite novels," he said, "and besides, this is my hotel. I'm staying here; where else am I supposed to sit?"

"Claire!" Tone looked behind the girl to see another girl standing at the bar. She was arranging some drinks to carry. "Come on, give me a hand!"

Claire turned around. "Yeah, OK, just a minute," she called, and turned back to Tone. "So is this you for the night, then?" she asked.

"That's the plan," Tone answered.

"We're heading into town for a bit of a session." She

137

gestured to a table where several girls, dressed for a night out, were sitting. "Why don't you come along?"

The suggestion was so spontaneous and Claire's exuberance was so invigorating that Tone was momentarily flustered. "Uhm, well I … oh, what the hell!" he said, finally. "Why not?"

The next morning, as Tone watched himself shave in the mirror, little fragments of the previous evening tumbled around in his head. There had been a lot of bars and a lot of alcohol involved in what had been Tone's first ever girls' night out. He could remember, with a fair degree of certainty, the first two or three bars, but after that the sequence of events became a little muddled. Some memories were more prominent than others: the Tequila slammers, dancing on tables, vodka shots, an impromptu folk session with stolen instruments. 'Quite a night,' he thought to himself. He turned to face the bed and to watch Claire's breasts rise and fall in time to her gentle snores. 'Quite a night, indeed.'

The early morning business meeting went smoothly despite Tone's wakening hangover and a deal was struck which meant that Tone did not have to travel all the way to Kerry that week. The Kerry hotel owner, however, insisted that Tone absolutely had to come down and stay some time and Tone insisted that he absolutely would as he tried to shake the image of Claire's breasts from his mind.

With the meeting concluded, Tone was eager to get back to his room, hoping that Claire would still be there. He had left her a note that said he wouldn't be long and also suggested some lunch together. He had already booked his room for an extra night, which had surprised him - perhaps he had caught some of Claire's spontaneity - and he had pictured a pleasant, lazy day in Dublin's fair city.

As he opened the door to his room he could tell right away that she was gone. The strength of his disappointment came as a bit of a surprise as he sat heavily on the bed. 'I mean, she was nice enough,' he thought, 'but -' It was then that he saw the note.

'Sorry, but I really had to go. Lunch sounds good. See you in the bar at one?' The little bubble of joy, again, came as something of a surprise.

'It's her personality,' Tone was thinking as he watched her approach. 'It actually makes her seem more attractive than she really is.' Claire's smile could be seen from the other side of the room: it grew bigger as she got closer. It was more than her smile, though, that intrigued Tone. Her entire face just seemed so alive, her entire manner so animated. It was as if she had a remarkable and quite ridiculous zest for life; an attitude that Tone would normally have dismissed with some contempt, but on Claire it worked. It worked beautifully.

"Not too late, am I?" she said, as she leant to kiss him on the cheek, and Tone was amazed at how comfortable he felt in her company.

"Not at all," Tone assured her. "What do you fancy doing? We could eat here or go out and find somewhere."

"Here's fine with me. Are we having a few drinks first?"

"A woman after my own heart. Do you have much on the rest of the day?"

"Not a thing," she told him.

"Well, after lunch I thought we could take in the sights of Dublin," Tone suggested.

Claire looked at him and cocked her head to one side. "I thought after lunch we could grab a bottle of wine and head up to your room."

"Now, why the hell didn't I think of that?"

"So, you're a student?" Tone was sitting up in bed watching Claire pull two cigarettes from the pack on the little dressing table. She tossed a cigarette to him and lit her own. She then walked across the room and handed Tone the lighter. She sat on the edge of the bed.

"Sort of," she said. "Not a professional, full-time type of student. My boss sent me on a course for work. It's only for six months. I stay in Dublin when it suits my lectures. What about you? What's your story?"

"Oh, it's all very boring, really. I'm a sales rep for a firm up north. They import genuine Irish linen from China and I flog it on to the tourist trade down here."

Claire smiled. "You sound like a desperate old cynic, so you do."

"You can call me a cynic if you want, but it's true." He set his cigarette down in the ashtray and gently brushed a fingertip across her nipple. She reached over to the side table and picked up the book that Tone had been reading. "I thought he only wrote plays," she said.

"Beckett? He wrote a lot of things."

Claire opened the book and read out the first line. "'The sun shone, having no alternative, on the nothing new.' Sounds like a barrel of laughs."

"Actually," said Tone, "I think you'll find that it is. It's one of the funniest books I've ever read."

"Do you read a lot?"

"I stay in hotels a lot, so there's usually not much else to do."

"I have a bit of a passion for literature," Claire said as she climbed into the bed and snuggled up to Tone. "Sometimes, though, it all seems a bit, oh, I don't know, overwhelming? Does that make sense?"

"Nah, you're gibbering there, love."

She laughed and gave him a nip. "It's just that there never seems to be enough time to read all the books that I want to read, do you know what I mean? When the hell am I ever going to read *Moby Dick* or *Middlemarch* or, well, forget about *War and Peace*, but you know what I mean, don't you?"

"You don't have to read everything, you know; there's no set list."

"Yeah, but there are so many books that I feel I should read, and it's not a pretentious thing, before you make a snide comment; it's just that these books are so famous that there must be something to them. I don't know, maybe it's just curiosity."

"Well, don't spend your life regretting," Tone said. He reached for the wine bottle and poured what was left into their two glasses. "Not that you appear to be doing that anyway. You seem to be living life to the full."

Claire laughed and took her glass of wine from him. "That's what life's for, isn't it? No, it's like, well, for example, I once read somewhere that *Middlemarch* was considered to be the greatest novel ever written in the English language. So, I mean, that's got to be worth reading, hasn't it?"

"Oh, I'm sure you'll read it some day and you'll be dazzled at the sheer achievement of it, but I think you'll find it all a bit dry."

She turned her head to face him. "Have you read it then?"

"Once, yes."

"And you didn't like it."

"I liked it a lot, just not enough to make me want to read it again. Like I said, it's a stunning achievement, it's hard to believe she managed to write other stuff as well."

"I felt like that when I read *One Hundred Years of Solitude*," Claire said. "That book just blew me away."

"I have a friend who reads Marquez in the original Spanish."

"That's pretty cool."

"And Camus and Zola in French."

Claire laughed. "Well, now he just sounds like a real geek."

Tone laughed with her. "I wouldn't say that to his face, he can be a bit intimidating."

"Sounds scary."

"He's a working class hero."

"So tell me," Claire said, snuggling closer to Tone, being careful not to spill her wine, "what are your guilty book secrets? What books have you not read that you feel you should have?"

"Probably loads, there's a lot of Hemingway I haven't read. I've never read *The Catcher in the Rye*, I've never -"

"You've never read *The Catcher in the Rye*?" Claire sat up straight.

Tone shrugged. "Never got around to it."

"Right, that's it. I'm going to get you a copy of *The Catcher in the Rye;* you just have to read it."

"I can get my own cop -"

"Shut up! It's a present, OK; you just have to lie there

and take it."

"What, again?"

She laughed. "Have you read any Joyce?"

"Some. Not *Finnegan's Wake*, of course."

"*Dubliners?*"

"Yeah."

She lay down beside him. "I read it just before I came here. I've read it a couple of times since. That last paragraph is so beautiful, it gets me every time."

"Yeah, it's very haunting, isn't it? Are we out of wine?"

"Looks like it."

"It's starting to get dark. Do you have to be anywhere in the morning?"

"I've got a lecture, but it's not till half-eleven."

"Fancy some dinner?"

"Sounds good."

"And some wine?"

"Sounds good."

"And then -"

"Yeah, that sounds good too."

They laughed as they got dressed and went down to dinner. The sights of Dublin, for the time being, would just have to remain unseen.

Nineteen

Jamesy was still hesitating. He was chewing his fifth extra-strong mint while staring at the window display of a men's clothes shop. Behind him and across the street the Christians were singing and chatting to the passers-by. Jamesy was able to watch them in the reflection of the shop window. He could see the girl and she was smiling that smile. The smile that had brought out the poet in Jamesy. The smile that could melt icebergs.

Despite the cold, Jamesy was sweating. He swallowed his mint and psyched himself up once more. 'Right, this time,' he told himself. 'Just do it.'

To his surprise, he actually turned around and started walking. When he reached the little group, he stopped in front of the girl and gave what he hoped was a friendly smile.

"Uhm, hi," he said. "I don't know if you remember me but -"

"Didn't we see you earlier?" Greg interrupted. "Your friend was getting rather excited, wasn't he?"

"Well, yes, that's what I'm here for." Jamesy spoke directly to the girl. "I thought I should apologise for my friend's behaviour earlier and maybe -"

"He seemed to have a lot of anger," Greg continued. "I'd really like to meet him again, to discuss some of the issues that he has."

"Uhm, yeah, that might be possible." Jamesy turned back to the girl. "Look, what I'd really like to do is buy you a coffee. Delaney's is just there. Would you like to join -"

"That's a good idea," Greg said. "I think we all could do with a break. That's all right, isn't it?"

'Bugger!' thought Jamesy. "Of course, yes, that's fine," he said.

Delaney's café is a popular destination for Belfast shoppers. The combination of cheap but decent food and a calm, friendly atmosphere make it a favourite spot for people to take a break from the normal hustle of the city centre. Inside, the decoration is eccentric, with stuffed animals peering through exotic foliage at the diners seated in neat little rows of booths.

Jamesy was thinking, as he queued for his coffee, that things hadn't gone entirely to plan. It was true he had succeeded in taking the girl for a coffee; he just hadn't bargained on a bunch of born-again Christians tagging along.

'Still,' he thought, 'better make the best of it.' He sat down at a booth, with Greg and the girl sitting opposite. The other Christians were seated in other booths around the café. Everyone was chattering excitedly about the day's events.

"I'm sorry, but I don't even know your name," Jamesy said to the girl.

"Oh, of course, it's Hannah," said Hannah with a smile that gave Jamesy a surprising stirring in his loins.

"Hannah? That's a nice name," Jamesy told her and she smiled a thank you. Jamesy almost dropped his coffee.

"Like I was saying," Greg began. "I found some of your friend's arguments quite interesting, but ultimately a little facile."

"What? Oh, right," said Jamesy. "Yes, he can come across a bit aggressively, but his heart's in the right place."

"I don't know about that," Greg replied. "If he has

banished Jesus from his heart then it can hardly be said to be in the right place." He gave a little snort of laughter and Jamesy couldn't stop himself from thinking that Tone was right. Greg apparently did need his teeth kicked in.

"Of course, it is still possible that he can be saved." Hannah assured Jamesy. "The Lord turns no one away."

"Yes, but he must want to be saved, you understand," Greg added. "He seems to be in a very dark place in his life."

"He's had some troubles, I suppose," Jamesy agreed. "But, like you say, no one is beyond redemption."

"What about you?" Hannah asked Jamesy. "Have you been saved?"

"Well, I'm a Christian," Jamesy, who'd never really given it much thought, replied. "Probably not as good a Christian as I should be, but then we can't all be perfect. Perhaps I've been a bit too absorbed in my studies to fully realise the depth of my faith."

"You're a student?" Hannah asked.

"Yes," said Jamesy. "I suppose my chosen field covers quite a broad spectrum of disciplines, from archaeology to the structures of early societies. Generally speaking, though, the term *ancient history* is a fair enough description."

"I would have thought," Greg said, "that you can find all the history you need to know in the Bible."

"Well, yes, of course," said Jamesy in an ingratiating tone, "but, with all due respect to the Bible, it tends to focus on just the one geographical area; it doesn't mention the Greeks much, for example."

"There could be a very good reason for that," Greg informed him. "It could be that God considers the contribution of the Greeks to be irrelevant. They did worship false gods, remember?"

Jamesy considered what Greg had just said to be probably the most objectionable statement he had ever heard. He suppressed his objections, however.

"But don't you think," he calmly replied, "that the more we uncover, not just in history but in all fields of knowledge, the better we'll be able to appreciate the full breadth of God's creation?" Jamesy shuddered as he thought about how Tone would have reacted to that little sentence.

"The answer to that can be found in Ecclesiastes, 'He who increases knowledge increases suffering'." Greg smiled his smug little smile. Jamesy simply did not know how to react to that. He wondered if Greg was making some sort of joke. He decided the best course of action would be to remain silent and try to lose himself in Hannah's smile. She gave him a quick glance, then shyly looked down at the table.

"Right from the very beginning," Greg went on, "God has been warning us about our curiosity. He explains it all quite beautifully when he shows us how Eve brought about mankind's fall. We really must take heed of what God is telling us, that we can only find knowledge through God himself. Any other way is an offence to him."

"Hmmm," said Jamesy, "that's an interesting way of looking at it." He was trying to be as accommodating as possible, but Greg wasn't making it easy. He thought it best to try to steer the conversation away from the minefield of faith. It wasn't that Jamesy didn't believe in God, because he assumed that he did; it was the fact that the sheer number of different convictions that were held with regard to belief made it almost impossible to give an opinion without causing some offence, somewhere. It was safer to avoid the whole subject altogether.

"So, what about you?" he asked Hannah. "Do you work or study or whatever? I'm curious, really. I'd like to know more about you."

"I'm in my second year at Queen's," she replied. "Doing computing. It's a bit boring, really."

"I wouldn't say that. People reckon that computing is going to be the thing to get into. It's not something I know a lot about, but I'm always keen to learn new things. But let's hear more about you: what sort of things do you like to do in your spare time?"

"All of my spare time is taken up with doing the Lord's work," she told him, although Jamesy thought she seemed a little hesitant.

"And is that what you enjoy?" Jamesy asked. She seemed surprised by the question.

"It's the Lord's work," she answered. "What could be more important?"

"Oh, yes, of course you're right," Jamesy assured her. His level of toadying was beginning to sicken even himself. He decided to cut through all the waffle and just ask Hannah out. He would suggest meeting up somewhere in town after Christmas, for a meal, perhaps. He was forming the proposal in his mind when Greg spoke.

"I wouldn't have thought there'd be much ancient history left to learn," he said. "If, as we now know, the earth was created in 4004BC and then had to be started all over again after the flood, then surely there can't have been that many events that you would need to learn about."

Jamesy felt that, had he been a character in one of those old Warner Brothers cartoons, his lower jaw would currently be resting on the floor. He was speechless. He had heard about creationists before, but he had vaguely assumed they lived in small isolated groups and were entirely confined to some of the more backward states of America. To be confronted with one in the relative sanity of a modern European city was, for Jamesy, beyond comprehension. "I ... I'm sorry, what?" he finally managed to stammer.

"Well, you study history," Greg said, "so you've obviously heard of the work of Bishop Ussher."

"Who?"

"You know," Hannah prompted. "Bishop James Ussher? He was once the Archbishop of Armagh." Jamesy shook his head. "Back in the 1600s," Hannah continued. "You should really know this, you know, especially if you study history. He was a great scholar and it was his deep knowledge and understanding of the Bible that allowed him to work out the exact date of Creation."

"That's right," said Greg, "his work was also able to confirm the results of the work previously carried out by Dr John Lightfoot. This, obviously, removed any doubts there may have been about the accuracy of Dr Lightfoot's conclusions. It was an incredible achievement, to be able to pinpoint exactly the very moment of Creation. We owe a great debt to Bishop Ussher. Have you really never heard of him?"

"Uhm, no," said Jamesy, becoming increasingly bewildered, "and you're saying that the earth was created, when was it? 4000BC?"

"4004 to be exact," Greg corrected him. "On the 23rd of October."

Jamesy stared at the two people sitting across the table from him. They appeared to be perfectly normal human adults. They were both coherent and articulate, they obviously possessed a reasonable intelligence, they were able to move around and to use implements like a cup and a saucer, they exhibited absolutely no signs of erratic or abnormal behaviour. Why, then, were they saying things that most infants would dismiss as palpable nonsense? It was bound to be a joke, Jamesy decided. They couldn't seriously believe what they were saying, could they? "Let me make sure I've got this right," he said. "Someone has worked out, from the Bible, that the earth is less than six thousand years old, is that right?"

"Not just the earth," Greg informed him, "the entire universe."

Jamesy realised he would need to be careful about how he proceeded here. He didn't want to offend their beliefs, regardless of how offensive their beliefs were to him. "That sort of timescale, you understand, doesn't fit very well with the current scientific understanding," he said.

"Scientists!" Greg said derisively. "Scientists are just men, you have to remember. How can any man know more than God? If they choose to ignore the facts contained in the Bible then they're simply blundering around in the dark. They're just guessing, that's all."

"Well, they do point to certain evidence which gives them a fair degree of confidence in what they say. Starlight, for example, can take hundreds of thousands of years to -"

"Yes, so they say," Greg broke in, "but they can't prove it, can they? All they are doing is making wild claims that don't make any real sense. It's perfectly simple. If any of the claims made by scientists, or anyone else for that matter, conflict with what we are taught by the Bible, then those claims are wrong. They must be wrong, otherwise we would be disagreeing with God." Greg laughed at the absurdity of the notion. "I mean, come on, you can't seriously expect us to do that, can you?"

Jamesy decided to try a different approach. He was having trouble, though, forming rational arguments, still reeling, as he was, from the scale of the irrationality that confronted him. "OK," he began. "I can see how you could be satisfied by the information contained in the Bible; there's so much to take in, after all. But don't you think that life would be more interesting if you asked more questions? What about things that seem strange or puzzling, things that don't have an obvious answer, even in the Bible? Don't you think you'd get a genuine thrill if you had to search for an answer that had seemed far too elusive but with a lot of work and reasoning you were finally able to find it?"

Greg shook his head dubiously. "I'm not sure what it is that you're getting at," he said. "What sort of questions, exactly?"

"Oh, I don't know," Jamesy said. "How about, why can't dolphins breathe underwater? Or what causes the auroras? Or what -"

Greg held up his hand. "Look," he said, "things like that are irrelevant; why would you even want to know anything like that? You said yourself that we can be satisfied with the Bible and the answers that it gives us; nothing else matters. To be honest, actually, I would say that if it isn't in the Bible then God doesn't want us to know it. The fate of Lot's wife is a good example of where curiosity can lead."

Jamesy glanced at Hannah. She was looking at him strangely. What was that look in her eyes, Jamesy wondered. Scorn? Contempt? Pity? Jamesy felt a surge of anger; he rarely got angry and he tried to fight it. "Look," he said, "all I'm saying is that a lot of advancements for mankind have been made by science. If you're going to dismiss the scientific process then you have to dismiss the work of people like Pasteur or Fleming or -"

"No," said Greg. "You weren't listening. I said if the claims made by science contradict the teachings of the Bible, then it's OK for them to be dismissed."

Jamesy looked thoughtfully at Greg. "I shouldn't mention Charles Darwin, then, should I?"

Greg laughed. "Old Charlie Darwin, eh? He really fooled a lot of people, didn't he? I honestly don't know how any sensible person could fall for that nonsense."

"You do know, don't you," Hannah asked Jamesy, "that evolution is only a theory?"

"What?" Jamesy was aghast.

"I think a lot of people tend to forget that," she said.

"Oh, I see," said Jamesy, "you don't fully understand the meaning of the word *theory* when it's placed in a scientific context. What it actually means is -"

"Are you seriously trying to defend such an obviously flawed idea?" Greg interrupted. "How can you defend the indefensible?"

"But many Christians have accepted evolution," Jamesy protested. "There's just too much evidence to support it."

"No real Christian can possibly agree with evolution," Greg told him haughtily. "Evolution basically says that the Bible is all lies; it's an idea that could only have come from Satan himself. I've been told that most scientists have rejected it as false."

"Trust me," said Jamesy as he struggled to keep his temper under control, "you have been severely misinformed."

"I'm sorry," Greg retorted, "but you don't seem to have understood this at all. Like I said, it's perfectly simple, the Bible has been given to us by God and if we try to find fault with the word of God then -"

"Look," said Jamesy, rubbing his forehead in exasperation. "God didn't actually write the Bible now, did he?"

"Of course he did," Greg said confidently. "He wrote it with the Holy Spirit."

"Why?" Jamesy finally snapped. "Couldn't he find a pen?"

Greg stared at Jamesy as a cold silence descended around them. A few of the other Christians in the booths nearby were glancing over at them. Jamesy felt his anger fade and he was instantly apologetic. "Look, I'm sorry," he began, but Greg shook his head. "I think we need to get going," he said to Hannah. He turned around and signalled to the rest of the group that they were preparing to leave. "It's starting to get dark, we should probably call it a day." He stood up and let Hannah slide out of the booth behind him. He looked down at Jamesy. "Well, it's been interesting meeting you." He gave an insincere smile. "But we really must be getting along. I hope you have a pleasant Christmas."

Jamesy sat and watched them march out of the café. He felt emotionally confused and, judging by his reflection in the window, he looked dreadful. The colour had drained from his face as he sat in stunned disbelief at what had just happened. He sat in silence for several minutes while a waitress came and cleared the table. She wiped away some spilled coffee and, stealing a quick glance at Jamesy, she self-consciously tidied away a little strand of hair that had come loose from behind her ear. Jamesy didn't notice: he continued to sit in silence, staring into the middle distance. Eventually, he summoned up the energy to stir himself. 'Well,' he thought as he pushed himself out of the booth, 'that could have gone better.'

Twenty

"Snouts!"

The five boys were aged between seven and ten years old and they were the only ones around to witness the invasion. They had lived all their lives in the shadow of the peace line; the high, rusting fence on the far side of the tarmac 'pitch' that marked the boundary of their world, never meeting or even seeing the people who lived on the other side.

There were many names for those people, the people of the Shankill. They were Prods or Orangies, Snouts, Loyalists, Unionists or Huns, and now the boys watched in horror as they poured over in their droves to attack the peace-loving residents of the Falls Road. On Christmas Eve. The sneaky bastards.

The boys had grown up with all the songs and stories of Irish Republican heroes; men who, when the call came, were not to be found wanting. Men like Wolf Tone and Robert Emmet, James Connolly and Padhraig Pearse, men who were prepared to stand up to tyranny and to give their lives in the name of liberty.

The call now came to them. Five small boys faced their destiny. Perhaps this was happening all over Belfast? All over Northern Ireland? What would history say of the battle for the Lower Falls? Would it be remembered by Republicans with shame? No! The boys were determined. They would not be found wanting.

"Come on, lads," the oldest boy rallied his troops, "get stuck into them!"

They hunted the pitch for ammo: there were stones and broken bricks scattered around the area and they hastily gathered as many as they could. They stood and faced the enemy just as Ding-a-Ling dropped the last few feet to the ground. One of the younger boys wildly threw a few stones and then panicked. "There's too many of them," he shouted. "I'm going to get my da." And he fled.

The other boys waited nervously; they began to fidget and then they broke as Snatter jumped to the ground, rolling forward as he landed to take the jolt. The oldest boy was the last to flee. He was armed with a weapon much favoured by the discerning rioter; a half-brick or 'halfer'. He didn't want to waste it. With all his strength, he hurled the halfer toward the attacking horde before he turned to pursue his comrades in full retreat.

"Watch out, Snatter," said Ding-a-Ling, stepping to one side.

"What?" Snatter asked as he stood up and dusted his hands. The halfer hit the ground in front of him and spun up to strike his shin with a crack that made even Ding-a-Ling wince. Snatter, once again, went down.

Ding-a-Ling stood and listened to the profanities that poured through Snatter's gritted teeth. He took out a cigarette and lit it. "It's starting to get dark, you know?" he told Snatter.

"... fucking ... bastard ... broken ..."

"You know?" Ding-a-Ling continued. "It's just occurred to me, those wee fuckers must have thought we were Prods."

"... cunt and fuck ... wanking ... shin...."

"Right! You want to go and get a taxi?"

"... bastard ... bloody ... fuck ..." Snatter was rolling around on his back, clutching his leg, when Ding-a-Ling suddenly noticed something. He went to stop Snatter, but was fractionally too late. Ding-a-Ling grimaced as he watched Snatter's face roll into a patch of nettles. He grabbed Snatter and pulled him free. There were tears in Snatter's eyes now, but he had stopped swearing. Ding-a-Ling took this to be a good sign. He snatched up a handful of dock leaves and started to rub them into the angry red welts that had appeared on Snatter's forehead. "Just take a wee rest there, Snatter," he said, "and then we'll head on. OK?"

Snatter didn't respond. He sat up and began to gingerly roll his trouser leg up until, eventually, he revealed a nasty wound on his leg. There was a little blood, but it was the swelling and the bruising that worried Snatter most. And the pain, of course: the pain was excruciating. He looked up at Ding-a-Ling, his eyes pleading. "Seriously," he insisted. "I really need to go to casualty."

Ding-a-Ling nodded. "Yeah, I think you're right," he said. "Can you stand OK?"

He helped Snatter to his feet and, with Snatter leaning heavily on him, they both started to shuffle towards the Falls Road and the Royal Victoria Hospital which, they reckoned, had to be close by.

"Lucky it was on the same leg as your sore foot," Ding-a-Ling noted cheerfully, "otherwise you wouldn't be able to walk at all."

'Yeah,' thought Snatter grimly. 'I've got to be the luckiest bastard in the whole world.'

Twenty-One

Tone fished around for a cassette. The radio was getting on his nerves and he wanted some decent music to listen to. He was driving back from Cork and was planning to stay overnight at his usual hotel in Dublin. His ebullient mood intrigued him. Yes, he had arranged to meet Claire, but his sense of expectation, his almost childish excitement, seemed a little disproportionate. Meeting Claire was no big deal, was it? He found a tape he liked and popped it into the deck. Stiff Little Fingers came blaring out of his speakers with *Barbed Wire Love* and Tone tapped his fingers on the steering wheel in time to the music. He was making good time and, if he was being honest with himself, he could easily have made it back to Belfast for the weekend. But then he wouldn't get to see Claire, and Tone was beginning to realise that seeing Claire was becoming increasingly significant for him.

He began to mull it over in his head once more, trying to pin down just what his feelings for Claire really were. At first he had assumed that, as far as he and Claire were both concerned, they were having a simple fling. A very enjoyable fling, he admitted, but a fling nonetheless. Temporary and fleeting. No strings. Ships, as it were, passing in the night. And yet. 'Bugger,' thought Tone, 'what was it?'

Just what was it that made him grin involuntarily whenever an image of her flashed into his head? He had gone out with more attractive girls in his time and he had been with smarter girls, but there was something about Claire that made all those other girls seem like meaningless distractions. He couldn't quite figure out exactly what it was: the more he tried to analyse it, the more elusive it became. Like grasping smoke. 'Does it matter?' he asked himself. 'Do I really need to scrutinise it so much? No, sod it!' he decided. 'Just enjoy it while it lasts.' He felt happy and relaxed in her company and that, he concluded, was all he needed to know. He glanced at the book on the passenger seat; it was a copy of *The Catcher in the Rye* and had been a present from Claire. Tone couldn't help but smile whenever he thought about how he had received it.

He had been staying in Dublin for a few days the week before and, as he returned to his hotel from an appointment, he went to reception to fetch his key. He was pleased to note that the pretty girl with whom he occasionally flirted was on duty. He smiled at her on approaching the desk and was pleased to see a little blush of colour rise in her cheeks. 'Still got it, Tone,' he thought smugly to himself. 'You've still got it.'

The receptionist handed him his key and then stopped him as he went to turn away. 'Oh, here we go,' Tone thought. 'I'd better let her down gently.'

"Actually, Mr Maguire," the girl began, blushing even more, "there seems to have been a package left for you." Tone looked surprised; he couldn't think of anyone in the city who would leave a package for him. Except maybe ... Oh crap! Tone stared, appalled, as the receptionist brought a small parcel out from under the desk. She appeared to be embarrassed just to touch it. She put it on the counter and pushed it toward Tone. Tone had to force himself to look at it. It was a small, oblong-shaped parcel, fairly obviously a book; but it was how it was wrapped that caught the eye. Or, more to the point, repelled the eye. The wrapping paper was the most garish shade of electric pink that Tone had ever seen and this was complemented by an elaborate concoction of pink and lilac ribbons and bows. There was worse to come, however, for as Tone slowly peered closer he realised that on top of this gleefully cheerful two-fingered salute to good taste was a card. And on this card was a message, a message that was clearly visible.

The receptionist was furiously looking in any direction that didn't have Tone in it and Tone suddenly had the impression that even the doorman was avoiding catching his eye. Despite his better judgement, Tone leaned a little closer so that he could read the message that apparently most of the hotel staff had already read. As it turned out, it was actually worse than he was expecting. The message read:

To Mr Anthony, Fluffybum, Maguire. For all those stolen kisses and so much more besides. For frequently letting me into your circle. With all my squidgy pidgy love. Yours forever, Derek. xxxx

Tone looked at the receptionist, who was now polishing a sheet of blank paper behind the desk. He picked up his package and gruffly cleared his throat. "Thank you," he said, and strode off toward the lifts.

He saw Claire later that night in a bar near the city centre and, still feeling angry from his humiliation, was planning to tell her off. As he started to reprimand her, though, and as he described exactly what had happened, he soon began to see the funny side, especially as Claire was doubled over in obvious discomfort with tears of laughter pouring down her face. "Stop it," she was saying. "Please, I can't take it any more." Her laughter proved to be so infectious that soon Tone was joining in. He started to make a joke of the whole thing. "Of course, I can never go back to that hotel," he told her. "I'm not even sure if homosexuality is still a crime or not in the South."

"Oh, God! Oh, God!" Claire was taking huge gulps of breath to try to ease the pain in her sides. "I can just picture the look on your face."

"I've blown my chances with that wee receptionist, you know? Thanks to you."

Claire collapsed into uncontrollable giggles; she couldn't speak any more. Tone watched her and grinned. It was impossible to be upset in the company of such expansive and unfettered joy. Claire's simple, overwhelming love of life seemed to overflow from her and pour out in waves to engulf those around her.

Later, as they walked back to the hotel, Claire turned to him and asked. "Are you going to let me into your circle tonight?"

"Are you mad, woman?" Tone replied. "What would Derek say?" They were still laughing when they reached Tone's room where, luckily, there was no sign of Derek.

Tone reached the outskirts of Dublin just after three in the afternoon and arrived at his hotel not long after that. Once he had checked in, he went up to his room to get ready for the night ahead. He had arranged to meet Claire in the Temple Bar area of the city just south of the river and, if he was being perfectly honest, he was having some misgivings. Not about meeting Claire, but about meeting in Temple Bar on a Friday night. It would be crowded, he realised, and noisy and vibrant and exciting, and what the hell was his problem? He knew he joked about getting old, but that was just a joke: he was still in his early twenties, for fuck's sake. He was at the perfect age to party in Temple Bar on a Friday night, but he just couldn't work up the enthusiasm for it. It began to dawn on him just what he would prefer to do that night, and it made him a little uneasy. He realised that he would much rather have a few quiet drinks in the hotel bar with Claire before they both adjourned to his room to enjoy a long and leisurely private evening together with wine, cigarettes and lots of gratuitous nudity. 'Jesus, I'm turning into Jamesy,' he thought. 'Only there's sex involved.'

It turned out to be an extremely enjoyable evening, although, deep down, he had always known it would be. After a couple of drinks, he started to unwind as he chatted and joked with Claire. She had brought a few friends from Trinity with her and Tone chatted and joked with them too. After a few more drinks, Claire dragged Tone up to dance and, in his mind, he was the best dancer there. As the drink flowed, the evening began to cascade. They lurched through the night from one bar to another, dancing along the cobbled streets with music blasting all around in varying levels of volume, the bars blurred into one another: the bars, the booze, the music, the faces, the dancing, the bars and the booze.

Tone opened his eyes. It took a while to recognise his hotel room. There was no sign of Claire, although it was a few moments before he could turn his head to verify that fact. There was some light coming through the window, which suggested it was morning, but it was a dull and greyish light that suggested it was not quite an acceptable point of the morning to be awake in. Suddenly Claire put her head round the bathroom door. She appeared to be wet and, from what Tone could see, naked. Tone had a vague notion that he should be taking a much greater interest in that fact than he actually was.

"Wicklow Mountains, then?" Claire said cheerfully.

'What? Oh, she's still pissed,' Tone thought. 'Poor bitch just can't hold her liquor.' He put his forearm over his eyes and waited for the time to become a little more reasonable.

"What time do you think we should leave?" Claire had come into the room now and was drying herself with a large towel.

"Maybe you should think about sobering up before we do anything," Tone murmured from the bed.

"What?"

"What?" Tone asked, and then it struck him that 'What?' might not be enough. "What do you mean by 'leave'?" he elaborated.

"Don't you remember?" Claire knelt on the bed. "Last night? You promised to take me to see the Wicklow Mountains today."

"Oh, that?" Tone lied. "Of course I remember. Just give me a minute."

It probably would have been quicker to take the main coastal road past Bray, Tone thought, but they were in no hurry, so he took the slower, minor roads to Glendalough.

Where the hell this idea had come from he couldn't remember, but the closer to the mountains they drove the more he was looking forward to it. It was a beautiful autumn day. The sort of day that Ireland had been made for. The sky was blue with a few immature clouds that were childishly teasing the mountain peaks in the distance.

"Nice day for it, at least," Tone said to Claire. She was rummaging around in the glove compartment, searching through Tone's cassettes.

"Jesus, Tony," she said, "don't you have any music that's a bit more up to date? I don't think I was even born when some of these things were made."

"You weren't born? So what are you? Five?"

"OK, so I'm exaggerating; but really, Tony, people still make music today, you know?"

"Bloody philistine!" Tone said. "Everybody knows that music died the day The Clash broke up."

Claire sighed and slipped a compilation tape into the deck. Squeeze came on, singing *Up the Junction*.

"You see, now?" said Tone. "Proper music."

"You're a sad old fart; you know that, don't you?"

"And bloody proud of it, let me tell you. So what do you want to do? What do you think about a picnic for lunch?"

"Sounds like a good idea, but we haven't brought anything, have we?"

"No," Tone conceded, "but there's a blanket in the boot and we can stop somewhere and load up with supplies; what do you reckon?"

"A picnic lunch in the Wicklow Mountains? Sounds very romantic."

"Oh, you stick with me, kiddo," Tone said, "and I'll romance your ass off."

They parked the car in the little town of Glendalough and, loaded up with food, drinks and blanket, they headed into the hills towards Glendalough's Upper Lake. The scenery they passed through was pretty, if unremarkable, and Claire said that it reminded her of the Glens of

Antrim. Claire did most of the talking on the walk and Tone was happy to make the occasional comment while doing most of the listening. They arrived at the shores of the Upper Lake and Tone began to arrange the blanket on a flat stretch of ground. He noticed that Claire had gone quiet and turned to find her staring at the lake.

"Christ Almighty!" she exclaimed quietly. "It's absolutely stunning." Tone followed her gaze and nodded.

The mountains, as if aware of their own beauty, had gathered to stare at their reflections in the still, clear water, while the entire scene was framed above and below by a deep and flawless blue.

"Yeah," said Tone. "But it'll look a lot better if you get some liquor down your neck and put some food in your gob."

Claire laughed. "Is that you romancing my ass off?"

"Come on, admit it," Tone replied. "You're turned on, aren't you?"

They sat on the blanket and Tone served up the food and poured the drinks: wine for Claire and a weak shandy for him. After they'd eaten, they sat side-by-side, smoking cigarettes and admiring the view. When Tone had finished his cigarette, he lay back with his hands behind his head, his gaze fixed on the sky above.

"Well," he asked Claire, "are you having a nice day?" He watched her shoulders shrug. "I've had worse, I suppose," she said casually and Tone laughed. She then added her cigarette butt to Tone's in the empty shandy can and turned around to lie on top of him. "It's been an OK day so far," she said, biting his lower lip. "Can you think of any way we can improve upon it?"

Tone managed to think of something.

"It's getting late," Tone said, eventually. "We should really think about making a move."

"Mmmm," Claire murmured. Her head was resting on Tone's chest. "You're right, it is getting late." She snuggled closer to him. "Just a wee bit longer," she suggested.

"OK," Tone replied, and reached down to rub her back. "What do you fancy doing this evening, then? Fancy going out for dinner?"

"Dinner sounds good. Then what?"

"Oh, I don't know, whatever you want, really. We could visit the theatre or go see a film; we have the whole of Dublin to play with. What do you think?"

"I think we should have dinner and then spend the rest of the night drinking, smoking and having sex."

"Well, at least I put up the pretence of being cultural," Tone said haughtily, and Claire laughed. "I know," she said, "but how often do we see each other? A few days a month? We need to make the most of it, don't you think?"

"Absolutely," Tone agreed. "Life is short and bitter, after all. We should cling to whatever respites we find along the way." Claire looked up and frowned. "That was a gloomy thing to say."

"I know, I'm sorry," Tone said. "I can't help being a miserable old git sometimes. Being with you helps, though."

"Are you getting all soppy on me there?" Claire teased, and settled back down to rest her head on Tone's chest. "What do you know about life, anyway? You're only twenty-four, for God's sake."

"What the hell has age got to do with it?"

"You know what I mean; it takes a while to build up life experiences."

"Depends what you mean by life experiences," Tone said. "I mean, a friend of mine was only eight-years-old when he saw his ma's head get blown off."

"Really?" Claire looked into his face.

"Yeah. Oh, it's by no means the most tragic story to come out of Northern Ireland, but he was certainly affected by it."

"So, what happened?"

"Well, as far as I know, he was off sick from school, mumps or something, and he was lying on the sofa in the front room. His ma brought her ironing board in so she could watch the TV and do her ironing at the same time. Then, just outside, apparently, a couple of IRA men who were moving some weapons were surprised by an army foot patrol and there was an exchange of gunfire. Nobody was hurt except my mate's ma, who was killed when a stray bullet came through the window and took the top of her head off."

"Jesus," Claire whispered, and she shivered slightly as she pressed closer to Tone.

"My mate once told me," Tone continued, "that the only thing he could really remember about it was thinking just how mad his ma was going to be when she saw the state of the wallpaper." Claire said nothing; she simply hugged Tone more tightly.

"There's more," Tone said flatly. "My mate's da took it badly. He hit the bottle pretty hard and for a while my mate had to look after himself and his da on his own. Although, to be fair, he had aunts and uncles who helped out and eventually his da started to come out of it. He stopped drinking and cleaned himself up and things seemed to be going well. Then he was hit by a police Land Rover that was chasing a joy-rider and was killed instantly. My mate was fourteen."

Claire remained silent for a few moments and then spoke. "You're right," she said.

"I'm right? About what?"

"We should cling to whatever respites we find along the way."

Tone remained thoughtful for a while and then he shook Claire. "Come on, woman," he said. "We have to go." They stood up and Claire stretched as Tone folded the blanket. She then gathered up all of their rubbish into a plastic bag and, making sure that they left nothing behind, they both started to walk back to the town.

"You're mate's OK now, though, isn't he?" Claire asked as they walked.

"Oh, yeah," Tone reassured her. "He got a big claim from the government and he runs his own shop these days, doing very well by all accounts."

"He's not the one that reads Marquez in Spanish, is he?"

Tone laughed. "No," he said. "He's a whole different story. He actually went to Inst., you know?"

"Inst.?" Claire asked incredulously. "You know somebody who went to Inst.? You're kidding me, aren't you?"

"Hard to believe, isn't it? But, yeah, he really did. Hated it, though."

"Is he, like, a real brainbox?"

"Not especially, no. I mean, he's bright enough, don't get me wrong, but -" Tone thought for a moment, "but I think there's something wrong with his brain."

Twenty-Two

There was something wrong with Joker's brain. Not necessarily in a negative way; but there was something about Joker's brain that made it function differently from other, more conventional, brains.

It first became noticeable at primary school, where Joker's teacher, Mrs Donohue, noticed how the young Joseph Anderson would consistently find solutions to simple problems a little bit faster than his classmates. Mrs Donohue then gradually provided Joker with more challenging problems which Joker, to the delight of Mrs Donohue, proved able to solve. Joker was hailed as a prodigy, a child with a God-given gift of above-average intelligence: a genius.

This turned out not to be true. It later transpired that Joker was just as stupid as everyone else; it was just that, when it came to problem solving, Joker's brain would simply take a different route to finding the solution than the brains of any of his peers. He wasn't a genius, he was just a bit strange.

Joker was born into a typical working class family in South Belfast, in the staunchly Loyalist area of Sandy Row. This labelled him instantly as a Protestant and a Unionist, although, in Joker's case, the reality was a little different. Joker's father, Davy Anderson, was, at first glance, a stereotype. Hard-drinking and pugnacious, he appeared to fill the role of the standard Belfast working man. Davy Anderson, however, was also a highly principled socialist and a committed and militant atheist. He was scornful of all religion, which he regarded as just another burden on the working class. Religion, as far as Davy was concerned, was the single greatest con in the history of mankind, and he would scathingly denounce it at every opportunity. This was something that Joker's mother, who preferred to hedge her bets when it came to God, once found out to her cost.

Katherine Anderson was a lively and cheerful woman who, while not being openly religious, was not as close-minded as her husband when it came to spiritual matters. She had been raised as a Presbyterian, but did not feel any strong ties to that denomination. She had always believed that, with so many varieties of Christianity to choose from, the path to salvation could be a deeply personal decision.

Her son and her husband would always be the two most important things in Katherine's life, but she also believed there should be a place in her life, and, by extension, her family's life, for faith. It was this reason that made her persuade Davy to accompany her to the local Church Hall to hear The Fury.

Nigel Linsey Smith was The Fury, a preacher from Ballymena who preached in the old style. He would stand and yell from the pulpit, berating his congregation, condemning them as sinners and vividly describing their future in the fires of hell. The path to salvation, he would declare, was not an easy path to take. It required determination and sacrifice; the feeble minds of man in the aftermath of the fall were easy prey for the demons of temptation and it took a strong will to turn away from these whores of seduction.

The hall was packed on the evening The Fury came to preach to the sinners of Sandy Row. Katherine had dragged her reluctant husband along to hear the famous orator deliver his sermon. She was curious to hear for herself the fiery brand of Christianity that had captivated thousands all over Northern Ireland and beyond; perhaps this would be the light she was seeking that would illuminate her path to the Lord.

Davy had grumbled the whole way there, but he couldn't deny that he was also a little curious to hear what this 'Fury' had to say. And so they had arranged a babysitter for Joseph, and had come along as good Ulster Protestants to be told what wicked sinners they were. The hall was already full when they arrived and they had to be content to stand at the back.

There was a hush as The Fury entered and slowly and deliberately took his place at the lectern, facing his congregation. He paused and looked around the expectant faces, then looked down as his hands clenched the sides of the lectern. He smiled inwardly as he relished the ease with which he would carry these simple people to the very gates of eternal damnation, the horrendous images he would place before their eyes, the unspeakable agonies they were sure to face, the burning, roasting, everlasting torture of hell, and how he would, inch by tantalising inch, bring them back from the brink. Back with *him* as their guide, leading the way to salvation, to God and to Paradise. He cleared his throat and began. " 'But the cowards and the unbelievers'," he shouted, and watched with satisfaction as the entire congregation visibly jumped, " 'the abominable, and murderers, and whoremongers, and sorcerers, and idolaters, and all liars, shall have their part in the lake which burneth with fire and brimstone; which is the second death'." He paused for effect and to let the words sink in, and then, unbelievably, just as he was about to continue, The Fury was faced with his first ever heckler.

"Look," a voice called from the back of the hall, "why don't you just tell us how much fucking money you want us to give you and we can all go home early."

The shock around the hall was obvious in the audible gasps and cries of disbelief. Katherine took a tiny step back and to the side, then another and another as she jostled her way through the crowd until she felt she was at a safe enough distance from her husband to be able to tut and shake her head along with the rest of the congregation.

"That's just shocking, so it is!" she said to the old woman she found herself standing nearest to.

"Yes, Katherine," the old woman replied drily. "I've always thought so."

The Fury was speechless. He had thought he had the measure of these people, these lower classes of Sandy Row. They were meant to be God-fearing and pliant; no match for his own soaring intellect. So what the hell were they doing with an opinion?

The Fury tried to work himself up to a show of righteous indignation; the crowd, after all, seemed to be as outraged as he was; but he was flustered and he only managed to stammer something about doing the Lord's work.

"Can't the Lord do his own work? The lazy bastard!" the voice called from the back. Many of the people in the congregation knew Davy Anderson and they knew him for what he was. He was a man you could trust, a man who would unflinchingly help his neighbour and spurn any gratitude. There were many in that hall who had been helped out by a timely and surreptitious gift of cash or had been grateful for Davy's strength when moving house or doing a bit of building work, and in return Davy would shake his head and say, 'Ach, you can buy me a pint the next time you see me.' Davy Anderson was a man of his community. A man of the people. But The Fury, it had to be admitted, was a man of God.

The boos and cries of 'shame' became louder until Davy had to admit defeat. He shook his head in disgust and stormed out through the main doors behind him. Katherine decided to stay and listen to the rest of the sermon and, when it finally ended, she could see no irony in the collection plates that were passed around the crowd. As the plate came to her she realised that no one had been prepared to suffer the social stigma of insulting God with a few paltry coins and so she was forced to give away the last pound note she had in her purse. It was to help with God's work was how she justified it to herself. You couldn't put a price on that now, could you?

Joker grew up with the influence of both his parents. His mother would supplement the religious teaching he received at school with her own indistinct and gentle interpretations of the message of Jesus Christ, while his father would simply provide him with an alternative set of ideas, content to let his son come to his own view of the world, in his own way and in his own time.

Joker, for his part, was more interested in his father's stories about the heroes of his own family. Davy would tell his son about his own father and grandfather who had worked in the shipyards, building ships that would sail all over the world. He would tell him of the working men from Katherine's side of the family, men who had grafted in the mills and foundries of Belfast to provide for their families. "Working men," Davy would tell Joker, "have to fight for everything their whole lives because no bastard is ever just going to hand them anything."

"That's right." Katherine, who enjoyed a bit of sarcasm,

would nod sweetly. "It's the women who get everything handed to them. The women in your family have always sat quietly at home waiting for their big strong men to bring them all the things they need. Women aren't very good at anything, you see."

Davy would bite his lip. He knew that Katherine's mother had worked twelve-hour days, six days a week, in the flax mills of North Belfast, while his own mother had once led a riot to improve the conditions for the men at the shipyard. Occasionally, therefore, he would admit that the role played by the women in the family was just as important as that played by the men. Only occasionally, though, because, despite his socialist principles, he was still a bit of a chauvinist at heart.

Joker's grandfather, Davy's father, had once sat Joker down in front of the fire in the living room and told him about his time in the army during the war. "Oh, aye," he said, "there was a wee gang of us, you see. All from Northern Ireland. A real bunch of madmen we were. And the Brits, of course, were desperate."

"Is this you and your mates winning the war on your own again, da?" Davy called from the kitchen.

"I'm telling the story!" Joker's grandfather testily replied.

"Well, be sure and tell Joseph there were other people involved."

"Yes, don't worry, I will."

"The Yanks were there, for one thing," Davy said mischievously. "And the Canadians, and the Poles, and -"

"Yes! Yes! OK!"

"And the Scots, and the Welsh. Even the English managed to -"

"All right, I know!" Joker's grandfather threw up his hands in exasperation. "Of course, your da's right," he told Joker. "There were loads of other people there too, but, to be honest," he said, lowering his voice, "between me and you, they just got in the way." And Joker laughed.

"Yeah, there was a bunch of us," his grandfather went on. "Good mates we were. There was wee Scotty from Limavady. Of course, nobody could understand a word that he said, but he was a good lad. There was Geordie Rice and Gerry McCann from North Belfast, and Billy Cavendish from Londonderry." Joker's grandfather was momentarily lost in his own reverie as the memories engulfed him. "I'm sure there was a photo of us all together, you know," he said finally. "Couldn't tell you what happened to it, though." And he went on to tell Joker of how he went off with his mates one summer's morning to steal a French beach and win a world war.

Joker loved to hear these stories; stories that were filled with humour and spirit, stories that set the honest, working man against a myriad of enemies. Against both the Nazis and the faceless demons of the ruling classes.

In the streets around Sandy Row, Joker played with the children of other working families; he grew up in the confusion of the troubles and he learned of other faceless demons: demons who wanted to kill him and his family and who were intent on destroying Northern Ireland itself. The Fenians.

"Who are these Fenians, da?" Joker once asked his father. Davy sat his son down and told him.

"The Fenians are Catholics, son, and Catholics are the same as us. They've been conned the same way that we've been conned. The only difference is that their conmen want to be in control of everybody; they don't want to be ruled by a different set of conmen and that's why they're causing all this trouble. Now I work with Catholics and they're good men; like I said, they're working men like we are, but if it comes down to it, then I'd have to choose our conmen over theirs. At least we know where we are with our lot."

Davy worked in Mackie's foundry in West Belfast, where he mixed with Catholics from working class backgrounds from across the city. He regarded them as decent working men and there were many he would call friends, but, despite his socialist ideals of a united working class, he would fight against any notion of a united Ireland. A united Ireland meant an Ireland that was ruled by the Pope in Rome, an idea that was simply unthinkable, and so Joker was taught not to hate the Catholics, like most of his friends did, but to disagree with their ideology. Essentially, Joker was taught to think for himself.

It was the Royal Belfast Academical Institution, or Inst., that opened Joker's eyes, and what he saw terrified him. It was Joker's contrary brain that had secured him a place at the prestigious school in the centre of Belfast, and Joker became something of a celebrity in his little community. Someone from Sandy Row, it was said, was going to make a name for himself.

Katherine stood and watched through tears of pride as Davy walked their son to school for his first day. And Joker was excited. He had often passed the RBAI in his youth: it was one of the more obvious landmarks of the city centre, and he had stared through the railings at the grand building beyond, wondering at the mysteries it contained; curious about the swaggering, confident boys that he watched file through those famous gates. Now

Joker was to join the privileged ranks, the sons of the rich and the powerful; the elite, the best that Northern Ireland had to offer. Bastards.

It took only a week for Joker to come to the conclusion that he didn't belong. The other boys came from a different world, a world that Joker simply couldn't comprehend. These boys possessed a natural confidence, an unswerving belief in themselves and their place in the world and Joker came to understand that they despised him. The boy from the slums trying to mix with his betters. Joker could feel their eyes staring at him in unfeigned disgust.

He was wrong, of course; he was making it all up. His alienation existed entirely in his imagination. The boys of Inst. were no more aloof than the boys from any other school. There were assholes, obviously, but there were assholes in every school.

Inst. did not have a monopoly on assholes, but Joker needed something to push against. He needed something to focus on, something that could turn his fear into something more positive: anger. Because Joker was afraid. He was afraid of the brash self-belief that these boys possessed, their cockiness, their blithe acceptance that their future would be spent in the boardrooms of industry and the corridors of power. The faceless demons of the ruling classes were not so faceless after all. So Joker became withdrawn; he wanted no part of the world that his schoolmates inhabited, because he didn't understand it. He kept his head down and quietly passed his school days focused only on the classroom. The world of study and learning became his domain and he excelled. Latin, a stumbling block for generations of schoolchildren, was, for Joker, a living and vibrant language. His brain revelled in the subtle complexities inherent in the structure of Latin and this helped him to completely master the modern languages of French and Spanish. He was also in the top ten percent in all of his other subjects; so, when he announced that he was planning to leave school at the age of sixteen to become an apprentice in the shipyard, his teachers were appalled.

"But, but you can't!" they cried. "What about your 'A' levels? What about university? You can't just waste your talent. Please think it through, think of your future." But Joker *was* thinking of his future; he had always known what he wanted to do, what he wanted to be. He was working class and that was a fact that filled him with pride. He wanted to work with his hands, to strain the muscles of his arms and back, to build and to sweat and to feel alive. He'd had enough of school and so, at the first opportunity, he left.

The glory days of the Harland and Wolff shipyard were long gone, though there was still enough work around for Joker to be taken on as an apprentice in the metal shop. He was there for just over a year - a time that Joker would come to regard as one of the happiest of his life - when he fell victim to one of the rounds of redundancies that were increasingly sweeping through the yard. He was devastated. For a while he moped around on the dole, feeling restless and useless; until, finally, he scrounged some money from his father, bought himself a coach ticket and went to find his fortune in London.

He'd been given a contact number from a friend back in Belfast and with this he was able to get a labouring job helping to build London's new orbital motorway. Life soon settled into a happy routine for Joker. He moved into a house with some of the guys that he worked with and, with the rent being shared, he was able to save a reasonable proportion of his wages each week. He spent several years in London, working, drinking and fooling around with girls; living the life of a young bachelor with money to spend and not much to worry about.

He was friendly with all of his housemates and there were two in particular that he spent a lot of time with. One of these was Danny, a young man whose parents had arrived in London from Jamaica just before he was born. Danny introduced Joker to reggae and marijuana, which would become two of Joker's greatest passions.

For his part, Joker introduced Danny to the Ulster fry with potato farls and soda farls, which Joker managed to find in a small store in Kilburn. Joker also taught Danny the anthem of the Orange Lodge and of Ulster Loyalists: *The Sash My Father Wore*, and they would sing it during drunken weekends in a deliberate attempt to rile their fellow housemates. Most of the other guys who were staying in the house were from the Irish Republic, from the western counties of Galway and Donegal. They were the strong-backed sons of the sons of the navvies who had torn up swathes of English soil to provide the arteries of the British Empire and they were not the type of people you would want to rile. The atmosphere in the house, however, was always good-natured and the banter between the young men never got out of hand.

It was Danny who persuaded Joker to shave all his hair off. Joker had been becoming increasingly concerned about his receding hairline.

"For Christ's sake, Danny, I'm only twenty," he would moan. "And look!"

"If you want my advice," Danny told him, "then just shave it all off and be done with it."

"Become a skinhead, you mean? How the fuck is that going to help?"

"It may feel a bit drastic to begin with, but you'll get used to it, trust me. At least you'll never have to worry about your hair again, man. Hey, it might even suit you, you know what I mean? You aren't bad looking for a white man, are you? What do you think the ladies will prefer, anyway? A guy who is going bald before his time? Or a guy who has the confidence to do a Yul Brynner?"

Eventually, Joker was persuaded to take the plunge and it turned out that his new, streamlined hairstyle did suit him and he, Danny and their other friend, Francie, decided to take it for a test drive down the local pub. It was there that Joker hooked up with a girl who sat on his lap and couldn't resist rubbing the little bit of fuzzy stubble on Joker's scalp. It turned her on, she said, and Joker became a confirmed and committed skinhead.

Francie, the other member of Joker's triumvirate, was from Glengormley, which was in Northern Ireland, just north of Belfast. Francie taught Joker and Danny a whole variety of complicated ways in which they could give all of their wages to Bookmakers. He showed them doubles, trebles, yankees and all sorts of accumulators, though, after a few weeks of having no money at all, Joker and Danny decided they weren't cut out for gambling.

"It's just an insidious tax on the working man," Joker would declare sanctimoniously, although he did help Francie spend his winnings one weekend when four horses romped home and landed Francie with over eight hundred pounds.

As much as Joker enjoyed his time in London, he always knew he'd go home. He supposed it was the same for Irish people the world over. No matter how far away they were or how long they had been away, the assumption was the same: at some point they would go home.

"What the fuck happened to your hair?" were Davy's first words to his son. But then he gave Joker a hug to welcome him home and Katherine fussed over the son who had returned to her.

When he first got back to Belfast, Joker wasn't bothered too much about finding a job. He had saved enough money from London to be able to take things easy for a few months and he felt that he needed a breather after the hectic lifestyle of the capital. He signed on the dole and gave his assurances that he would actively look for work, and then he prepared himself for a time of chilling out and relaxing in the familiar surroundings of his home town.

He began seeing a local girl and was even thinking of moving in with her. In general, therefore, Joker's life settled into a placid monotony: comfortable, secure and maybe a little dull.

One annoying condition of receiving dole money was that Joker would occasionally have to attend job interviews arranged by the dole office. Joker considered it only a minor inconvenience and, besides, it was practice for when he started looking for a job in earnest. And so one afternoon Joker went along to an interview for a job that he had no intention of landing. It was at a newsagent's shop in the city centre.

Joker noted with satisfaction the looks of dismay on the faces of the two interviewers as soon as he entered the shop. It was just after lunch and the shop was quiet.

"Good afternoon, it's Mr Anderson, isn't it?" Snatter asked politely. He was looking at a clipboard he was holding in his hand. On it was a form, forwarded by the dole office, which contained Joker's details. "My name is Mr Green and this is my associate, Mr Lingfield."

"Linfield? I'm a big fan. I -"

"Not Linfield, LINGfield," Ding-a-Ling interrupted. "With a 'g'."

"Oh, sorry," said Joker. "My mistake."

"So, you're a Linfield fan, are you? Does it bother you that me and Snat … er, me and Mr Green are both Cliftonville supporters?"

"Bother me? Not at all, I've had my tetanus jabs." Joker was surprised to see Mr Lingfield appear to stifle a grin. He decided that he might as well have a bit of fun.

"No, it doesn't bother me," he said. "In fact, when I was a kid I used to have this football game and I painted one of the teams to look like Cliftonville. There was a terrible accident, though, when the coach taking them to Windsor inexplicably caught fire. No survivors. Shocking, it was. Striker, the game was called, do you remember it?"

"You had Striker?" Ding-a-Ling asked excitedly. "I used to love Striker. I had the World Cup edition and everything, all the accessories. The game with 'real kicking action', wasn't it?"

"Yeah," Joker replied. "I never really got into all that Subbuteo crap. I thought it was just fancy marleys, but Striker needed skill."

"I've always said that," said Ding-a-Ling. "You really had to judge your pass, didn't you?"

Snatter let his clipboard drop in exasperation. He turned to look at Ding-a-Ling and then back again to look at Joker. He was incredulous. "Excuse me!" he said. "But can we just be serious here for a minute. You can't really be comparing Striker to Subbuteo! That's ridiculous. Subbuteo was by far -"

"Oh, yeah," Ding-a-Ling said, "I'd forgotten you were always a big Subbuteo fan. Well, tell me this, Mr Smartass, what about the night that Man United beat Liverpool 48-nil in the FA cup final?"

"What the hell has that got to do with anything? That was when you played your sister; you told me all about it in school the next day. But, anyway, I'll repeat the question, what the hell -"

"Are you Man United fans?" Joker asked.

"Yeah," said Ding-a-Ling. "Why?"

"Well, put it there, lads." Joker shook hands with them both. "We haven't had much to cheer about in a while, but we should stick together, at least."

"You're right about not having much to cheer about," Snatter said. "I'm starting to think I'll never see them win the league. Not in this lifetime anyway."

"Ah, you can't think like that. Liverpool can't win it every bloody year." Joker tried to cheer him up. "I have an aunt who thinks she's Bobby Charlton."

"Really?" Ding-a-Ling was intrigued.

"Well, no, I just made that up," Joker admitted. "But that would be cool, wouldn't it?"

"That *would* be cool," Snatter agreed. Ding-a-Ling turned to Joker. "Do you remember the 1979 cup final?" he asked.

"Are you kidding? I'm still recovering."

"Well, me and Snat ... um, I mean Mr ... oh, fuck it! Me and Snatter here watched it round at my house with another mate of ours. There was just the three of us in the house and when Alan Sunderland -"

"Frizzy-haired bastard," Joker broke in.

"Exactly!" Ding-a-Ling said. "When he scored I was so worked up that I grabbed my ma's clock off the mantelpiece and fucked it at the TV."

"Jesus!" Joker exclaimed. "What happened?"

"Nothing good," Snatter told him.

"The TV exploded," Ding-a-Ling elaborated. "The three of us just stood and stared for a second and then we turned and ran like fuck."

Joker threw back his head and laughed and Snatter and Ding-a-Ling joined in. "The worst thing about it, though," Ding-a-Ling continued after a while, "was that the clock was an anniversary present my da had given my ma. Waterford crystal it was. Worth a bloody fortune."

The three of them laughed even harder and the banter flowed easily between the three until, as the laughter began to die away, Ding-a-Ling made a suggestion. "Hey, Snatter, I think we should give Mr Anderson here the job. What do you say?"

"You do seem to be the most suitable applicant that we've seen," Snatter told Joker.

"No other cunt bothered to show up," Ding-a-Ling explained.

"So, Mr Anderson, what do you say? Do you want the job?"

Mr Anderson reached across to shake hands. "Call me Joker," he said.

It was a few years later that Joker met Carol. Joker knew that he wasn't a bad looking bloke. Despite the years of alcohol abuse, his physique was still in good nick; he liked to keep trim, and his rugged facial structure had been likened to that of James Dean, so Joker was aware that he had a lot going for him. But Carol was something else. Carol was from a different planet.

He first saw her in the Speakeasy bar of Queen's student union. It was a Friday afternoon and Joker and Ding-a-Ling had taken the day off to go on a bit of a session. Joker was standing at the bar when Carol walked in. She was with a group of friends, but Joker didn't notice them because Carol stood out so much. She stood out from everyone in the bar. She stood out so much it was almost embarrassing. It wasn't that she was beautiful, although she was hardly unattractive. It was everything about her. It was the way she moved, it was the way she dressed, it was the way her face came alive when she smiled, it was the way she smiled, it was -

"Are you fucking deaf?"

"What?" said Joker with a jolt.

"I said that'll be £1.60, please."

"Jesus," said Joker, reaching into his pocket. "80p for a bloody pint. Your prices are catching up with the rest of the bars. I thought you were meant to be subsidised."

The barman didn't reply; he took Joker's five-pound note and went to the till. When Joker got back to the table where Ding-a-Ling was waiting, he had worked himself up into quite an excited state. "Did you see your woman, Ding-a-Ling?"

"No, Joker, I didn't," said Ding-a-Ling taking his pint, "because not only am I blind, I'm also a homosexual and I'm made out of fucking concrete."

"Point taken. Do you think I've got a chance?"

"You're not serious, are you? You should count yourself lucky she lets you be in the same room as her."

"That's a no, then?"

"Joker, I'm not being funny, but look at her. She is effortlessly cool. This is a woman who oozes class from every perfect pore; she is panache personified, she has élan, she has style. Let's be honest here, she makes every other person in this bar look like a bucket of shit."

"What are you trying to say?"

Ding-a-Ling stared at Joker and shook his head. "Go for it, mate," he said. "Don't let me stand in your way. I'll be waiting for you when you get back."

"Listen." Joker tilted his head as a song started to play over the tannoy system. It was *A Rainy Night in Soho* by the Pogues and it was one of Joker's favourite songs. "That's a sign, it's got to be," he said. "The most beautiful song ever written for the most beautiful woman in the world."

"Oh, dear God," Ding-a-Ling muttered. Joker gazed over at the vision on the other side of the room, willing her to glance in his direction. When she did, Joker gave her a friendly wink and what he thought was his most charming smile. She smiled back.

"Won't be a minute," Joker said to Ding-a-Ling as he got up and strolled over to the most beautiful woman in the world. He came back with her phone number.

It was never going to work. It was probably the happiest six months of Joker's life, but there was always a subtle and underlying problem: Joker felt inferior.

At first he dismissed it; he tried to see it as immature jealousy and, in time, it would go away. He then tried to disguise it as something else, deciding that Carol's relentless perfection was boring and that he needed some stimulation. But he was lying to himself and he knew it. He knew that he would always feel the need to measure himself against her and he knew that he could never hope to reach her heights. Whenever they were introduced to anyone new, Joker was convinced he knew what they were thinking. They were thinking that he must be part of some sort of care in the community project that Carol was involved with. What other explanation could there be for them being together? This was all in Joker's imagination, but it was growing, and it was growing to such an extent that something had to give.

It finally came to a head one night when they got back to Carol's house after a party. Carol had insisted that they leave early and Joker had brooded on that fact the whole of the way back to Carol's place. The argument had started as soon as they got into the house, with Joker accusing her of being a control freak and of trying to distance him from his friends. At first Carol was taken by surprise, but she had then become resigned and she just let Joker rant until he got tired and collapsed, unconscious, onto the sofa. She had seen it coming too. It was never going to work.

The relationship struggled on for a while, but they both knew the end was inevitable, and so it came as no surprise when they finally acknowledged it was over. Joker was devastated.

His accusations against Carol were, he knew, not just unfounded but laughably ridiculous. Carol was the nicest, sweetest, most wonderful person he could ever hope to meet. She was perfect. Any deep, scarring faults in their relationship were all down to him. Joker had a relationship with an unbelievable woman, a woman who was special in every way, and what had he done with that relationship? He'd crumpled it up and thrown it away.

But then, as many people suspected, there seemed to be something wrong with Joker's brain.

Twenty-Three

"Right! Up against that fucking wall!" The voice that barked the command came from behind them and Snatter groaned. 'Now what?' he thought.

They were about to turn around when they were pushed roughly up against the gable wall of a derelict house.

"Aye, that's two of them." A young boy's voice could be heard. "The rest must have scattered."

"What?" Ding-a-Ling began. "What the fuck?"

"Shut it!" Snatter and Ding-a-Ling felt their feet being kicked apart as a hand was run up between their legs, searching for concealed weapons.

"Where's the rest of you fuckers?"

"Seriously," said Ding-a-Ling. "What?"

"You two cunts came from the other side of the peace line, didn't you?"

"What? Well, yeah, but -"

"There was fucking loads of them," the young boy said. "I saw them."

"OK now, there's something going on here and I'm going to … is that you, Gary?"

Ding-a-Ling turned his head. "Frankie?"

"Aye, fucking hell, what the fuck are … it's OK, Paddy, you can let them go."

Snatter and Ding-a-Ling felt the hands that were pressing them against the wall relax and they turned around to see the young boy who had thrown the halfer. He was standing beside two anachronisms.

Frankie and Paddy could easily be identified as two men who had sacrificed a large part of their youth to the paramilitaries. There were men like Frankie and Paddy all over Northern Ireland and they were easy to spot, for they all wore the same uniform. The uniform of the seventies.

When the sectarian tensions in Northern Ireland had finally erupted into full-scale violence at the end of the 1960s, young men, on both sides of the divide, flocked to join the ranks of the paramilitaries. They were desperate to defend their own communities and, at the same time, to either preserve the union with Britain or to free Ireland, once and for all, from the tyranny of British rule. The paramilitary organisations, however, struggled to cope with the scale of the influx and, as their numbers swelled, the various groups became unwieldy, with a basic lack of both discipline and security. It became routine for the security forces to round up and prosecute many of these young and inexperienced volunteers and the prison population grew accordingly. Now, in the 1980s, these men, their sentences having been served, were being released and they were being released to wardrobes that were no longer fashionable.

Frankie and Paddy were both wearing bell-bottomed jeans with a high waistband, shirts with huge collars and brown anoraks. They also had shoulder length hair, sideburns and handlebar moustaches.

"What the fuck do you mean there were loads of them?" Ding-a-Ling turned to the young boy. The boy suddenly realised that he may have made a mistake and, spinning round, he beat a hasty retreat.

"Did you really come over the peace line?" Frankie asked.

"Yeah," Ding-a-Ling replied, "had a bit of a run-in with some real nasty bastards."

"Shit, to hear that wee fucker you'd have thought the whole bloody Shankill Road was attacking."

"Ah, you know what kids are like." Ding-a-Ling smiled. Snatter rolled up his trouser leg to take another look at his shin.

"You all right there, mate?" Frankie asked. "Looks bad, that."

Snatter looked up and grimaced. "Is the Royal far from here?"

"No, it's not far at all," Frankie informed him. "You going to casualty?"

Snatter nodded. Frankie hit Ding-a-Ling a friendly slap on the back and smiled. Snatter could smell beer on his breath.

"We're heading back that way. We were in The Laurel Leaf, you see," Frankie explained. "We'll dander along with you as far as the Falls."

So Snatter and Ding-a-Ling once more set off for the hospital, only this time they were escorted by the IRA from the 1970s.

Twenty-Four

"It's a bit bloody obvious, isn't it? I mean, Marcia Brady? Everybody fancied Marcia Brady, for fuck's sake."

"OK then, smartass, who was *your* first crush?" Bobby felt a little disgruntled. Joker thought about it for a second. "Remember the *Double Deckers*?" he asked. Everyone nodded. "Well, I used to fancy the wee kid with the stuffed tiger."

"She was only about six, you bloody pervert!" Sean said in disgust.

"I wasn't much fucking older than that myself," Joker said in his defence. "I mean, it wasn't a sexual thing or anything like that. I just thought she was, well, you know, pretty."

"Ah, that's so sweet," said Tone mockingly. "Did you want to hold her hand? Did you want to share your sweeties with her?"

"Piss off!"

"What about you, Tone?" Bobby asked. "Who did you fancy when you were a kid?"

"Not really sure," Tone replied. "I mean, apart from Marcia Brady, obviously. I seem to recall a good-looking girl in *Black Beauty*. Remember? The TV series?"

"Oh yeah, I fancied her too," Sean said. "And Marcia Brady, obviously. And the older one in *The Little House on the Prairie*, Mary, wasn't it?"

"Didn't she go blind?" Bobby asked.

"Yeah, but what the fuck has that got to do with anything?"

"Nothing, I'm just saying, that's all."

They were now in White's Tavern, one of Belfast's oldest bars, and like all the other bars they had been in, there was a noisy, festive atmosphere. When they had first arrived there was no room to sit down, so they had stood at the bar. As they waited for a table to become available, they had to hold their drinks close to their chests as the crowd at the bar swayed around them. Joker had a brainwave. He reached over and plucked a straw from a box that was sitting on the bar. He was then able to sip his beer without any danger of spilling it.

'Classy,' thought Tone with a smile. Eventually, Sean managed to procure a table and they all sat down. Joker brought his straw with him.

"Become attached to that, have you?" Bobby asked him.

"You can't go wrong when you've got a straw, Bobby," Joker told him solemnly. "You just never know when it'll come in handy." And he popped it into his pocket.

The first round of drinks was coming to an end as they discussed *The Little House on the Prairie*, and Joker and Sean went off to get the next one. When they returned, Bobby handed cigarettes to Joker and Tone and they lit up. Tone leaned back, relaxing, as he exhaled his first draw. "Did Jamesy ever tell you about the great plan he has for his life?" he asked around the table. No one spoke; they either shrugged or shook their heads. Tone continued. "I was out with him a while back when he told me what his dreams for the future were. He was saying that he wants to be a professor, lecturing at either Queen's or Trinity, or maybe even somewhere across the water."

"Lecturing in what?" Joker asked. "Ancient history?"

"Well, yeah," said Tone. "You know the way he's always banging on about that hero of his, don't you?

Themi … Themis …"

"Themistocles?" Sean suggested.

"Yeah, that's him. I think Alexander the Great is a bit too racy for Jamesy. Anyway, in Jamesy's fantasy, he'd come home every evening to his wee wife and they'd sit in front of the fire and chat about their day."

"Aye, that's Jamesy for you," Bobby said, "always shooting for the stars."

"Well, that's the thing," said Tone, leaning forward. "At first, I was just as cynical. I said to him, rather wittily, I thought, 'So, essentially, Jamesy, you want to be Mr fucking Chips?'"

"Yeah, very funny, Tone," Sean said.

"But then," Tone carried on, "I thought, that's just the sort of pragmatism that should be admired, not mocked. I mean, why shoot for the stars if you're only going to fucking miss?"

Bobby looked thoughtful. "I'm not sure if that's a worthy sentiment or just a bloody depressing one," he said.

Tone glanced over at the door. "Speak of the devil," he said. "Looks like Jamesy's had his eyes opened." They all turned to see Jamesy approach. He had a look of utter desolation on his face.

"Things not go well, then?" Tone asked.

"Bloody hell, I just don't believe it," Jamesy muttered in reply. "She thinks the Bible should be taken literally. You know, Adam and Eve and all that stuff?" He sat down. "Jesus! I actually feel a bit sick."

"You just need a drink, that's all," Tone assured him. "Joker, go and get Jamesy a pint."

"I've just got back from the bar," Joker complained. "Why should I go?"

"Because, if you don't," Tone explained languidly, "I'll twist your dick off and make you eat it."

"Well," Joker said as he stood up, "you can't say fairer than that, eh, Jamesy?" As Joker went off to the bar, Tone could see the dismay in Jamesy's eyes. "So, she's a creationist, is she?" he asked. Jamesy nodded. "Let me guess," Tone continued. "She thinks the universe is six thousand years old?"

"Yes," Jamesy said miserably. "Bloody hell, can you understand that level of ignorance?"

"Have you got a problem with ignorance, Jamesy?" Bobby asked, smiling. He was trying to lighten Jamesy's mood, but he had misjudged the depth of his feeling.

"Of course not, Bobby," Jamesy replied sharply. "Everybody is ignorant about something, but it's wilful ignorance that I don't understand. How can anybody actually choose to be ignorant? To just ignore the perfectly obvious? I … I can't get my head around it."

Joker came back from the bar with Jamesy's drink. "There you go, Jamesy, get that down your neck and you'll soon forget all about your woman."

"I'm not sure I will," Jamesy said as he took his pint. "I mean, what if that was it? Seriously, I've never felt like that before. I really thought that she was the one, you know? The one and only, so-called, fucking love of my life. And what if she was? What if my 'one and only' turns out to have had her brain wiped clean? To have had all independent thought sucked out of her? To be just another mindless drone spouting from a ready-made script? What the fuck do I do then, eh?"

"OK, Jamesy, take it easy," Joker said. Jamesy rarely swore, which made it all the more shocking when he did.

"You've really got it bad, haven't you?" Tone added.

"Well, there's nothing we can do about it now, except to keep on drinking. It does pass, Jamesy, trust me."

"Yeah, cheer up, Jamesy," Joker said. "Do you want to see my straw?"

"What?"

"So, Jamesy, do you want to give us all the gory details?" Sean asked. "What exactly did she say?"

"Well, for one thing she said that evolution was just a theory."

"Yeah," Tone said. "They don't like Mr Darwin at all, those types. He really pissed on their parade."

"Greg was doing most of the talking, though."

"What the fuck was Greg doing there?" Tone exclaimed.

"Who's Greg?" asked Sean.

"Greg invited the whole bloody lot of them," Jamesy explained. "There wasn't much I could do about it."

"Who's Greg?" Sean repeated.

"He was in *Scooby-Doo*," Joker told him.

"Greg reckoned the Bible was written by God and the Holy Spirit. It's funny, you know," Jamesy went on, "but I've never really thought about it before. Just what *is* the Holy Spirit? I don't think anybody's ever actually explained that to me."

"It's like everything else in religion," said Tone. "It means whatever you want it to mean. If you ask ten religious experts, you'll get ten different answers. The Holy Spirit is an essence, it's a type of mist, it's God's butler, it's a twenty-foot tall rhinoceros with banjos for ears; it doesn't really matter because it isn't fucking real."

Sean stiffened at Tone's remarks. Sean's faith played a large part in his life and he was often exasperated when

Tone so easily dismissed something that Sean felt was important. He kept quiet, however, and concentrated on his beer.

"When I was a kid," Joker said, "I used to think the Holy Spirit was God's nickname for his dick." Everyone stared at Joker as if he had suddenly sprouted antlers.

"Have you been drinking out of the toilet again?" Tone asked him.

"No, seriously," Joker protested. "Doesn't it say in the Bible somewhere that God impregnated Mary using the Holy Spirit? Well, when you're a kid you -"

"Oh, Christ!" Sean exclaimed, looking up to the ceiling.

"Why would God even need a dick?" Jamesy asked.

"Obviously for just such an occasion," Joker informed him.

"For fuck's sake!" Sean cried. "I think we can safely assume that the Holy Spirit is not some bloody euphemism for God's wab."

"Why's that then, Sean?" Tone asked. "The Bible has always been and always will be interpreted in hundreds, if not thousands, of different ways. I think Joker's idea is just as valid as any other."

"Bollocks!"

"Well, presumably, yes."

"I think Jamesy raised an interesting question," Bobby said. "I mean, we're supposed to be made in God's own image, right? So does that mean that God would have a penis?"

"Or a belly button?" Joker suggested.

"Yeah," Tone joined in, "you can just picture God sitting up there in heaven wondering just what the fuck his nipples are for." Sean put his head in his hands.

"Anyway," Tone continued, "if you subscribe to evolution, then the whole 'God's own image' idea becomes meaningless."

"Why?" Bobby asked.

"Because we're still evolving, that's why. A million years ago we didn't look the way we do now, with the possible exception of Joker, and a million years from now we'll look different again. So at what point in our evolutionary development is 'God's own image'?"

"Maybe the phrase refers to the soul," Sean suggested. "Maybe the essence of God is in harmony with the human soul."

"Jesus, Sean, with that sort of convoluted, twisted, fucked-up, nonsensical bullshit you could join the priesthood," Tone snorted.

"Yeah, well at least I'm not twisted with bitterness, Tone!" Sean snapped. "At least *I* don't hate God."

"Who hates God?" Tone asked. "I certainly don't hate God. I might as well hate Thor or Isis or the bloody pixies that play with the elves in fairyland. As you know, I don't believe there is a God, but, to be honest, I couldn't give a shit either way. If there is a God or Gods, then you can fucking guarantee they bear no resemblance whatsoever to the vicious asshole portrayed in the folk tales of the Middle East. The existence or non-existence of any supreme beings is of absolutely no concern to me."

"Then what's your bloody problem?"

"My problem is the snivelling, grasping, lying bastards who claim to know what God wants," Tone said. "This bloody country's been going downhill ever since St Patrick came. Jamesy, what's the name of that Greek bugger?"

"Could you be more specific?"

"You know the one; he wrote about the Celts."

"Strabo? Is that who you mean?"

"That's the one," Tone said. "He was writing about the Celts before Jesus Christ ever came along, and he described them, with admiration, you understand, as people who were madly fond of war. Our ancestors were mental bastards apparently, even the women; just look at Boadicea."

"Boadicea?" asked Bobby. "Wasn't she English?"

"It's more likely that her name was Boudicca," Jamesy informed him. "And no, she wasn't English. England didn't exist back then. Boudicca was a British Celt."

"That's right," Tone went on. "Then along comes St Patrick and tells us that we should all be on our knees. And we've been crawling ever since."

"That's a ridiculously simplistic way to -"

"Yes, OK, Jamesy," Tone interrupted. "OK. The point I was stumbling towards is the impossibility of religious uniformity. It's like I said, the Bible, like any other book, can be interpreted any way you want. For every single religion on Earth there are hundreds of thousands of shades of opinion on how the holy words should be interpreted. That's because we're all individuals with individual ideas and there's nothing wrong with that. Take you, for example, Sean; you consider yourself to be a good Catholic, right?"

"Yeah, so?"

"But you still use condoms, right?"

"Yeah, but that's -"

"I'm not having a go. I'm just saying that you've tailored the teachings of the Church to suit your individual needs. Everybody does, to one extent or another, and that's fine, because everyone's different. But it's the priests, the vicars, the rabbis, the mullahs and imams, the druids, the shamans, the self-important shit-talkers who think that *their* individual beliefs have to be forced on everybody else that piss me off. Show me someone who claims to know exactly what God wants you to do and I'll show you a damned, bloody liar. 'My God wants you to do this. My God wants you to do that. My God, coincidentally, has exactly the same political agenda as I do.' These people should be shunned, but they're not, are they? No, they're treated not just with respect but with fucking reverence. They're treated like they actually do have a direct link to God. We let them dress up in fancy dress and rape our kids, we let them -"

"Oh, fuck off, Tone!" Sean was getting angry. "Most of these people you're talking about have had a calling from God; it's a vocation they couldn't ignore. You can't dismiss that. People all over the world rely on them for guidance; they gain strength and a sense of morality from these people that you're so fucking contemptuous of. I've met loads of priests who were really sound, Tone, and so have you."

"Yes, that's true," Tone agreed, "but we've both known a lot of priests who were total bastards. Do you not remember, Sean, that time in school when Rubber beat the crap out of you against the lockers in D Block?"

"Rubber?" asked Joker.

"Catholic Gestapo," Tone told him. "Yes, Sean, it's true there are a lot of priests who are genuine and decent human beings, but they would be that way whether they were priests or not. There are good and bad people in every walk of life, but the Church, taken as a single entity, has to be, by its very nature, controlling and manipulative."

"What the hell are you talking about?"

"You just have to look at the Republic, or the Free

State as it was then. The Unionists were right to fear the Catholic Church becoming the real power because that's effectively what happened. The Church, right from the beginning, dominated just about every part of life in the country. And what was one of the first things the Church did, Sean? They started banning books, didn't they? The land of saints and scholars actually banned more books than the fucking Soviet Union. And you know why a regime feels the need to ban books, don't you, Sean? It's because they're not confident in their own ideas. It's because they're shit scared that the people, given the opportunity, will start thinking for themselves. The Church is terrified of rational thought, because it's always relied upon ignorance and superstition to keep its grip on power. Reason is the biggest fucking enemy the Church can ever have."

There was a brief, tense silence as Sean thought about his reply. Joker had taken the straw from his pocket and was twirling it between his fingers. He turned to Jamesy, who was just putting his pint to his lips. "Have you ever bubbled a frog?" he asked. Jamesy managed to spit most of his beer back into his glass. The rest, however, came down his nose.

"It's easy to focus on the negative, Tone," Sean said coldly. "The Church has had a long history and, of course, mistakes were made; but what about the achievements and the advances the Church has made? In art, in architecture and even in science?"

"They'd fuck all choice after Galileo!"

"I've never done it myself, like." Joker was continuing as Jamesy tried to clear the rest of the beer from his nostrils. "But I'm aware of the procedure. Apparently, you take a straw and -"

"Yeah, well, like I said, mistakes have been made, but at least the Church is trying to acknowledge them. You won't recognise that, though, will you? You refuse to see any of the good the Church does; not just Catholics, either, but all religions. What about all the charities founded by religious people all over the world?"

"Those people would do good works whether there was any religion or not," Tone replied. "Or maybe they wouldn't. And if that's the case, then what sort of people does that make them? Who would you consider to be the better person, Sean? The Christian who performs good deeds because they either want a reward from God or they fear a punishment, or the atheist who performs good deeds out of nothing but sheer bloody human decency? Of course, there's always morality, isn't there? Isn't that what you Christians like to bleat about? Where do we get our sense of morality from, if not religion? Well, would you agree that one of the strongest bonds throughout the animal kingdom is the bond between a parent and a child?"

Sean leaned back in his chair and sighed. "Well, yes, obviously. What's your point?"

"Well, the fact that we can see this bond all over the animal world must show that it's a biological urge or some sort of evolutionary device, right?"

"Yeah, OK. And?"

"So what is the only thing that can counteract this normally overpowering urge to safeguard your offspring? Apart from any psychological problems, that is."

Joker put his hand up. "Oh! Oh! Oh! I know! I know!" he cried excitedly. "Is it religion?"

Sean shook his head and gazed upwards. "There's a surprise," he muttered.

"Very good, young Anderson," Tone said. "Because it's only with religion, isn't it, Sean, that parents can not only stand by and watch someone mutilate their infant son's penis, but they can fucking celebrate the fact. It's only with religion that parents can send their teenage daughter away to have her clitoris ripped off because some ignorant fucking wankstain has decided it's a sin for women to enjoy sex."

"Oh, come on, Tone, you're talking about -"

"And it's only with religion," Tone interrupted, "that parents can sit and watch their child die and do nothing except mutter meaningless crap at an empty sky."

"I would imagine, though," Joker concluded to Jamesy, "that it's not something you'd want to do if you've got your best clothes on."

"What's your answer then, Tone?" Sean asked angrily. "If you ruled the world, what would you do? Ban all religion?"

"Of course not. I think that it's a basic human right that people should be free to believe whatever they want to."

"Then what the fuck -"

"What I *would* do, though," Tone continued, "is ban religion for anyone under the age of eighteen."

"What?"

"Think about it: children should be free to have a childhood. They should be free to become accustomed to this life without having to worry about the possibility of a next one. It should be no more acceptable to impose religion on kids than it is to force-feed them whiskey. I mean, let's face it, religion has killed more people than booze, cigarettes and sex combined, but it's considered OK to expose newborn babies to it. I say that once someone turns eighteen, then they should be shown all the religions of the world and told they can choose whichever one they like. Or, if they can't find one that suits them, then they're perfectly free to invent their own. Of course, they'll also have the option to choose no religion at all. Now you can't deny that that is a perfectly reasonable idea; but can you imagine the uproar? Religious leaders all over the world would squeal like fucking pigs because they'd know the game would be up. Without the impressionable minds of small kids to fuck around with, then all religions would wither and die."

Joker suddenly roared with laughter. "Tone, that's brilliant! I think you've really got something there. You can just picture it, can't you? All these eighteen-year-old blokes going, 'Hand me those scissors, I've decided to become a Jew.' You and me, Tone, we should start a campaign."

"I can imagine there would be some blokes attracted to the misogyny of Islam," Tone said, "but how many women do you think there would be? How many eighteen-year-old girls are going to think, 'Yes, I like the idea of being put in a sack for the rest of my life and the risk of being stoned to death for having a shag just adds an element of danger'?"

Tone stood up. "Anyway," he said, "it's my round. Who wants to give me a hand?"

"I will," Bobby said. "There's something I want to talk to you about." He got up and followed Tone to the bar.

"Well, Tone didn't seem to have anything to say about eighteen-year-olds accepting Christianity," Sean commented to Jamesy and Joker. "Do you think that's a flaw in his great plan to wipe out religion?"

"Course not," Joker said as he lit a cigarette. "Weren't you listening? On turning eighteen, you'd be presented with every religion in the world. That's the beauty of it, don't you see? Christianity is no more plausible than any other religion, so why should it stand out? Did Tone ever tell you about the founding of Mormonism?"

"Yeah, he did," Sean replied wearily. He knew where Joker was going.

"And what did you make of the story?"

"That it was an obvious con, perpetrated by a convicted conman."

"Yeah, we can see just how blatantly false the whole thing was because it didn't happen all that long ago. But, think about it, Mormonism is growing all the time and in time there's no doubt that it'll be just as established as any mainstream religion. In fact, in America, it already is. Now Tone's point is that the founding of Mormonism is no different to the founding of any other religion. Actually, I think Joseph Smith nicked the whole dictation idea from the Muslims."

Sean sighed. "I hate arguing with Tone," he said. "I mean, I know he's wrong, he bloody has to be wrong, but he's so clever at twisting arguments around so much that you don't know where you are."

"Really?" Joker asked. "I think Tone just tells the truth."

"What about you, Jamesy?" asked Sean. "Are you turning into one of these mad atheists?"

"I don't think so, though I wish I'd had Tone with me in Delaney's," Jamesy said with a sad smile. "No, I think religion fulfils some sort of spiritual need that humans have and to that extent it's probably necessary. Having said that, though, I think Tone has a point about how religions can go too far. Basically, religion, or more correctly faith, is believing in something that has absolutely no evidence to support it. That means there are no limits to what you are free to believe and that means that religion has no parameters. There is no system in place to rein in the wildest excesses that religions, being man-made, can be prone to. Yes, I know that female circumcision is technically illegal in this country and human sacrifice is generally frowned upon, but things like that do still happen because somewhere there will always be someone who truly believes that it's what his God wants."

"So what's your solution then, Jamesy?" Joker asked him.

"I don't think there is one. In fact, I don't think that one is needed. Religion may well have been woven into human nature from the very beginning of human sentience. Maybe it's just the way we are."

"Well, that's depressing," Joker said.

Tone and Bobby returned from the bar and passed around the drinks. Cigarettes were distributed and everyone settled down once more.

"You were just talking about religion there, Jamesy," Sean began, "but isn't that missing the point?"

"You mean God, don't you?" Jamesy asked.

"Well, yes, obviously."

Jamesy shrugged. "There are just as many Gods as there are religions. Actually, probably a lot more."

"I don't know how you can say that. The biggest religions in the world are all monotheistic, so it stands to reason that they all worship the same God, and that's just the one God."

"I don't think Jamesy's talking about polytheism, Sean," Tone said. "Let me put it this way. I've met Christians who believe that their God wants homosexuals to be killed. Is that the sort of thing that your God would be interested in?"

"Oh, you're just talking about interpretation again, aren't you?" said Sean. "Yes, OK, different people will always have different ideas about God, but that doesn't mean that God doesn't exist."

"That's true," Tone conceded. "But what about *your* God, Sean? Which particular variety of God is the one that floats *your* boat?"

"There is only one God," Sean said grumpily. "The God that gave us the Ten Commandments."

"You think the Ten Commandments are important?"

"Of course they're important," Sean cried. "They're the most profound moral guidelines we've ever received. They form the basis of all of our laws. They -"

"Name them."

"What?"

"These profound moral guidelines," Tone said. "If they're so intrinsic as to how we conduct ourselves, then you should be able to name them."

"Well, I can't. Not off the top of my head at least."

"I'll get you started with some clues. The first commandment should be a good one, right? It should get the ball rolling with something fundamental, something that absolutely nobody could argue with. In other words, something like this. 'Thou shalt not physically, mentally or sexually abuse children in any way, shape or form. Under any circumstances. Ever.' Does that ring a bell, Sean? Does that sound like the first commandment?"

Sean said nothing; he just lifted his pint and took a drink. Bobby looked around the table. "That's weird," he said. "I had to learn the Ten Commandments for Sunday School, but I can't remember what the hell they are, apart from 'Thou shalt not kill', of course. Everybody knows that one."

"That commandment should really read, 'Thou shalt not murder someone without a valid reason'," Tone said.

"Is that right, Tone?" Sean asked. "So you can just rewrite the bloody commandments, can you? It's the most clear-cut and simple of all the commandments; it doesn't need any elaboration from you."

"OK, so the Bible is clear on that, is it? Killing is not allowed? Then what about 'Whoever does any work on the Sabbath must be put to death', from Exodus, or 'All who curse their father and their mother must be put to death', from Leviticus? Seriously, Sean, I could go on all day listing the types of people that the Bible insists must be killed. 'Thou shalt not kill' is the one commandment that the Bible couldn't give a flying fuck about."

"Fondling your neighbour's ass," said Joker. "Isn't that one of them?"

"Don't you mean covet?" asked Jamesy.

"Covet. Fondle. What's the difference?"

"Good point."

Sean buried his face in his hands. "Jesus Christ!" he muttered.

"Ah!" said Tone. "Now that *is* one of the commandments. 'Thou shalt not take the Lord's name in vain.' Now we're getting somewhere."

"OK, Tone," Bobby said. "It's bugging me now; just tell me what the first one is, then I'm sure I'll remember the rest."

"I'll tell you the first four, actually, because they tell us a lot about Sean's God. Number one is 'Thou shalt have no other Gods before me', right? Number two is 'Thou shalt not worship any idol', or it could be 'craven image' or a load of other stuff, but you get the gist. Number three is 'Thou shalt not take the Lord's name in vain' and number four is 'Remember to keep holy the Sabbath day'. So, God uses up the first four of the ten most important laws for humanity to live by, all on himself. The selfish wanker!"

"For fuck's sake, Tone, you can't say that," Sean groaned.

"Yeah, Tone," Bobby agreed. "I'm not especially religious, but some things have to stay sacred, don't they?"

"You vicious bastard, Tone," Joker cheerfully joined in, "picking on God like that. You know he can't defend himself."

"Oh, whatever!" said Tone, lighting another cigarette. His attention was drawn to a striking-looking girl who seemed to be coming their way. There was another girl with her, a girl that Tone thought he recognised. Was it Karen, Ding-a-Ling's sister?

"Right!" said Karen, as they reached the table. "Where the fuck are they hiding?"

"I'm sorry?" Tone replied.

"Gary and Seamus; we know they're here. What the fuck have you done with them?"

"Karen," Sean began. "Hi, Rosie. Actually, they're not here."

"What the fuck are you talking about? They were meant to be meeting up with youse cunts, weren't they?"

"Yeah, they were," Sean agreed, "but they never showed up. I mean it; we haven't seen them all day."

Karen, puzzled, turned to face Rosie. Rosie was looking pale, she thought. She turned back to Sean. "So where the fuck would they be? Have you no ideas at all?"

Sean shrugged. "No," he said, "to be honest, we know as much as you do. We haven't heard anything since I talked to you earlier on."

Karen looked thoughtful; she wasn't sure if she should be worried or not. She tried to reassure Rosie. "Don't worry, Rosie love, they're bound to turn up somewhere. And when they do -" she turned back to the table. "You can tell our Gary if you see him he'll be getting my fucking toe up his hole! All right there, Jamesy love?" Karen had a soft spot for Jamesy. She turned and took Rosie's arm and they both strode off towards the door.

"Lovely turn of phrase, Karen has," Joker said. "Don't you think?"

"So that was the future Mrs Green?" Tone asked.

"Yeah," said Sean. "That's Rosie."

"Not exactly Snatter's type, I would have thought."

"Yeah," Bobby added, "she looked like she could eat Snatter for breakfast."

"You've been very quiet about this whole business, Sean," Tone said. "Is there something you're not telling us?"

Sean put up his hands. "None of my business, Tone." He stood up. "I'm away for a piss."

Joker leaned over and tapped Tone on the shoulder. "Black," he said.

"What?"

"The colour of her hair. It's black."

Twenty-Five

"Rosie's pregnant." Snatter was surprised at how easy it was to say out loud and how natural it sounded. "I'm supposed to keep it all a big secret till after Christmas, but, fuck it, what difference can it make?" The casualty department of the Royal Victoria Hospital would certainly have heard much more shocking statements, but Snatter had expected more of a reaction from Ding-a-Ling.

They had been waiting in casualty for almost two hours and were finally getting ready to go. Snatter's various wounds had all been tended to and they were now waiting to get the news from his leg x-ray. Snatter glanced at Ding-a-Ling, who was staring straight ahead. "Well?" Snatter asked. Ding-a-Ling seemed startled. "What? Uh, I mean, are you sure it's yours?" he blurted out.

"What the fuck do you mean by -"

"All right, all right. I don't mean anything by it; it's just a figure of speech, OK? It's just that, well, it came as a bit of a surprise, that's all."

"Yeah, well."

"So that's what all the marriage talk is about then?" Ding-a-Ling asked. Snatter nodded. "Rosie's idea," he said. "It's all taken on a life of its own. I really could have done with a day out with the lads today, you know? They must be wondering where we are. Do you think we should ring somebody? Ding-a-Ling, are you even fucking listening to me?"

"What? Uhm, yeah, yeah. Ring? Ring who?"

"I don't know, your Karen, maybe. Find out what happened to Harry, at least. Or your folks. Somebody may have phoned them to find out where we are, so they may be worried."

"Yeah, you're right. I'll go and make a few calls." Ding-a-Ling got up and walked over to some payphones that were attached to the far wall. A nurse came and called Snatter to the treatment room. When he got back, he found Ding-a-Ling sitting with his elbows resting on his knees. He was staring at the floor.

"Well, it's not fractured," Snatter said.

"What? Oh, right. That's good then. Ready to go?"

"Yeah. What I think we should do is grab a black taxi into town and then just get a private taxi straight to the Bot. There's no point trying to intercept them before that. I don't think I'm up to it anyway. At least we know they'll end up in the Bot sooner or later."

"Yeah, I think you're right, come on."

Ding-a-Ling walked and Snatter limped to the exit. When they got outside, they were surprised to see it was snowing. "I suppose it's been cold enough today," Snatter said. "A white Christmas, eh?" Ding-a-Ling didn't respond. When they reached the Falls Road, they crossed over at the traffic lights and stood by the roadside, waiting for a black taxi to come along. The Falls Road black taxis operated like a bus service, following a set route to ferry people from the Nationalist community of West Belfast to and from the city centre. Snatter, shuddering against the cold, turned to Ding-a-Ling. "So, did you get through to anybody?" he asked.

"What?"

"On the phone."

"Oh, yeah, I was talking to my ma. Turns out Karen, Harry and Rosie are on the warpath. They've headed into town to try and find us."

"Fuck!" Snatter suddenly looked worried.

"You don't seem all that excited about becoming a da," Ding-a-Ling ventured.

Snatter hesitated. He looked up and watched the falling snowflakes. "To be totally honest," he said, "it's my worst fucking nightmare. I don't want to get married. I certainly don't want to have a kid." He shook his head. "But I just don't seem to have any say in anything. I just don't know what to do. It's like I'm watching my life being taken away and there's fuck all I can do about it."

Ding-a-Ling was watching him carefully. "Sounds like you needed to get that off your chest," he said. Snatter sighed and closed his eyes. Ding-a-Ling went on. "I assumed that you and Rosie were happy together." Snatter looked at him and let out another sigh. "Not really," he said. "*I'm* not happy anyway, and I'm pretty sure Rosie isn't all that happy either. I'm not really sure how the hell it all happened; it's like it all happened to somebody else, you know? I mean, one minute I just bump into her in the street and the next minute I'm on the verge of having a fucking wife and kid."

Ding-a-Ling seemed to be about to say something, but he spotted a black taxi approaching and he put out his hand. As the taxi drew up to the kerb, he turned to Snatter. "Yeah," he said, "bit of a bugger, that, isn't it?"

Twenty-Six

It was almost seven when they got back to the hotel. Claire, in the car's passenger seat, yawned and stretched. "Can't we skip dinner?" she asked. "And just go straight to bed?"

Tone looked at her and shook his head. "No, I'm starving," he said. "And you just need to get your second wind. A good meal, a drink of wine and an invigorating cigarette should do the trick."

"Will you carry me into the hotel?"

"The answer to that question would have lots of swear words in it, not to mention some violent, slapping actions, so I'll pretend I didn't hear you."

Claire laughed. "My hero."

"Come on; like I said, I'm bloody starving."

They had dinner in the hotel restaurant and then adjourned to the bar where Tone had a pint of lager and Claire had a glass of wine. They each lit a cigarette and sat back in quiet contentment.

"So, did you get around to reading *The Catcher in the Rye*?" Claire asked casually.

"Yeah," Tone replied. "I enjoyed it."

"I thought you'd like it; you remind me of him."

"What? You mean Holden?"

"Yeah." Claire smiled. "You both take everything so seriously. No, wait, that's not exactly what I meant. I think it's more that neither of you are prepared to suffer fools gladly. You know what I mean? People annoy you, don't they?"

"Well, I wouldn't say that. That seems a bit harsh."

"But they do; oh, I know you try and hide it, but it's

obvious. At best, I'd say that you just about manage to tolerate people, but there's a real resentment there, isn't there? Is resentment the right word? Disgust, maybe?"

"Are you just making this stuff up? I thought it was journalism you were studying, not psy -" Tone stopped abruptly as Claire suddenly leaned forward, her elbows resting on her knees.

"I want to find out what makes you tick, Mr Maguire," Claire said fervently. "I'm going to analyse you; I'm going to explore the murky depths of your soul."

"That sounds like a fun evening," Tone said lightly and Claire laughed.

"It will be," she reassured him. "I just think you're worth getting to know, that's all. There's more to you than meets the eye."

"I'm worth getting to know?"

"Well, let's just say that I'd like to get to know you better. I'd like to make the effort."

"You're not getting all soppy on me there, are you?" Tone gently mocked and Claire smiled a little nervously. She then lowered her head and gazed at him through her eyelashes. "Maybe I am," she said softly, and Tone felt his heart beat faster. "What do you want to know?"

"Everything!" Claire exclaimed. "Now go and get a couple of bottles of wine and we'll head upstairs. We've got work to do."

"It was a normal enough childhood," Tone said. He was sitting in the one chair in his hotel room while Claire faced him, sitting propped up on pillows on the bed. "Or at least as normal a childhood as you can have, growing up in the Divis Flats in the seventies. My parents were pretty old when they had me; I think I may have been an accident. They already had a son, you see: my brother, who's about ten years older than me. He lives in Australia now and we don't hear from him very often."

"Does that bother you?" Claire asked.

"Not even slightly. Nice try though." Tone smiled and took out a packet of cigarettes. "No, I think there was too much of an age gap for us ever to be close," he said, as he handed a cigarette to Claire. "I was only about twelve when he left, so I never really got to know him. Maybe that's something for the future; some big reunion where we finally get to know each other after all these years." Tone shrugged. "At the moment, though, I don't even think about it."

Claire looked thoughtful for a second and then she reached for the wine. She topped up her glass and passed the bottle to Tone. "So there's no big juicy childhood trauma that we can dredge up and pick over?"

"Sorry," said Tone.

"But there *is* something that rattles your cage," Claire persisted, "and I'm going to find it. Let's see, I know you've got a bee in your bonnet about religion; I can tell that from all the bitter wee comments you make. I don't think that's the problem, though. But, what the hell, we've got all night, so tell me about that. What's that all about? What have you got against religion?"

Tone took a sip of wine and lit his cigarette. He studied Claire's face and then he sat back with a sigh. "You're going to make a big deal out of this," he said.

Claire was suddenly intrigued. "Really? Well, come on, let's hear it."

"To be honest," Tone said, "I'm not really sure what it is you're looking for, but I don't think this is it. But, as you say, what the hell. I met this girl when I was at university in England, OK? She was part of an obscure Christian sect that doesn't believe in modern medicine. Well, to cut a long story short, she died because of that belief. She probably would have lived if she'd gone to a hospital but -" Tone shrugged. "Well, there you go. Is that what you're looking for?"

"Jesus!" Claire said quietly. "Did you love her?"

"What? Oh, I don't know. Maybe things were going in that direction, but who knows? No point in thinking about it, really; and, to be honest, I think about it less and less."

"And you blame religion? All religion?"

"Of course I blame religion. Wouldn't you?" Tone waited for an answer, but Claire remained silent. He sighed. "I'd never really thought about religion," he continued. "It was just something that was there; you know, something that everybody has to some degree. But when Emily died then -"

"Emily? That was her name?"

"What? Yes. Look, do you want to hear this or not?"

"Sorry." Claire smiled. "Go on."

"Well, when she died, I sort of lost the plot a bit, did the usual old clichés; you know, drink and drugs? But eventually, after I'd got back to Belfast, I took more of an interest in religion. I did a lot of research and stuff and I have to admit it was a bit of an eye-opener. It all just seemed to be such an obvious con."

"What do you mean, 'a con'?"

"Well, it seemed to me that every religion in the world was started for a reason. Either for social manipulation or a way of making money."

"What about God?"

"What's God got to do with anything?"

Claire tilted her head to one side and gave a sardonic smirk.

"Seriously," said Tone, "when it comes to religion, then I think that God is irrelevant. Think about it. What are you? Church of Ireland?" Claire nodded, and Tone continued. "Well, if you go to a bishop or even an archbishop for advice or guidance, then do you think their reply is coming directly from God?"

"I suppose not."

"Of course not; all you would be getting is one man's opinion. You may as well ask a greengrocer or your postman. God, like I said, is irrelevant. Even Shakespeare said, 'In religion, What damned error but some sober brow, Will bless it and approve it with a text, Hiding the grossness with fair ornament'."

"Quoting Shakespeare means you're either cool or a pretentious prat."

Tone laughed. "I like to think Shakespeare was a closet atheist. Or an agnostic, at least. Wasn't it Hemingway who said that all thinking men are atheists?"

"Now you're quoting bloody Hemingway? Anyway, to get back to the point. You say that you may as well ask a postman. Well, OK, but aren't the clergy trained? Isn't it some sort of vocation they're meant to be on?"

"It's just a job," Tone said. "And when you say they're trained, then trained in what? Trained in vagueness? In the unverifiable? The supernatural? It certainly isn't anything practical like carpentry or plumbing; they're trained to have an opinion on ancient mythology, that's all. But they're treated as if they -" Tone leaned back in his chair and sighed. He took a last puff from his cigarette and stubbed it out. "Oh, I don't know," he said. "I'm getting tired of the whole argument."

Claire studied him for a while. "It's certainly touched a nerve with you, hasn't it? But I think you're right: I don't think it's the main problem."

"What makes you think there *is* a problem?"

"I don't know." She smiled. "Maybe I'm wrong, but I just get this feeling." She stood up and walked towards him. Standing in front of Tone, she reached out and ran her fingers through his hair. "I just get this feeling there's something twisting you up. Does that sound stupid?"

"Yes."

Claire laughed and gave Tone a playful slap on the side of his head. She jumped back onto the bed and picked up her wine from the table. "OK," she said, as she made herself comfortable, "so Christianity is a con, is it? How do you work that out?"

Tone smiled. "It's only my opinion," he told her. It was true, he thought, he *was* getting tired of the argument; all he wanted to do just then was to crawl into bed beside Claire and help her out of her clothes.

"Well, I'm being nosy," Claire said, "so let's hear your opinion."

"OK." Tone sighed. "Christianity was founded by a bloke called Saul of Tarsus, who'd never even met Jesus."

"Saul of Tarsus? You mean St. Paul?"

"Yeah," Tone said. "He changed his name after his *miraculous* conversion. Don't you think it's strange that God only appeared to individuals, and only in private? Anyway, I reckon he changed his name so that less people would associate him with the Saul of Tarsus who was a known persecutor of heretical Jews."

"Heretical Jews?"

"Early Christians, you could call them. Don't get me

wrong, I'm sure Saul did have a revelation on the road to Damascus, but I think it was more of a financial opening of the eyes than a spiritual one. He was a big fan of opening up Christianity to non-Jews by telling them they weren't required to follow the old Jewish laws like circumcision and avoiding certain foods. This obviously would have hugely increased the potential resources he would have access to. His letters in the New Testament are nothing more than fancy begging letters."

"But wasn't he arrested and killed for his beliefs?"

"He was arrested, yes, and tradition suggests that he was beheaded, but I don't see what you're getting at. Are you trying to say his arrest and execution make him somehow more genuine?"

"Maybe; oh, I don't know, I'm just trying to play devil's advocate."

"Yeah, well, it's impossible to know what really went on back then; we're talking about events that have had two thousand years of rose-tinted gloss applied to them. When you try and look at it all logically, it just doesn't make any sense."

"Isn't that the point, though: faith and faith alone is all that's needed?"

"Then why do these people make such a big deal about so-called miracles? Why do they need to see moving statues or miracle cures or the face of Mary in a bloody hedge?" Tone shook his head sadly. "I think it's the awful waste of human potential that bothers me the most. Just imagine what we could achieve as a species without religion constantly trying to keep us in the Dark Ages."

"I'm not sure I know what you mean."

"Look at the universe," Tone said, raising his arm to the window. "Look at the scale of it. The scale of the solar system is incredible enough; the scale of the galaxy we're in is mind-boggling; but the entire universe is, and I don't care who you are, way beyond human comprehension. Factor in the immensity of time and you've got yourself a whole lot to think about. But religion only wants us to dwell on events that occurred in a very limited ... well, put it this way. Imagine an incredibly beautiful beach; it's got the lot: palm trees, crystal clear seas, everything. Now imagine focusing all of your attention on just one grain of sand. That, for me, sums up religion. I think it was Carl Sagan who once asked, 'Why bother with the supernatural when the natural is super enough?'"

"Yeah, that's very nice, Tony," Claire said, "but don't you think you're massively over-generalising. To say that religion is trying to keep us all in the Dark Ages is, I think, a bit too dramatic. I mean, don't you think your antipathy towards religion has been blown out of proportion. When I think of the clergy in the -"

"Conmen."

"What?"

Tone smiled. "A friend of mine - actually the one I told you about, went to Inst. - well, his da is a bit of an outspoken atheist and the word that he uses for the clergy of any religion is conmen."

"Sounds like you two would get on very well together."

"Yeah." Tone laughed. "I've only met him the once, but, yeah, we did get on well."

"That reminds me," Claire said. "I meant to ask you earlier. Didn't you say there was something wrong with your mate's brain? What did you mean by that?"

"Oh, nothing really; it's just that, well, I don't know if it's some weird form of autism or whatever, but there do seem to be some things that he's unnaturally gifted at. For example, he's very talented at modern languages."

"A cunning linguist, eh? I'm a fan already."

"You, my dear, are incorrigible. I've never met anyone who was so incapable of being corriged."

Claire laughed and held out her glass for Tone to top it up with wine. "What does this mate of yours do with himself, then?"

Tone paused, then shook his head. "He's on the dole at the minute." Claire was suddenly alert. She leaned forward. "Well, *that* hit a nerve," she said.

"What?" Tone asked. "What are you talking about?"

"You flinched just before you answered. I mean, it wasn't very obvious, but it was there. Now why would you do that?"

"Are you drunk already?"

"Now you're being defensive," Claire said. "Tell me about him, tell me about your mate."

"Christ!" Tone muttered. He stood up and paced along the floor. "There's nothing to tell." He let out a deep breath and ran his hand through his hair. "Like I said, he's very gifted at certain things. Of course, at other things he's just an asshole." Tone smiled, but Claire thought it was a nervous smile. "What else do you need to know?" he asked.

"So he's got a talent that he doesn't use; is that what you're saying?"

"I'm not sure he even wants to use it." Tone shrugged. "He's just drifting, you know?"

"Is he happy?"

Tone leant against the bedside cabinet. He looked down at his glass and swirled the little drop of wine around in the bottom. "He shouldn't be," he said finally. "He's just prepared to settle, and what he's settling for is nothing. Is he happy? He probably is, but that doesn't make it any less of a waste."

Claire was silent for a few seconds while she made up her mind whether to ask the question or not. What the hell, she thought. "Are you talking about him or you?"

Tone jerked his head around to stare at her. "Oh, spare me the amateur bloody psychology," he snapped. Claire jumped off the bed, her eyes wide and her anger flaring. "Well, you bloody tell me, Tony," she barked. "Just what *is* the problem, because I just don't get it? What is it that's holding you back? It's obvious you hate your job, you bloody moan about it enough; so what the hell is the problem? As far as I'm aware, you don't have a wife and kids back up north, or do you?"

"Of course not."

"Then come on, Tony, tell me; you must be on a decent wage and you don't seem to have too many expenses. You must have some money in the bank, so what's stopping you? There must be something you want to do with your life besides selling bloody tablecloths, so why not just do it? Why not just -" Claire slumped onto the chair, her anger fading. "Just grasp the fucking nettle."

Tone looked down at her. He knew she was right; he'd been thinking the same thing himself lately. What *was* holding him back? Was it fear? He was aware that Emily had already started to blur in his memory, but was there something else that he had lost in Bournemouth? And if so, what was it? His drive? His ambition? His self-belief? He watched Claire as she stared at the carpet, sulking. "Did you find what you were looking for?" he asked sheepishly.

"Maybe I'm just too nosy for my own good," she replied, not looking up.

"You know that cheesy old phrase, 'You look beautiful when you're angry'?" Tone asked her. Claire looked up at him, her expression guarded. She remained silent.

"Well, *you* don't," Tone continued. "In fact, you look like shit." Claire leapt up from the chair and snatched a pillow from the bed. She rushed at Tone, brandishing the pillow as a club. She managed to catch Tone with a blow to the head before he grabbed her around the waist and they struggled and wrestled with each other across the room. They wrestled each other and they wrestled each other's clothes off and they wrestled each other down onto the floor.

Where they remained for quite some time.

Twenty-Seven

Jamesy drained his glass and placed it on the table. "We're not staying for another one here, are we?" he asked.

"No," Tone told him, "we should probably make a move. You knocked that back quick; what's the rush?"

"I just fancy a walk, that's all. Get a bit of air, you know?"

"Yeah, OK. Do you want some company?"

Jamesy looked at Tone and nodded. "If you don't mind," he said.

"Course not." Tone knocked back his drink and stood up. As he pulled on his coat he spoke to the three who were still finishing their drinks. "See you in The Crown, then?"

"Yeah, we shouldn't be long," Sean said. "I can't see us having time for The Elms this year."

"Probably not," Tone agreed. "Right, Jamesy, let's go. We'll see you in a bit, then?"

"Yeah, see you," Sean answered for the three of them.

"Jesus!" Tone said as they stepped outside. "Bloody cold enough for snow, wouldn't you say?"

"It is, yeah."

"So, Jamesy, how are you feeling now?" Tone asked, as they made their way through the dwindling crowds. Most of the shops were now closed and those people still in the city centre were either making their way home or were, like Tone and Jamesy, heading for a bar. Parties would be erupting all over town as the end of the working day signalled the official start of the countdown to Christmas. The city centre still had a buzz to it as the crowds milled around the bus stops and taxi ranks. Alcohol-fuelled sing-songs were springing up everywhere amidst the laughter and the excited chatter.

The Christmas lights completed the festive scene, which had the giant Christmas tree at the City Hall at its heart. Jamesy barely noticed the tree as he and Tone walked past. He had answered Tone's question with a non-committal grunt. He knew it was unfair of him, and Tone, he thought, deserved better. He also knew, though, that Tone would understand if he needed to be quiet for a bit. As they got closer to The Crown, he began to feel the need for some conversation and turned to Tone as they walked.

"Do you think I'm overreacting?" he asked.

"No, Jamesy, I don't," Tone replied. "I really can sympathise, you know?"

"I think I'm still in shock, actually." Jamesy gave a little laugh. "The more I think about it, the less I actually believe that it happened. Can they really believe those things they were saying? How can they? I mean ... seriously? How?" Jamesy shook his head in wonder.

"Yeah, I know, Jamesy. I've heard just about all the extreme, crackpot beliefs there are and, still, they never cease to amaze me. To be fair, though, most Christians don't believe in that crap. Young-earth creationists are about as extreme as Christians get, but as long as they don't try to infest the school system they're harmless enough."

"Bloody hell, Tone!" Jamesy laughed. "You've mellowed!"

"Yeah, well," Tone said, "perhaps I weary of the fight."

"That would be a shame," said Jamesy. "The world

needs more people like you, Tone. More people to stand up and question things."

"Are you flirting with me?"

Jamesy laughed again. He was beginning to feel better. "There was one thing that Greg said that I thought he may have had a point with, though."

"What was that?"

"He said he couldn't believe that anyone could believe in evolution and still be a Christian."

"So?"

"Well, it just made me think that his beliefs may be more valid because he refuses to compromise them."

"It sounds like you're starting to question your own beliefs."

Jamesy nodded silently. "Maybe I need to take a closer look at what I actually do believe," he said.

They walked on in silence for a while until Tone piped up. "Of course, you're right about Greg," he said. "I wish that all Christians thought like him because they'd paint themselves so far into a corner they'd have nowhere to go. Do you think the Catholic Church would still be around if they were still insisting the sun went round the earth? No, mainstream Christianity is a much more fluid beast than that. It needs to be to survive. It has to constantly adapt and to constantly find ways to reconcile what it teaches with whatever new scientific insights come along."

"They evolve, in other words?"

"Yes, Jamesy," said Tone laughing, "they evolve. And they've got very good at it, too. Slippery wee bastards."

Jamesy suddenly sighed. "I'm still really depressed about Hannah, though."

Tone held open the door to The Crown and let Jamesy

enter first. "Well, it's like I said, Jamesy, my old mate," he said as Jamesy went past him, "it'll pass."

"Oh, shit!" Joker exclaimed as they got up to go. "I forgot to get my ma a bottle of vodka."

"Bit late now, Joker," Bobby said. "Everywhere's closed by this time."

"There's an offy beside The Crown," Sean pointed out. "That should be open."

"I might know a better place," Joker told them. "Let's get going."

They walked out into the cold, shivering as they adjusted to the temperature. They remained silent as they walked, feeling it was too cold to waste energy on idle chat. As they turned onto Royal Avenue, Bobby stopped and gave a loud wolf whistle. Some girls who were waiting at a bus stop turned round and started laughing. "Bobby!" they called, and began waving to him. One of the girls broke away from the group and, walking over, she gave Bobby a warm embrace.

"Hello, beautiful," Bobby said happily. "You going to be calling round tomorrow?"

"Of course," she replied. "Probably late afternoon." Behind him, Bobby heard Joker theatrically clear his throat. "Oh, right," Bobby said with a laugh. "You've already met Sean, haven't you?" She nodded to Sean and smiled. "Well, this is Joker," Bobby went on. "Joker, this is Claire."

Twenty-Eight

Tone and Claire had found a run-down little bar not far from O'Connell Street in the centre of Dublin. It was late afternoon and the place was starting to fill up with traders from the nearby market in Moore Street. Tone could guess how cold it was outside by the actions of the newcomers. They would rub their hands and stamp their feet as they made their way to the bar to order a pint of Guinness and a hot whiskey.

"Do you want another one?" Tone asked Claire as he pointed to her empty glass.

"Oh, yes, please," Claire replied happily. "I could get very settled here."

Tone smiled, then picked up the two glasses from the table and went to the bar. They had spent much of the day strolling around Dublin, finally getting around to seeing the sights, but the temperature had dropped suddenly, forcing them to take refuge in the first suitable place they could find.

Claire watched Tone walk back and place the drinks on the table.

"Pretty rubbish Christmas decorations, aren't they?" she said, nodding to the bar.

Behind the bar, a single length of straggly silver tinsel was pinned up. It swayed half-heartedly each time the door opened.

"Yeah, I noticed that," said Tone. "To be honest, though, I think it suits this place. You know, understated?"

"Understated?" Claire laughed. "Do you think that's their mission statement?"

"You never know with bloody theme pubs these days," Tone said. Claire lit a cigarette and sat back. "This year's just flown in, don't you think?" she said. "I can't believe it's only two weeks till Christmas."

"Got any plans?"

"For what? Christmas?"

"Yeah, for Christmas."

"Oh the usual, you know? A traditional family affair. I'll be staying with my parents, the same as every year. Nothing out of the ordinary, but I like it, you know? The whole corny Christmas thing. What about you?"

"Same for me really. I stay at my own flat, but I spend all of Christmas Day at my folks' place. We sit around, chat, have a few drinks, watch TV, the usual stuff.

Any chance we could meet up over Christmas? If we're both going to be in Belfast then -" Claire shook her head. "I'd love to," she said, "but I'm not going to have any time for myself at all when I'm back home. You know what families are like. Plus, I'll probably have to call into the *Telegraph* at some point. The way the news is at the minute it seems hard to keep up. I still can't believe the Berlin wall has gone."

"Yeah, that was a bit of a shock," Tone agreed. They had both watched the news coverage, in the early hours, in Tone's hotel room a few weeks back. "I noticed you got a wee bit emotional during it."

Claire laughed. "Of course I did, and so did you."

"I don't know what you're talking about," Tone said dismissively as he took a drink.

"Oh, yeah, right!" Claire teased him. "What was all that - 'I'm just off to the bathroom here to do some man's stuff'? - I heard the quiver in your voice."

"Nonsense, woman!" Tone protested. "It was just like I said: it was bloke's stuff; the sort of stuff that women just don't understand. And, to be honest, it's probably best that you don't know, what with all the scraping and poking and scooping involved; it's all very unpleasant."

Claire nudged him in the ribs with her elbow. "Are you trying to tell me that you didn't feel a lump in your throat when all those people were dancing on the wall?"

"Course not!" Tone sniffed. "I'm a bloke, remember?"

"Yeah, OK, I believe you," Claire said mockingly. "But doesn't it give you some hope for Northern Ireland? I mean, if that can all work out, then there must be hope for us all, right?"

Tone shook his head as he drained his pint. "Not really," he said. "The more you know about Northern Ireland the more you realise there is no bloody hope at all."

"Oh, it's Mr cheery optimist!" Claire laughed.

"Mr miserable bloody realist, you mean," Tone replied. "Anyway, drink up and we'll go and see if we can find dinner somewhere."

"So, what about you?" Tone asked. "I've told you all about the tragic farce that passes for my love life; it's your turn to dish the dirt. Anyone waiting for you back in Belfast?" Tone tried to make it sound like a casual inquiry, as if the answer was of no more than a passing interest to him. He was aware, however, of just how anxious he was feeling, how much expectation he was placing on the reply. Claire hesitated and Tone's heart sank. It was now late in the evening and they were both lying in bed in Tone's hotel room. Somehow the conversation had stumbled onto the subject of past relationships, and Tone had told Claire about the variety of different girls that had passed through his life, none of whom, apart from Emily, had created much impact. And now he waited with grim anticipation for Claire to reveal her story. A few more moments passed as Claire framed an answer.

"To be perfectly honest," she finally replied, "I'm not really sure." She laughed. "That doesn't make any sense, does it?"

"Oh, I don't know," Tone said. "There have been times when I wasn't too sure if I was in a relationship or not."

"It's something like that, I suppose." Claire lit a cigarette and sat up straighter in the bed. "We grew up together, you see. We met in primary school and just became friends right from the beginning. It sort of grew from there, you know? We'd call round each other's houses and hang out together. We had this wee gang and we'd do pretty much everything together and things just went on from there. We had our first teenage fumblings together, experimenting and all that stuff, but I never thought there was anything serious to it. As we grew up I had other boyfriends and he had other girlfriends, but we always seemed to end up back with each other, some sort of unspoken thing, I don't know.

Then he went off to Queen's and I went off to Jordanstown, and I think at the time I just assumed that we'd drift apart; that's what normally happens, isn't it? But it's weird, it's like we never managed to get around to drifting apart, you know? So, that's it. I'm not really sure where things stand at the moment."

"Do you love him?" Tone blurted out and then silently cursed himself. Again Claire took a little time to thoughtfully compose her answer. Eventually she nodded.

"I love him for who he is," she said carefully, "for his goodness. That's not too corny, is it?" She smiled. "He's always been there for me, so I love him for that, you know? For his friendship. He's a genuinely lovely person;

so, in that way, yes, I do love him. In other ways, though." Claire shrugged. "Does that answer your question?"

"Yeah." Tone pulled her down to lie beside him. 'Yeah,' he thought. 'Because he sounds like a bit of a wab.'

Twenty-Nine

"Nice meeting you, love." Joker nodded to Claire and turned to Bobby and Sean. "I'm going to nip off here. I want to get that bottle of Smirnoff for my ma. I'll see you in The Crown, all right?"

"Yeah, see you in a bit, Joker."

Joker took off. He knew of a little off-licence round the back of the City Hall where he could get cheap spirits, and his mother's vodka was the last and indeed the only present he needed to purchase tonight. He assessed his level of drunkenness as he crossed at the lights. 'Not too bad,' he thought. 'Feeling pretty damn good, actually.' He walked past the City Hall's Christmas tree and was cheered by the sight. 'You just can't beat Christmas,' he told himself.

The back of the City Hall was quieter than the busy retail area that blazed brightly down the length of Royal Avenue. Most of the buildings here were comprised of office blocks, closed now for Christmas. Joker found the off-licence in a quiet little side street.

"Just in time," the elderly man behind the counter told him. "Be closing up any minute now."

"Yeah," Joker said, "you'd want to be home by this time on Christmas Eve if you'd any sense."

"That where you're off to then?"

"Oh no, but then nobody would say that I had any sense." Joker laughed. He wished the old man a Merry Christmas and set off for The Crown, a plastic carrier bag containing the vodka clutched in his hand. He shivered briefly and quickened his pace, eager for the warmth, the comradeship and the beer on offer in The Crown. He knew a shortcut from here to The Crown that would take him down a twisting alleyway.

The entrance to the alley was formed, on one side, by a tall office block and, on the other side, by the remains of an old and recently demolished warehouse. At this time of day, and with the rubble from the warehouse casting grotesque shadows, the alley would be dark and uninviting. Silent and spooky in the darkness. Not that Joker was worried, of course. It was Christmas Eve, after all.

Sticky Mickey watched from the back of his car. Jippo, his right-hand man, sat in the front passenger seat.

"I wanted the two of them together," Sticky Mickey said grimly; "it's getting too fucking late now."

"I'm sure they were meant to meet up earlier," said Jippo defensively. He had been following Joker for most of the day, waiting for Ding-a-Ling to show up so that he could contact his boss and get everything moving. Ding-a-Ling, however, had failed to show. "I don't know what's happened. There's been a balls-up somewhere."

"You got that right."

"So what do you want to do?"

Sticky Mickey thought about it; he had really wanted this out of the way before now, but he had been busy lately and this was the first chance that he had had to sort this out. Just getting one of them, however, seemed messy and unfinished. He would have preferred to get the whole business cleared up in one go and so, had it been entirely up to him, he would have left it for another day. He had made promises, however, which meant he felt obliged to do something tonight.

Now was the perfect opportunity, he felt. The streets around the back of the City Hall were deserted and there was a dark alley up ahead that Joker was approaching.

He was still thinking it over when Jippo suddenly stirred in his seat.

"Wait a minute!" Jippo said. "Who's that?"

Sticky Mickey looked and saw someone stop and talk to Joker; they appeared to know each other. "Fuck it," Sticky Mickey said to Jippo. "I don't care who it is, we're getting this over with now. Give the word."

Jippo quietly got out of the car and gave a signal to a group of men who were waiting in the shadows on the far side of Joker and his companion.

"Hey, Joker, my main man!" the voice came from behind Joker and stopped him in his tracks. Joker stood with his eyes closed, muttering silently to himself.

'Please don't be Johnny Gee! Please don't be Johnny Gee!' "Johnny Gee? It *is* you, isn't it? How's it going? Last-minute shopping, I see." Johnny Gee had his hands full with shopping bags. Joker had only met Johnny Gee once before and that, as far as Joker was concerned, had been one time too many. Johnny Gee came round to face him. "Same as you, I see," he said, gesturing to Joker's carrier bag. "So, where are you off to now?"

"Nowhere in particular," Joker said, matter-of-factly. He was already trying to think of a way he could break off from this encounter as quickly and as politely as possible. He certainly took no heed of the three men he could see approaching from behind Johnny Gee. Johnny Gee, in turn, paid no attention to the three men who were walking up behind Joker.

"Listen, Johnny Gee," Joker began, but he was startled when an arm was thrown around Johnny Gee's neck and, with a hand clamped over his mouth, Johnny Gee was dragged backwards along the street. Before Joker could react, his right arm was grabbed from behind and pushed up his back. A hand covered his own mouth and he was thrust roughly forward in the direction that Johnny Gee was now taking. Both Joker and Johnny Gee were forced into the dark alleyway and were pushed, faces first, against a brick wall. Someone spoke.

"Is this the other one?"

"Let's see. Fuck. No, I don't know who the fuck this is."

"Shit!"

"What do you want to do?"

"Just hit him a slap and tell him to fuck off."

Joker heard a cry and managed to turn his head enough to see Johnny Gee reeling to the end of the alley. It was beginning to dawn on Joker just what was going on.

"Mr Anderson, I take it?"

"Let me guess," said Joker. "You're Sticky Mickey?" Joker's head was pushed hard against the wall and his arm was shoved further up his back. He felt the carrier bag containing his mother's vodka being wrenched from his hand. The blow to his head had left him a little dazed and, as he turned to face his inquisitor, he struggled to focus.

"Nobody fucking calls me that!" Sticky Mickey said angrily. "Especially not a pointless piece of shit like you."

"I'm sorry," said Joker. "What do you prefer? Just Sticky? Or Mr Mickey?"

A fist was driven into Joker's back, causing him to wince in pain. He made a mental note to keep his big mouth shut.

"Where's your gobshite mate?" Sticky Mickey asked.

"Could you be more specific? I've got loads of gobsh-" Again Joker's head was banged hard against the wall. This time he could feel a trickle of blood run down his nose. 'You really must shut the fuck up,' he told himself. He turned his head and finally managed to get a glimpse of his tormentor. He was shocked. Sticky Mickey was tiny. He had small, delicate features, which Joker thought would not look out of place on a young girl, and his smooth, stubble-free complexion only added to his distinctly feminine appearance. Joker looked beyond him, trying to fully appreciate the situation he was in. He could see one hood at the end of the alley, about thirty feet away, and two more standing by Sticky Mickey. If he added the two who were holding him against the wall, then Joker reckoned the odds were six to one. Not great. Sticky Mickey made the situation seem a lot worse when he pulled a black automatic pistol from his pocket.

"Aye, I had one of them too when I was a kid," Joker said. "Does it fire wee bits of potato?"

Joker then received a violent slap, which made his head ring. Despite his bravado, he was starting to have serious misgivings about the whole business.

"My wife wants me to cut your balls off and bring them back to her," Sticky Mickey said.

"She sounds lovely."

"She took it as a personal insult when you broke her brother's arm, so you can understand her being upset. And when she's upset I have to fucking sort it out, you know? She made me promise to bring your balls and your fucking dickhead mate's balls to her on a plate. To be honest, I thought that was going a bit too far, though; just a good fucking kicking should be enough."

The hood at the end of the alley had been rummaging around in some building debris and had found a three-foot long piece of broken banister, which he was now weighing up in his hands. Joker didn't want to think about what the hood might have planned for his makeshift weapon, but he wanted to think about his balls on a plate even less.

"But your dickhead mate's not here, is he?" Sticky Mickey went on. "And that fucks things up a bit."

"Well, if it's easier for you to wait and do us both together then -"

"Shut it!" Sticky Mickey waved his gun in front of Joker's face. He was about to tell Joker what he was planning to do, when a shout came from the end of the alley.

"Hey, who ordered the fucking gorillagram?" the hood called out with a laugh.

Everyone turned to look at the new figure that had entered the alley; his face was in shadow, which made it impossible to make out his features. Joker, nevertheless, grinned.

"You couldn't give us a hand here, could you, Harry?"

Thirty

The Crown Liquor Saloon was well aware of Thomas Edison's new-fangled electric light bulbs, but wanted no truck with them. There was nothing wrong with gas lighting, it was decided. Gas lighting was honest and easy to understand. What could be more natural, it was argued, than pumping combustible material into your premises and setting fire to it? Electric lighting was clearly nothing more than witchcraft, and so Mr Edison, a minion of Satan if ever there was one, could go fuck himself.

The gas lighting also gave the bar a distinctive yellow glow, which instantly provided Bobby and Sean with a feeling of warmth as they stepped out of the cold. The Crown had a central floor space which was surrounded on three sides by a series of enclosed booths, or 'snugs', and on the fourth side by the bar itself. The central area was crowded with people standing, smoking, drinking and chatting, but Sean spotted Tone waving to him through the open door of one of the snugs. Sean and Bobby pushed their way through the crowd and stepped into the snug.

"How did you manage this?" Bobby asked. When The Crown was busy it could often be difficult to acquire one of the snugs, which, not counting the stools at the bar, contained The Crown's only real seating.

"We just squeezed in beside some people who've only just gone," Tone said. "Bit of luck, really. Where's Joker?"

"He had to go and pick up a bottle of vodka," Sean replied. "Ready for another one?" he asked, gesturing to the two almost-empty glasses on the table.

"Yeah, cheers," Tone said, and Sean went off to the bar.

"I thought Joker would have been here by now," Bobby said as he sat down. "He left us a while ago, we were talking to -"

"There's an off-licence just outside," Jamesy pointed out. "Why didn't he go there?"

Bobby shrugged. "This is Joker we're talking about. I think he knew somewhere cheaper."

"Yeah," said Tone, "that sounds like Joker. So, Bobby, you and Sean will be normal, civilised human beings next year? Not the work-shy, scrounging bastards that you are at the minute."

"That's one way of putting it," Bobby said. "You know we've both got placements in the same firm, don't you?"

"Yeah, but isn't Sean planning on going abroad?"

"The Far East, yeah; it's still with the same firm, though. They've got places all over the world."

"You and Sean building skyscrapers, eh? Never thought I'd see it."

Sean came back from the bar and passed the drinks around. "Did I just hear my name being mentioned?"

"Tone was just pointing out that we won't be lazy bastard students any more, after next year," said Bobby. Sean rolled his eyes. "I don't know why you keep having a go at students, Tone," he said. "Although, having said that, I can't remember you ever giving Jamesy any jip."

"Oh, you know I'm only messing about," Tone said. He then lit a cigarette and sat back. "Actually," he went on, "I'm considering a return to the academic world myself."

"You?" Sean asked. "Back at university, you mean? To do what?"

"Not sure yet," Tone replied. "English? Drama? I don't know. Like I said, I'm still considering it."

"It's about time, Tone," Jamesy said with a smile.

"What's brought this on?" Bobby asked Tone. "It's a bit out of the blue, isn't it?"

Tone shrugged. "It's just something that somebody said, that's all. So, yeah, I'm looking into becoming a mature student."

"At Queen's?" Jamesy asked.

"Probably."

"Well, that's good news," Jamesy said. "You finally getting your life back on track?"

Tone, drinking his beer, gave Jamesy a wink. He then put down his glass and stretched out his arms, yawning at the same time A few flakes of ash fell from his cigarette.

"Starting to feel the pace there, Tone?" Sean asked.

"A bit, yeah," Tone replied. "Getting old, you see."

"Aye, well, you'll be twenty-five next year, which is just the same as being dead," Sean said, and Tone laughed. "You're right, Sean," he said. "But I'm looking forward to it. I wonder where we'll all be this time next year."

"Right here, hopefully," Bobby said. Tone lifted his pint and gave Bobby a salute. "Yes, Bobby, here's hoping." He took a drink and glanced over at Sean. "Bloody hell, Sean, take it easy!" Tone watched as Sean drained his glass.

"Some of us can still take the pace," Sean said, and waved his empty glass at Tone.

Tone looked through the door of the snug into the bar. "Where the hell is Joker?" he muttered. "It's his round, isn't it?"

"Fuck knows whose round it is," said Sean. "But, yeah, that's a point, he should be here by now."

"It does seem a bit weird," Bobby agreed. "It's not like Joker to be late for a drink."

"The same with Snatter and Ding-a-Ling," said Jamesy. "There's still no sign of *them*, is there?"

"Maybe somebody's bumping us off one by one," Sean suggested. "And who's going to be next, eh? Maybe we should all make sure that we stay together."

"Is this some elaborate ploy, Sean, to get somebody to go into the bogs with you and hold your willy?" Tone asked. "Because I've always -"

"Do you think we should ring somebody again?" Jamesy broke in. "See if we can find out what's going on?"

"I think I'm too drunk to care," Bobby said. "Does that make me a bad person?"

"Yes, Bobby, it does," Tone told him. "But to get back to more important matters, what are we going to do about the whole drink situation? It's nearly time for another round; do we hold on for Joker to get here or do we just say 'fuck him'?"

"'Fuck him' sounds good to me," Sean said. "It's what Joker would have wanted."

"OK," said Tone. "I'll get the drinks in." He stood up and pushed open the door of the snug. "I'll come with you," said Sean, getting up.

"All right, but no holding hands."

Tone and Sean stood side-by-side at the bar and waited for one of the bar staff to become available. Tone got the impression that Sean had accompanied him to the bar for a reason, but he sensed that Sean was being hesitant.

"What's on your mind, Sean?" Tone asked.

"Oh, I don't know," said Sean; "it may not be anything, but I just need to tell somebody."

"Is this about Snatter?"

"How did you know?"

"You've been acting a bit cagey all day, Sean, whenever Snatter's engagement came up."

"Yeah, well, I don't like to gossip, but sometimes some things need to be said, you know?"

"OK, so spill it."

"Well," Sean began. "It was back in August at the Ardoyne fleadh; this was before Rosie appeared on the scene. I'd arranged to meet up with Snatter one night in the GAA; there were some good bands on that night, you know? Well, Snatter had been on the sauce all day and he was rightly by the time I got there: he kept calling me Tommy Gun, for Christ's sake. Anyway, we're sitting there in the GAA with Snatter rambling away - you know what he's like - and, all of a sudden, he blurts out that he thinks he might be gay."

"Really?" Tone was surprised at how unsurprised he was at the news.

"And you know what sort of men think that they might be gay, don't you?" Sean continued.

"What sort of men?"

"Gay men," said Sean.

"You an expert, are you?"

"Oh, come on, Tone; have you ever thought that you might be gay?"

"Yeah," Tone replied. "I once thought of becoming gay, but then I thought, 'Why bother my arse?'"

"Oh, that's very funny, Tone, yeah. Quality material, mate, really hilarious; but don't you think this is serious? This is a mate we're talking about."

"Yeah, you're right. Has Snatter mentioned it since then?"

"No," said Sean. "I don't think he even remembers saying it. I ended up carrying him home that night; he barely remembers even being in the GAA. And I never mentioned it to him because I thought, well, you know, it's his business. If he wanted to talk about it, then OK, but I wasn't going to force it. But then Rosie bloody shows up out of nowhere."

Tone managed, at last, to catch the attention of a barman and he placed his order. When the barman had gone off to pour the drinks, Tone turned back to Sean. "So what the hell is Snatter doing getting engaged? Unless … unless … Am I thinking what you're thinking?"

Tone looked at Sean for more information, but Sean just shrugged. "Are you saying that Snatter," Tone went on, "has got some girl pregnant and has now decided that he has to marry her? Even though he's gay? That's a bit of a fuck-up, isn't it?"

The barman returned with four drinks and Tone paid for them. He was about to pick up two of the glasses when Sean stopped him. "There might be something else," he said.

"Jesus!" said Tone. "Now what?"

"It may be nothing," said Sean, "but do you remember Weasel from school?"

"Of course, how could I forget?"

"Well, I bumped into him in town a few weeks back and we got chatting, you know, just small talk; but he was telling me about this party he was at, down the Markets."

"Charlie's party?"

"Yeah, you weren't at it, were you?"

"No, I was meant to go, but, well, something came up that night."

"Right, well, anyway, Weasel was at this party." Sean related Weasel's story as they walked, each carrying two drinks, back to the snug. As they reached it they could hear Jamesy inside, trying to reassure Bobby that he wasn't a bad person. Tone and Sean paused before opening the snug's door. "But you can't be sure?" Tone asked Sean.

"Well, no, but I just put two and two together."

"It's not like you to jump to conclusions, Sean," said Tone.

"No, it's not, but it's like I said," Sean told him. "I know Rosie from way back."

Thirty-One

Harry would never have considered himself to be a violent man. It was true that he was prone to what some people would call violent outbursts, due to his rather short temper, but, essentially, Harry saw himself as a peaceful, easy-going type of guy. It didn't take much to keep him happy; all he asked for was a couple of evenings a week to enjoy a few drinks round The League with his mates. That's where he should be now, he was thinking, not traipsing around the city centre on some wild-goose chase. What the fuck did Seamy Green's whereabouts have to do with him? Nothing, that's what! Harry's mood had been getting darker as he had been walking around, thinking about the injustice of it all. Now, at least, it looked like he had found the pub-crawl, or a bit of it anyway.

Joseph Anderson, in Harry's opinion, was a decent enough bloke. They didn't know each other very well, just to say hello to, really, but Harry thought that Joseph was OK.

More importantly, Joseph was a friend of Karen's brother, which, in Harry's view of things, made him a part of the family, and Harry didn't like the thought of anyone threatening his family. He didn't like it at all. Now, just who was this asshole?

Clint Eastwood. That's the picture that Sticky Mickey had in his mind as he posed in the middle of the alley. The pistol sat loosely in a hand that rested, ever so coolly, on his right hip. Clint Eastwood facing the Tiger tank at the end of *Kelly's Heroes*. Sticky Mickey was feeling arrogant: he had two men behind him who were pinning Anderson to the wall, Jippo was to his left and he had another man on his right, while, further down the alley, and behind the newcomer, was a fifth man. Besides, he thought to himself, he was armed. He took a casual step forward.

"I don't know who you are, mate, but this is none of your business. So, do yourself a big favour and just -"

Harry, with surprising speed, reached out and clamped his right hand over the front of Sticky Mickey's head and, as he picked him up by his face, Harry threw a straight left towards the hood that had been to the right of Sticky Mickey. The hood walked right into Harry's fist and, as he made his way towards the ground, he realised that his cheekbone had been fractured. He determined, therefore, that, on reaching the ground, he would close his eyes and would take no further part in proceedings.

Sticky Mickey dropped his gun as both his hands instinctively flew to his face. His delicate fingers clawed at the huge hand that was smothering his entire face in its grip. His legs were flailing wildly below him and, occasionally, he would connect with Harry's thighs. Not that Harry seemed to notice, though. Still holding Sticky Mickey, he thrust him at the oncoming Jippo. The back of Sticky Mickey's head and Jippo's nose came together with a pleasant crunching sound and Jippo dropped in a searing flash of agony.

Harry knew that an attack from behind was imminent and, as he spun around, still holding a gyrating Sticky Mickey, he realised he had timed it perfectly. The piece of broken banister came down hard on the back of Sticky Mickey's head and Harry felt him go limp. He dropped him and grabbed the banister from the hood, who stared, horrified, at what he had just done.

In the meantime, the two hoods holding Joker had been

agonising over whether they should risk releasing their captive to join in the fight or just bide their time and see how things worked out. It soon became obvious, though, that things weren't working out well at all. They both let go of Joker and went after Harry. Joker, now free, reached out and grabbed a handful of one of the hood's hair as he ran past. The hood's head jerked backwards, exposing his bare throat to Joker's free right hand. Joker chopped down on the hood's Adam's apple and at the same time let go of his hair. The hood pitched forward, choking and retching and gasping for breath. He fell to the ground, holding his throat, where he crouched on all fours, just in front of Joker. Joker accepted the invitation. He swung his right leg back and then brought it rapidly forwards to force the toe of his DM boot into the hood's unsuspecting genitalia. The hood seemed to freeze for a second and then, with the tiniest of whimpers, he slumped onto his side.

While this was going on, Harry thrust one end of the banister into its former owner's face. The hood staggered back, his mouth a mess of blood and broken teeth; and in almost the same movement, Harry turned quickly with the banister held at arms length.

The second hood who had been holding Joker caught it full on his lower jaw and, as he went spinning into the wall, he was sure he felt his jaw dislocate.

"All right there, Joseph? Have you seen our Gary and Seamy Green?" Harry was not a man who was easily flustered.

"What? Uhm, bloody hell, what?" Joker stared at Harry. "That was bloody cool, Harry."

"What was?"

Joker simply gestured at the carnage in the alley. "Oh,

right," said Harry. "Who were they anyway?"

"Have you ever heard of Sticky Mickey?" Joker asked, as he picked up his carrier bag. He was surprised and delighted to see his vodka was still intact. He looked around for the gun, but couldn't see it. 'Fuck it,' he thought. "Come on, Harry, let's go."

"Sticky Mickey?" Harry asked, as they both walked down towards the end of the alley. "Never heard of him; should I have?"

"Oh, yeah, he's a top hood. Bit of a reputation in some areas; even the paramilitaries can't touch him."

"Really?"

"That's what they say."

"Imagine."

"Uhm, Gary and Seamy?" said Joker, getting back to Harry's earlier question. "To be honest, there's been no sign of them all day. We were expecting them ages ago, but something must have happened. We heard you had a wee bit of trouble with the cops earlier."

"Yeah, but, as far as I know, Gary and Seamy went to get the bus. Hours ago."

"Then I don't know, Harry. If they were in town they would have found us by now. Your wife managed it."

"You saw Karen?"

"Yeah, her and Sna … Seamy's girl nabbed us round in White's, so they know Gary and Seamy aren't with us. Look, I'm heading to The Crown; have you time for a quick one?"

Harry looked tempted, but he declined. "Nah, I'd better meet up with the women and get them home. Doesn't seem to be much point hanging around town."

"OK. Here, look, thanks for helping me out back there." Joker grabbed Harry's hand and shook it. "Seriously, I thought I was fucked."

"Ah, don't worry about it," Harry said. "Right, I'm going to take off, here. I'll see you later, Joseph."

"Yeah, Harry, see you." Joker mopped a little blood from his forehead and set off for The Crown.

Thirty-Two

Ding-a-Ling and Snatter had finally arrived in the city centre and were now making their way to a taxi firm that they knew to be fairly reliable. Snatter was still limping, though it wasn't as pronounced as before. The snow was still swirling around in the air, not falling heavily enough to lie, and the wind had dropped, which made the evening reasonably pleasant to walk in.

From the outside, the taxi rank was uninviting, with sheets of painted plywood nailed across the front that had once been shop windows. The inside was slightly more welcoming, with a few plastic chairs dotted around an otherwise empty room. High up on the wall that faced the entrance was a square window, behind which sat the taxi controller.

"Where to?" a disembodied female voice asked as they entered.

"Could we have two taxis please, love?" Ding-a-Ling called up to the window. Snatter shot him a glance. "What the -" but Ding-a-Ling held up a hand.

"One going to The Botanic Inn and one going to Ardoyne."

"They'll be about twenty minutes."

"Aye, love, that's dead on."

"What the fuck's happening?" Snatter demanded.

"Come over here and sit down," Ding-a-Ling told him. "There's something you need to know." They sat down beside each other and Ding-a-Ling leant forward. He started to rock slightly as if trying to find the right way to begin.

"I'm not sure how you're going to take this," he said, "but, well, you know how I've always felt about Rosie, don't you?"

Snatter leaned back in his chair and took a deep breath. For some reason he could feel his heart start to race. "Yeah," he answered, "since we were kids. Why?"

"Well, there was a party in the Markets a few weeks back. You didn't go; you weren't well, apparently."

"Charlie's party? Yeah, I remember that night. I'd a real bad dose of the Gary Glitters. In fact I was -"

"Jesus, OK, Snatter, thanks for filling in the details, but I'm trying to bloody tell you something here."

"OK, OK, Charlie's party, what about it?"

Thirty-Three

It was actually a double house party. Charlie lived next door to his cousin and they had opened up both houses, as well as the two large back gardens that lay side-by-side and were linked by a small gate. Most of the neighbours in the little cul-de-sac had also been invited and, as they moved to and fro between the party and their own homes, the boundaries of the party became blurred, making it seem more like a street party. Ding-a-Ling and Joker were standing chatting with some people in one of the kitchens, while the rest of the party sprawled all over the rest of the two houses and gardens.

On the whole, it was turning out to be an extremely good party, though Joker had decided that at some point during the evening he was definitely going to punch the dickhead who had been talking to him non-stop for the past fifteen minutes. Ding-a-Ling, Joker decided, was also due a bit of a slap for introducing him to the little prick. 'You knew what you were doing, you bastard,' he was thinking as he looked over at Ding-a-Ling's innocently smiling face.

"Joker, my old mate!" Ding-a-Ling had shouted eagerly when Joker strolled into the kitchen. "Come over here and meet somebody."

'Should've known better,' Joker told himself, 'should've fucking known.'

"Joker, this is Wea … er, Johnny. We were at school together."

"Johnny Gee, actually," Johnny Gee corrected.

"All right there, mate?" said Joker, shaking hands; he didn't see Ding-a-Ling slip quietly away to the other side of the room, where he now stood, having a pleasant conversation with a perfectly normal-looking young man and woman.

"Here, Joker, you'll love this," said Johnny Gee. "Why did the pervert cross the road?"

Joker shook his head dumbly; he wasn't sure he could take much more of this.

"He couldn't get his dick out of the chicken!" Johnny Gee threw his head back and laughed the laugh that had been making Joker's skin crawl for a quarter of an hour.

"What do you call a rabbit with a bendy dick?" Johnny Gee continued. Joker just stared into the middle distance. "Fucks Funny!" Johnny Gee roared.

'Right!' thought Joker. 'Fuck this!'

"Hey!" he shouted, while pointing through the open door that led into the garden. "That's the woman that stole my hat!"

Joker then set off in pursuit of his imaginary hat, pausing only to grab a few cans of beer from the fridge. Ding-a-Ling watched Joker's audacious escape with admiration, then suddenly dropped to the floor in a panic as he realised that Johnny Gee's head was swivelling round in his direction. As the couple he had been chatting to looked all around in consternation, Ding-a-Ling crawled through the crowd towards the door to the hall.

'Bollocks,' he thought, as it dawned on him that he was getting further from the fridge, and again he had to admire the thoroughness of Joker's plan. Once he was out in the hall, he got to his feet and made his way to the front door. He decided to make his way to the house next door, as he was sure that Joker would be there and, besides, he needed to find another fridge.

Next-door's kitchen was crowded and Ding-a-Ling had to force his way through to the fridge. He took a four-pack of beer and headed out to the back garden for some breathing room. He couldn't see any sign of Joker, so he put down three of the beer cans and lit a cigarette. He leant against the back wall of the house; it was a pleasant evening, and he was enjoying just chilling out. Along the wall from him, at head height, was a small frosted window, giving off a weak yellow light. It drew Ding-a-Ling's eye as the light went off. A few seconds later the window opened and Ding-a-Ling was amused to see Joker's head appear. Joker wriggled and squeezed through the tiny gap until, finally, he fell through onto his hands and finished with a forward roll into the garden.

"Yeah, I get fed up with those old fucking doors too," Ding-a-Ling called to him. Joker stared at him, then ostentatiously turned away. "Can't you see I'm busy?" he said, as he walked off.

"Did you get your hat?" Ding-a-Ling called after him.

"Fuck off!"

Ding-a-Ling picked up his beer and hurried to catch up. "So what is it that you're doing?"

Joker stopped and turned. He poked a finger in Ding-a-Ling's chest. "Not that it's any of your business," he said, "but I happen to be helping a toilet queue to assert itself."

This wasn't an answer that Ding-a-Ling had been expecting and he was left momentarily speechless, as Joker turned and continued on his way. Ding-a-Ling followed. "Well, would it be possible for me to observe?"

"It's a free country."

"That's a matter of opinion."

Joker walked around the side of the house and went in through a side door, with a curious Ding-a-Ling close behind. He then made his way through to an interior corridor, where a line of people stood waiting by a door.

There was a small, spiky-haired punk rocker at the head of the line who seemed startled when Joker strode up to him.

"Been waiting here long, mate?" Joker asked.

"What?"

"Been here long? It's just that I saw a bloke go in there earlier and he didn't look well at all. I mean, he looked at death's fucking door." Joker then banged on the bathroom door, which caused the punk to jump. "Oi, you, OK in there?" he shouted. Silence. He banged again. Silence.

Joker turned back to the punk. "Seriously, mate, I think something's wrong. He might have fucking collapsed or something."

"What do you think we should do?" asked the punk. He seemed concerned.

Joker appeared to ponder the dilemma and then he snapped his fingers. "I've got an idea." He studied the young punk. "You look about the right size. Well? What do you think? Do you think you're ready to fill your boots?"

"What?"

"Good man!" Joker exclaimed. "Good man, yourself! You're a legend! You know that? A fucking legend. Come with me."

Joker led the bewildered punk around to the back of the house, where he pointed to the open window. Ding-a-Ling was close behind.

"You could squeeze through there, couldn't you?"

"Well, I -"

"Come on, I'll give you a hand." Joker bent his knees, leant his back against the wall and let his hands form a cradle in front of him. The punk seemed unsure about what to do, but Joker's manic grin persuaded him that the best course of action would be to stay on the good side of the tall skinhead. And, besides, he was desperate for a piss. He put his foot in Joker's hands and heaved himself up. He was halfway through the window when he paused. "Hang on," he said. "I can't really see anything."

"What was that? You need a shove?" Joker threw up his hands and the punk disappeared into the darkness beyond. There was a muffled yelp, followed by a loud clatter as the little punk collided with the collection of shampoo and bubble bath bottles that Joker had carefully positioned earlier. Joker dusted his hands and turned to Ding-a-Ling. "My work here is done."

"And fine work it was too," said Ding-a-Ling, handing Joker a beer. "It's a service you provide, son, you know that? A service." They strolled into the garden.

"Where's your wee mate?" Joker asked.

Ding-a-Ling laughed. "Sorry about that," he said. "We used to call him Weasel at school, although he seems to prefer, what was it? Johnny Gee? Don't know why, though. His name's Kevin."

Joker laughed. "Yeah, that actually makes sense."

"Carol not here yet?"

"Haven't seen her. Doesn't mean she's not here though." They were standing close to the end of one of the gardens, just in front of a large hedge. A sudden noise made them both turn round in time to see a young couple come careering past the hedge. The couple saw Ding-a-Ling and Joker and burst into a raucous, drunken laughter. They staggered on past, up the length of the garden, towards the house. Curious, Ding-a-Ling and Joker peered through the hedge. "Fucking hell," said Joker. "You wouldn't know that was there, would you?" Behind the hedge, almost hidden from the house, was a fairly sizeable garden shed.

On closer inspection, it looked more like an outside room than a garden shed. There was an old sofa along the far wall and a few garden chairs were dotted about. There was also a coffee table and some rugs were scattered on the floor.

"Very cosy," Ding-a-Ling commented.

"Maybe me and Carol could sneak in here later on," Joker said.

"Oh please, let me be there when you ask her!" Ding-a-Ling laughed. "Fancy a shag in a shed, love?"

"I like to think I'm a wee bit more suave than that."

"Oh, you are, Joker, you are. Well, most of the time, anyway." They were both laughing as they drifted back towards the house. It was almost time for another visit to the fridge.

The kitchen was almost empty when they entered; a couple of girls were at the workbench, topping up their glasses with vodka, while a young man was asleep under the table. Joker and Ding-a-Ling went to the fridge to search for some beer. One of the girls turned round on hearing the fridge open and gave a sudden gasp. Ding-a-Ling threw her a glance and froze. "Rosie?" he exclaimed. "What are you doing here?"

Rosie quickly regained her composure and regarded Ding-a-Ling with what he thought was distaste. "I didn't know you were going to be here," she said, almost haughtily.

Joker straightened up with his beer and took out a packet of cigarettes. He offered one to Ding-a-Ling and took one himself. As he lit the cigarettes, he looked quizzically at Ding-a-Ling.

"Oh, Joker, this is Rosie, Snatter's girlfriend," Ding-a-Ling explained.

"Right there, love," said Joker. "Is Snatter with you, then?"

Rosie rolled her eyes and tutted. "Still using those stupid nicknames, Gary? You're not bloody kids any more, you know?" she turned to Joker. "His name's Seamus and no, he's not here. He's … he's not feeling very well tonight."

"Who are you here with, then?" Ding-a-Ling asked.

The girl beside Rosie turned round. "This is Sheila," Rosie told him. "She's an old friend from Derry."

"Aye," said Sheila, "living in the Short Strand these days, though." She looked at Joker. "Fuck, you're a big one, aren't you?"

"You don't know the half of it, love," said Joker, giving her his best leer. Sheila laughed. "Fucking typical isn't it, Rosie, love? Here we are at a party with two good looking fellas and we're both fucking spoken for."

Rosie was about to reply when a small group of men came into the kitchen and made for the fridge. An absurdly elegant woman came in behind them and suddenly the kitchen began to fill up.

"All right there, Gary?" One of the men recognised Ding-a-Ling.

"Oh, hiya, Joe. How's it going?" Ding-a-Ling answered. "Still at the *Irish News*?"

"Yeah, still working away. What about you? I heard you got your balls cut off."

"What?" Ding-a-Ling asked, surprised. "Where the fuck did you hear that? No, I think I would have noticed that."

"Oh, right, OK," said Joe. "You still at that place in Royal Avenue?"

"Nah, I got laid off a couple of months ago. I'm sort of stuck on the dole at the minute. That's life, I suppose."

"I'm sure something will turn up," Joe said. "Anyway, see you later, OK?" Joe and his mates drifted into the back garden, having stocked up on drinks, and the kitchen emptied once more. Ding-a-Ling couldn't help noticing that Rosie and Sheila had gone. Joker was chatting to the elegant woman.

"Hiya, Carol," Ding-a-Ling said. "How's it going? Feeling any better?"

"Hiya, Gary; not too bad at the minute," said Carol. "I've got the doctor again on Tuesday, so fingers crossed. I'm just explaining something to Joseph."

"Yeah, get this," Joker said, a look of disbelief on his face, "she say's she doesn't want to spend the evening standing in a stranger's kitchen watching me drink beer. Can you believe that?"

"Ah, she's only messing you about, Joker. I mean, you'd need to be some sort of weirdo not to want to do that."

Carol laughed. "I'm planning to have a few drinks here, then I'm going to have to drag him away, if that's OK?"

"Aye, go on, Carol, love," Ding-a-Ling assured her, "he's only been holding me back anyway. Cramping my style, you know?"

"Style? What bloody style?" Joker cried.

"What do you want to drink, Carol?" Ding-a-Ling went over to the kitchen workbench that was piled with all kinds of drinks. "I'll be barman."

"Just a wee Bacardi and white, please, Gary." Ding-a-Ling poured Carol's drink and the three of them strolled out to the back garden, where a makeshift dance floor had been marked out. There were quite a few people dancing energetically to *Wings of a Dove* by Madness, and this proved to be such an entertaining spectacle that Ding-a-Ling, Carol and Joker were happy just to stand and watch.

Rosie watched from the house. She was standing by the window in the back dining room; Sheila had gone upstairs with her boyfriend.

"Are you sure, Rosie, love? You'll be OK on your own? I can tell Jim to fuck off if you want; it'll probably do him good to have to wait for a bit anyway, the horny bastard."

Rosie laughed. "No, go on, really, I'm all right as I am. You go ahead; you don't want to keep Jim waiting." And Rosie was indeed all right. She had had several vodkas and she was now enjoying the warm, slightly fuzzy feeling it gave her. She stood alone and watched Gary and his companions laughing together. She guessed that the tall skinhead was Gary's flatmate, Joseph, and the woman seemed to be his girlfriend.

Even from this distance, Rosie could see that the woman was a seriously class act: she made even Rosie feel a little shabby, and when she turned and leant on Gary's arm to say something in his ear, Rosie was astonished at the sudden pang of envy she felt. She took a sip from her glass and wished she had a cigarette. She had been trying to quit, on and off, for a few months now, though she secretly believed it was impossible. 'Oh, to hell with it!' she thought. 'I need a fag.' And she went off to scrounge some smokes.

"Don't you stay out late," Joker was telling Ding-a-Ling, "and don't drink too much. And stay away from strange women. You know, funny-shaped ones?"

"Carol, for Christ's sake, will you take this eejit with you?"

"I'm trying to, Gary," Carol said, as she pulled on Joker's arm. "Come on, you big bloody lump."

"And don't do anything that I'd be willing to have a bash at; you'd only injure yourself." Eventually, Joker was bundled into the back of a taxi and he and Carol left. Ding-a-Ling shook his beer can and decided that another trip to the fridge was in order. As he entered the kitchen, he was surprised to see it was empty; even the guy who had been asleep under the table was gone. The party by this time, Ding-a-Ling figured, was probably spread all over the cul de sac. He took a beer from the fridge and leant against the workbench as he opened it. As he took a swig, Rosie appeared. She gave him no more than a glance as she went to refill her glass.

"You settling back in OK, Rosie?" Ding-a-Ling asked. "In Ardoyne, I mean."

Rosie turned to face him; she was standing at the workbench on the opposite side of the kitchen. "Karen tells me you're scrounging off the dole," she said. Ding-a-Ling noted the disdain in her voice, but he thought he heard something else as well. What was it? Regret?

"Yeah, hopefully not for long, though," he said.

"Seamus is doing very well for himself, you know?" She said it almost defiantly.

"Yeah, I'd heard."

"He may even start looking out for more shops to run."

"Good for him."

There was a brief silence, which made Ding-a-Ling feel a little uncomfortable. Rosie was staring at the floor. She appeared to be almost simmering.

"How was Derry?" Ding-a-Ling asked, to break the silence more than anything. "I heard you didn't have an easy time of it."

Rosie shrugged. "It was OK; at least in Derry we didn't

have everybody laughing at us because our da was in fucking Purdysburn!" Ding-a-Ling felt hurt by the flash of anger in her eyes. He looked down at the floor. "Not everybody was laughing, Rosie," he said softly. Rosie felt suddenly chastised. She gave a brief smile.

"No, not everybody," she admitted, "*you* never did." Her face softened as she looked at him. "You and Sean and Seamus, you three never did. You always stuck up for me." Embarrassed, Ding-a-Ling took a drink of beer. Rosie looked at him and smiled a warm and genuine smile. It took him by surprise. It also took his breath away.

"You were my Three Musketeers," she said, and then blushed.

"What?"

"Nothing," she said, blushing even more; "just kid's stuff."

"No, go on."

"Well, do you remember the cartoon?"

"The cartoon?" Ding-a-Ling thought for a moment. "Shit, yeah! You mean from *The Banana Splits*? I'd forgotten about that." They both started laughing. "Wasn't there a really annoying kid in it? I think I remember hoping the wee bastard would be killed every week. He never bloody was, though."

"That's right," Rosie laughed. "It was my favourite show. I used to fancy D'Artagnan."

"Well, fuck, who wouldn't?" exclaimed Ding-a-Ling. "He was bloody gorgeous!"

They laughed long and hard, their childhood memories mingling and flickering between them, softening the harsh lines of the present. After a while the laughter faded, to leave a comfortable, if slightly awkward, silence. Which Ding-a-Ling shattered.

"I was gutted when you left, you know?"

Rosie's head snapped back as if she had been slapped. 'Fuck him!' she thought furiously. 'Fuck him! Why did he have to -' And suddenly she was kissing him.

'What the hell are you doing, you stupid bitch?' her mind was screaming. But the vodka was muffling those screams and, besides, her heart wasn't listening. All that Rosie knew was that she was in the arms of the one person she had never been able to forget, her childhood crush, the shoulder she had cried on, her defender and protector, her musketeer. Her D'Artagnan.

'One hell of a good-looking couple,' thought Johnny Gee as he watched them slip through the back door into the garden. He then raised a cigarette packet to his mouth and, using his teeth, he took out a single cigarette. He rolled it around between his lips while, with one hand, he slipped a match from its box and placed it in the crook of his forefinger. He then flicked his thumbnail across the match head to light the match. It had the desired effect: the match head burst into flame, but, unfortunately, it also flew off the matchstick and landed on the stair carpet, where it started a happy little fire. "Shit!" Johnny Gee muttered as he stamped it out. He took out another match and tried again. He made sure the match was sitting much lower in his forefinger, which prevented the match head from becoming detached. It also meant that he managed to burn a neat little hole in the flesh of his finger. "Fuck!" he cried, as he shook out the flame and ran to the kitchen sink. After he had run some cold water over the burn, he dried his finger and took out another match. He struck it against the side of the matchbox and lit his cigarette. He then languidly stroked the match several times through the air until it had gone out and he sauntered casually to the back door. Taking a slow puff from his cigarette, Johnny Gee flicked the dead match through the open door, sending a tiny trail of smoke spiralling into the garden. 'Cool as fuck, Johnny Gee,' he told himself. 'Cool as fuck.'

Thirty-Four

"In a fucking shed?"

"That's hardly the point now, is it?" Ding-a-Ling said quietly.

Snatter wasn't sure what he should be feeling right now; on the one hand he had been betrayed by his oldest friend and that had certainly shocked him, but on the other hand -

"She was bloody furious afterwards," Ding-a-Ling continued. "I mean, she went fucking mental. Told me never to breathe a word about it or she would never forgive me. Said she was fucking ashamed of herself. Can you believe that?"

Suddenly the full implications of what Ding-a-Ling had told him dawned on Snatter. "What the hell are you saying here, Ding-a-Ling? That you think the kid's yours?"

"I'd put money on it," Ding-a-Ling replied. "Look, Snatter, I know you. You put a condom on just to shake hands with a woman, for fuck's sake!"

And that is what had been bothering Snatter. His relationship with Rosie had not been overly physical, but on the few occasions when alcohol and loneliness had pushed them both over the edge, he had always been careful to use protection. Caution was almost an obsession with Snatter. He knew that no form of contraception was 100% effective, but fuck! Just how unlucky would he have had to be? Voicing these doubts to Rosie, however, had, so far, proved to be impossible. Had Ding-a-Ling just solved his problem?

"Wait a minute," he said. "Rosie isn't stupid; she must know the chances are that you're the father. So why the hell would she -"

"I've been thinking about that," Ding-a-Ling interrupted. He had been sitting with his elbows resting on his knees, staring at the floor. He turned and looked up at Snatter. "It's like you said, Snatter; Rosie's not stupid. Look at you, you're well on your way to making a success of your life and I'm, or at least I have been, just some waster on the dole." Snatter tried to speak, but Ding-a-Ling gestured for him to be quiet. "That's why Rosie wanted you to go round her sister's house today, isn't it? I take it the engagement was going to be made official?"

"Yeah," Snatter nodded. "I suppose that's why Rosie was so insistent that I keep quiet about the baby till after Christmas. Once we were engaged, then she probably thought that would be it. Nothing could stop it."

"Can you picture the look on her face when she found out you were going drinking with me all day?" Ding-a-Ling asked with a smile. "She must have fucking shit herself."

"What are you going to do?" Snatter had just remembered the two taxis. Ding-a-Ling stood up and stretched. He looked at Snatter and grinned.

"I think me and Rosie McCann need to have a wee chat," he said. "We've got some things to discuss."

"What about the pub-crawl?"

Ding-a-Ling looked suddenly thoughtful. "Maybe some things are more important than even the pub-crawl."

Snatter almost jumped to his feet to slap this imposter. This was a Ding-a-Ling that Snatter didn't recognise. "What about the lies she told? What she was trying to do was just so fucking, what's the word?" Snatter thought for a second. "Mercenary! And with *your* kid. Are you telling me you're OK with that?"

Ding-a-Ling sighed. "She hasn't had it easy." He sat

down beside Snatter and turned to look at him. "OK, OK, I know that doesn't make her unique; but, like I said, you know how I've always felt about her. I don't blame her for what she tried to do; she must have been desperate. But that doesn't matter any more; what does matter is that Rosie McCann is carrying my kid." The grin on Ding-a-Ling's face was so huge that Snatter could only smile. "I mean, this is the future, this is *my* future. Fuck me, Snatter, I've got a future."

"And the future's rosy, is it?" Snatter asked, trying to maintain a cool detachment. In reality, though, he was relishing the sense of relief that was flooding through him. Ding-a-Ling roared with laughter. "That's a good one," he said. "Yes, my old mucker, the future is indeed Rosie, and do you know what? I just can't fucking wait."

Snatter hadn't intended the pun, but he said nothing. He simply sat back and let himself bask in his friend's touchingly unrestrained happiness.

"Taxi for Ardoyne!"

Ding-a-Ling jumped to his feet. "Well, that's me!" He grabbed Snatter's hand and shook it. "Give the lads my regards; tell them … tell them …" He paused as he thought about it. He smiled. "Tell them I may not be able to play with them any more."

This was, indeed, a new Ding-a-Ling, a revitalised Ding-a-Ling, a Ding-a-Ling running through Bedford Falls at the end of *It's a Wonderful Life*. He strode out the door; then, after a few seconds, he reappeared in the doorway. He seemed a little concerned. "Uhm, me and you? We're OK, aren't we?"

Ding-a-Ling, Snatter had to admit, was no Jimmy Stewart, and Belfast was, by no stretch of the imagination, Bedford Falls. "Fuck off, asshole!" Snatter said.

Ding-a-Ling walked, grinning, to his taxi. 'Yeah, we're dead on,' he thought. 'Absolutely dead on.'

Thirty-Five

"What the hell happened to you?" Tone asked as Joker appeared.

"I bumped into Sticky Mickey," Joker told them. "But I could do with a beer before I can tell you any more than that. Did you know it's snowing out there?"

"Snowing?" asked Sean. "Is it heavy?"

"Nah, not really. Very festive, though. Really gets your bells jingling."

"I'll get another round in," Bobby said, and got up to go to the bar.

Joker sat down and dabbed at his forehead. "Does it look bad?" he asked.

"Well, it doesn't look life-threatening, if that's what you mean," Tone said. "We'd just about given up on you. We were going to head on."

"Well, thanks a bloody lot," said Joker.

After a while, Bobby came back with a tray of drinks. Tone looked at his watch. "It's knocking on a bit," he said. "We could do with drinking these up."

"What's the rush?" Joker protested. "I've just had a very traumatic experience, thank you very much, and I could do with a calm and relaxing period where I can chill out and savour this pint."

"Yes, and I'm sure you will be boring us all with the details of your traumatic experience but, seriously, we don't want to leave it too late to get to the Bot."

"Why not?" Joker asked. "And, anyway, it isn't that late, is it?"

"No, it isn't that late, Joker," Tone said, exasperated, "but we need to go soon because, for one thing, we need to get something to eat."

"Oh, for Christ's sake! If you're hungry then get a pint of Guinness," said Joker. "That's food, isn't it? Guinness is food."

"But I also happen to know," Tone continued, "that Janty will be finishing work shortly."

"Janty? The bouncer? But what does that … oh." Joker happened to catch a glimpse of himself in one of the little painted mirrors that adorned the inside of the snug. With his shaven head, black eye and bleeding forehead, he looked exactly like the sort of person who would not be welcome in a respectable nightclub. "That's a bloody good point, Tone," he said. "Right, everybody, drink up!"

Despite Joker's protests, they called into a nearby fast-food restaurant and filled up on burgers and chips, setting themselves up for the night ahead.

"Maybe we should get a couple of taxis," Jamesy suggested when they stepped outside. It was only a fifteen-minute walk to The Botanic Inn, but it was snowing and they were all drunk, so Jamesy thought that taxis would be a sensible option.

"Yes, Jamesy," Joker said, "that's a fine idea, except this happens to be a pub-*crawl*, not a bloody pub … bloody sitting in a taxi … thing."

"Beautifully put, Joker," Sean said, "but we're hardly going to be crawling up to the Bot, are we?"

"That's just the pedantic sort of thing that -"

"Will you all just shut the fuck up and start walking!" Tone was getting impatient; he was eager to get settled into the warm atmosphere of the final bar of this year's pub-crawl. He wanted to sit down and enjoy the end of the evening; and so he set off along the road with the rest of the lads grumbling in his wake.

Luckily, Janty was still on the door when they got to the Bot. He rolled his eyes when he saw Joker, but he nodded for him to go in.

"For fuck's sake, Joker, just find a dark corner and stay there, OK?"

Once inside, they made their way upstairs to the disco and found a booth which they decided to make their base for the rest of the night. Jamesy and Joker went to get the drinks, and Tone, Sean and Bobby made themselves at home. Tone had a look around.

The place wasn't too crowded, though there were a few people dotted here and there. Everyone seemed to be enjoying themselves: happy, smiling and laughing. The music was at a tolerable level and Tone felt it was the ideal place to end the night. Up on the dance floor, he watched a group of girls, no more than teenagers, gyrating and swivelling to the music, their slim figures balanced elegantly on high, slender heels. Joker and Jamesy came back from the bar with the drinks and everyone settled down. Cigarettes were passed around and glasses raised.

Tone was feeling very mellow; he was vaguely aware of Bobby chatting to him, but he wasn't really listening. He could hear little snippets of what Bobby was saying, but he could also hear snatches of Joker's conversation with Jamesy. Sean was singing to himself.

"… better watch out, you'd better not cry, you'd better …", "… lamped him so hard in the ging-gangs that his eyeballs popped out, swear to fuck, you can ask …", "… Santa Claus is coming to …", "… really going to have to meet her, so you are …", "… sees you when you're sleeping …", "… actually, the next time you're in Dublin …", "… no time to waste, though, because Harry was in trouble …", "… a course down there …", "… be good for goodness sake …", "… 'Joker, help,' he was shouting. 'Help me, Joker.' So I …", "… for the *Belfast Telegraph*, you see …", "… you'd better not -"

Tone's attention was suddenly focused. "What was that? What did you say?" he asked Bobby.

"What?" Bobby was momentarily thrown. "Oh, I was just saying you could meet up with my girlfriend some time when you're in Dublin. She's on a course there from the *Belfast Telegraph*. It's only a six-month journalism course." Tone felt himself rise from the table to go careering across the dance floor, to scatter the tottering, anorexic slappers into the vacant, dead-eyed crowd. "Claire's her name, Claire Masterson. You'd really get on well together." To hit the top of the stairs and spiral down into the night, to spin amongst the drunks and the dregs and the fucked-in-the-head. To lose himself, anonymous and alone. "I think I've got her number here somewhere. Her Dublin one, I mean." To need no one, to want no one. To puke and rage against an empty sky, to spew his frustration and his bitterness into a city that overflowed with bitterness, to pour his bile over the streets and over the silent fields, over the hatred and mistrust, the anger and the laughter and the love, over all the living and all the fucking dead. He picked up a cigarette from the table and put a light to it.

"Oh, yeah, you're seeing some girl down in Dublin, aren't you?" Bobby went on. "How's that going?"

"Have you ever read any Joyce, Bobby?" Tone asked.

"What? What the fuck's that got to do with anything? No, I haven't, why?"

"Oh, nothing. I always thought he was overrated, that's all. What were you saying?"

"This girl in Dublin, how's that going?"

"Dead and buried, Bobby, my old mate," Tone said. "Dead and buried."

"What? But I thought -"

"Nah, Bobby; it's over even as we speak."

"That's a shame, though, isn't it?"

Tone shrugged. "Wasn't meant to be, that's all. Just wasn't meant to be. Still, it's not your problem, is it?"

"Yeah, but I just thought … Oi! Get the fucking drinks in!" Snatter had arrived. Jamesy stood up. "Sit down there, Snatter; you look like you need a seat. I'll get this round." Jamesy went off to the bar and Snatter sat down.

"Where's Ding-a-Ling?" Joker asked.

"It's a long story," Snatter told him.

"Ah, fuck it then."

"Your girlfriend was looking for you earlier," Tone said to Snatter.

"Not my problem any more," Snatter told him happily.

"Really? False alarm?" Snatter looked at Tone in surprise. He smiled. "Not for Ding-a-Ling," he said.

"I see."

Jamesy came over, put some drinks on the table and went back for the rest.

"This calls for a toast!" Sean suddenly exclaimed.

"What calls for a toast?" Bobby asked. Sean looked confused. "OK then," he said. "I call for a fucking toast."

Jamesy came back from the bar and sat down. "A toast?" he asked. "What are we toasting?"

Sean raised his glass. "How about, 'Ireland united, Gaelic and free'?"

"I don't know," Bobby said. "Wouldn't the Unionists in the company find that offensive?"

"Fuck them."

"How about," Tone said, looking at Snatter. "How about, 'Freedom'?"

"Hmmm," Bobby pondered, "freedom from what, you see. I mean that -"

"Oh, give it a rest, Bobby!" Joker laughed.

'Freedom?' thought Snatter, as he lifted his first drink of the day. "Yes," he said. "Yes, I'll drink to that."

Epilogue

It was the sort of morning that, normally, Jamesy would have loved. A grey, cold and wet Sunday in mid-January. He would stand at his window and regard the deserted streets with smug satisfaction. The howling wind that would occasionally throw a smattering of rain against the glass would warm him to the very depths of his being. He could even be indulgent towards the raindrops; each one a perfect little sigh of melancholy, come to make a monochrome world all blissful and sad.

But now the little bastards were just making him wet.

As he stood and waited for the lights to change on the pedestrian crossing, a van sped past, splashing through a puddle and soaking his feet. Not for the first time that morning, he cursed Tone and Bobby.

Jamesy's mood was not helped by the fact he could feel a bit of a hangover coming on. That, he was sure, was down to all the whiskies that Snatter had insisted on buying him the night before. Jamesy was partial to the odd whiskey every now and then, but Snatter had seemed to be continuously forcing a glass into his hand. So here he was, trudging through a rain-swept Belfast on a miserable Sunday morning, getting more and more wet and feeling more and more nauseous. Still, he thought, it had been a pretty good night. They were all there, all of them, finally together in one place. For it was Ding-a-Ling's engagement party.

"So you're an actual, real-life homo?" Joker was standing at the bar with Jamesy and Snatter. They were in a private room, the entire upstairs of a city centre bar.

"It's certainly looking that way," Snatter said. "Why? Does it bother you?"

"Course not!" Joker said, slightly offended. "You're a mate, aren't you? I'm just curious, that's all. Do you know what you're supposed to do, for instance?"

Snatter raised an eyebrow. "What? You mean -"

"Oh, fuck, no, I don't mean the actual, well, fuck, you know. I'm talking about what your next move is. Like do you know any clubs or bars you can go to? That sort of thing, you know?"

"I've got a few contacts," Snatter said, "but it's working up the courage, that's the problem. I suppose it's something I can work on this year. I'm looking forward to it, but at the same time it's, well, you know."

"If you need anybody to come with you for a bit of moral support," Joker told him, "then just say the word."

"You, Joker?" Jamesy broke in, bemused. "In a gay bar?"

"Aye, no bother," Joker insisted. "Listen, Snatter, if I come with you then you don't have to worry, OK? I'll make sure none of those queers give you any jip."

Snatter and Jamesy smiled at Joker.

"Oh, you know what I mean," Joker said. Behind Jamesy, Snatter saw Rosie approach. As she looked shyly at Snatter, Joker tactfully nodded to Jamesy for them both to move a little further up the bar.

"Hi," Rosie said. "We haven't really had a chance to talk, have we?"

"No, it's been a hectic couple of weeks," Snatter agreed.

"I just wanted to make sure that we're, well, you know, that we're OK."

Snatter didn't know what to say, so he just walked

forward and embraced her. "Of course we're OK, Rosie," he finally said. "We'll always be OK. Look!" He turned her around to look across the room. Ding-a-Ling was entertaining a small group of people with a story that seemed to require a lot of elaborate arm movements. He looked to be in his element. "I can't remember ever seeing him so happy," Snatter said. "So how could we not be OK? I just want you to know that if there's anything you need, anything at all, then don't hesitate, and I mean it; do not hesitate to ask, OK?"

Rosie nodded, unable to speak as her emotions threatened to engulf her.

She had met Gary's closest friends one by one over the past few weeks and in turn they had all told her basically the same thing. 'Anything you need, just ask.' Even Joseph, who had initially been sullen at what he had called Ding-a-Ling's defection to the real world, once he had spent a little time with Rosie, had subsequently informed Ding-a-Ling that if he ever harmed that wee girl in any way then he would have *him* to answer to.

Snatter gave her another hug and Rosie was grateful for it as it gave her the opportunity to quickly wipe away the tears that were welling in her eyes.

"So, how's Din … Gary's job going?" Snatter asked. "I haven't had a chance to talk to him lately."

Rosie smiled as she used a knuckle to dab the corner of her eye. "He loves it," she said. "Him and Joseph are just like a couple of big kids with new toys to play with."

"You and him belong together, you know that, don't you?" Snatter told her. Rosie simply smiled and nodded.

"I know," Rosie said. "I've always known. It's just taken me a while to admit that."

"Jamesy! Come over here a minute!" Tone called out and Jamesy went over and sat down at the table where Tone was sitting with Bobby.

"What is it?" he asked.

"I was round at Bobby's flat during the week," Tone explained, "and his wee cousin was there; I don't know if you know him."

"Nah, you wouldn't know him," Bobby put in, "but he's doing Ancient History for 'A' level."

"Oh, right," said Jamesy. "Smart lad, then?"

"Yeah, well, anyway, he's doing something about Themistocles, is it?" Tone said, looking to Bobby. "And what his actual role was during some battle. What was it, Bobby?"

"Salamis, I think."

"Yeah, that's right," said Tone. "Salamis. Apparently, he thinks that this Themistocles bloke may have been a bit of a double agent at the time."

"What?" Jamesy was outraged. "Themistocles was one of the greatest men who ever lived. It's true that in later life he -"

"Yes, Jamesy, yes, OK," Tone stopped him. "This is me you're talking to and I don't give a shit, remember? The thing is, this guy's actually heard of you, from some lectures you've given, I think. So me and Bobby said that we'd introduce you to him. What do you think?"

"Of course," said Jamesy. "Someone needs to put him straight."

"Good man," Tone said. "We're all meeting up at Maggie's; you know, the coffee shop?"

"Yeah, in Shaftesbury Square?"

"That's it. So, ten-o-clock? Tomorrow morning?"

"What? Come on, Tone! Tomorrow's Sunday. It's

meant to be a bloody day of rest."

"I know, but I'm driving to Donegal on Monday. Come on, Jamesy; I'll buy you lunch afterwards. One of the hotels up round Queen's; we'll make a day of it."

"Well, I suppose. But, bloody hell, Tone!"

"You OK there, Rosie?" Ding-a-Ling had finally got a chance to talk to his fiancée. She had been sitting at a table having a chat with Karen, but Karen had now gone to look for Harry and she was left on her own. "You look a bit lost."

"I'm OK," she said. "I'm happy just sitting here."

"No worries then?"

"Worries? No." She looked around the room. Seamus and Bobby were standing at the bar talking to Sean, while Tony and James were laughing at Joseph, who was using a straw to blow bubbles into his beer. Rosie turned back to Ding-a-Ling. "Why would I have any worries?" she said, laughing. "I have seven musketeers."

Ding-a-Ling laughed with her. "That's right, love," he said. He put his arm around her shoulder and she turned her face to his and they kissed. 'That's right.'

Later on, Rosie found a quiet little corner of the room where she could sit by herself and be alone with her thoughts. She smiled indulgently at Gary over at the bar, laughing and animated, surrounded by his friends. She placed a hand on the growing bump of her stomach and gave it a gentle rub. 'You OK in there?' she asked her unborn child. 'We all can't wait to meet you, you know? You're going to love your da; he'll make you laugh with all the silly things he does. And all his friends are going to spoil you rotten. So we'll all be here to meet you whenever you're ready to arrive; but whoever you are and whoever you turn out to be, there's something you're going to need to know.' Rosie said the next words aloud. "Never lie and never steal, sweetheart." 'That's what I'll be telling you when I see you. I'll be telling you that a lot.'

'Bloody Tone and bloody Bobby!' Jamesy was soaked through as he approached the coffee shop. Just before he entered, he stood in the little hallway and shook himself like a wet dog. He wiped his nose, then he sniffed and shivered and pushed open the door.

He could tell right away that he'd been set up. There was no sign of Tone, nor of Bobby, nor of Bobby's bloody cous … Bobby's cousin? But then, how? Jamesy felt his head begin to swim; he couldn't seem to think straight. But what was -? His nausea was getting worse and he was beginning to shake. He stood in the middle of the floor, dripping onto the black and white tiles, sniffing and shivering and swaying.

And caught in the full and blinding glare of a smile that could melt icebergs.

"So tell me," Hannah said. "Why *can't* dolphins breathe underwater?"

Lightning Source UK Ltd.
Milton Keynes UK
25 August 2010

158968UK00007B/7/P